VILLAIN
Demons of Foxglove Grove, #1

Chani Lynn Feener

CHANI LYNN FEENER

ALSO BY CHANI LYNN FEENER

*For a list of YA books by this author, please check her website. All of the books listed below are Adult.

Bad Things Play Here

Gods of Mist and Mayhem

A Bright Celestial Sea

A Sea of Endless Light

A Whisper in the Dark Trilogy
You Will Never Know
Don't Breathe a Word
Don't Let Me Go

Abandoned Things

Between the Devil and the Sea

Echo

These Silent Stars

Call of the Sea

Devil May Care

Devil May Bleed

Devil May Fall

His Dark Paradox
Under the penname Avery Tu with Kota Quinn

CHANI LYNN FEENER

VILLAIN
Demons of Foxglove Grove, #1

Chani Lynn Feener

This is a work of fiction. Names, characters, places, and incidents are the product of the author's imagination, and any resemblance to actual events or persons, living or dead, is entirely coincidental.

Villain

Copyright @ 2024 by Chani Lynn Feener.

All rights reserved. No part of this book may be reproduced, distributed, or transmitted in any form without written permission from the author.

Front Cover design by INKBookDesign.

Printed in the United States of America.

First edition—2024

AUTHOR'S NOTE

Dear Reader,

Even if you've read one of my books before please do not skip this note. As some of the triggers couldn't be included on the books main listing, I wanted to take the time to include them here. If you're a close friend or family member...please don't read this ༼ ͠°⌓͠° ༽

Villain is the first book in a DARK Why Choose Romance. There are strong themes of bullying, mention of suicide, and dealing with the death of a loved one. Unlike with my other books, the MC Nix is involved with three men at once. There is NO cheating, and all of the men are in agreement.

I want to be clear that I don't condone anything that takes place in this book in real life. This book is purely fiction. These characters are not real and this takes place on a made-up planet in a made-up galaxy. None of my characters are human, though I sometimes use the word humanoid, and this galaxy is nowhere near ours. If you or someone you know is ever in a toxic relationship, please seek help. You deserve better.

The Demons of Foxglove Grove are spoiled and used to getting their way. They can get away with literal murder on their planet, and rule the school through a mixture of fear and morbid curiosity from the other students. While they all will fall for Nix in their own ways and time, there is no instant love for any of them. Basically, they aren't good people and they aren't above using someone for their own gain.

Nix is dealing with some pretty heavy emotions when he enters the school at the start of the book. He displays a range of them throughout whenever he thinks of his cousin, who he believes to have taken her own life. Some of these emotions are more negative than others, and some characters make comments on their own on the subject. Sometimes these comments are disrespectful or place blame on the wrong person. Please keep in mind these are characters, and again, their expressions or views of such heavy subject matter are not my own personal take. Having lost loved ones myself, I understand how hard this topic can be to read about, and want to be completely upfront about that running conversation throughout this, and the other books in the series. If this isn't something you think you can read about, please skip this and read something else.

Now, onto the rest of the triggers. **If you aren't easily triggered or you want to avoid potential spoilers, feel free to skip the rest of this note.**

I tried to note down all of the ones I can think of, but please keep in mind I may have missed one or two. Your mental health is important, if any of these do not sound appealing or may put you at risk, please skip this book. I have other MM books that don't fall under the Dark category that may be better suited for you.

Most, but possibly not all, notable triggers include: Noncon, dubcon, bondage, more than one lover, violence, death, mention of suicide (not shown on page), bullying, controlling male leads, manipulation, torture, murder, and graphic sex scenes.

I just want to reiterate there is no cheating in this book. The Demons do NOT share Nix with anyone else, and the series as a whole will have a HEA. That being said, the relationships in this book are twisted, toxic, and manipulative. I in no way, shape, or form condone anything mentioned above in real life. This is purely fiction.

This book is intended for a mature adult audience only.

Remember, your mental health and well-being are more important than reading this book. Always put yourself first and be responsible for your own triggers. You're worth it, and you matter.

PROLOGUE:

Dear Nix,

Where to start. If you're reading this, it's already too late for me. I'm sorry. Things got really bad really quickly, and I didn't know what else to do.

Maybe I should have confided in you sooner…

Maybe you hate me now and this letter won't mean anything to you…

Maybe you won't even read it.

Actually, that's probably for the best. I hope you aren't reading this. I hope it remains forever tucked away in the drawer of your ridiculous blue end table we painted the summer you turned eleven. Or it burns to ash in a bonfire you throw at our spot on Aunt Arla's orchard. I shouldn't even be writing this down, but I'm selfish.

I guess that's the first secret I'll share with you now. I'm selfish, Nix. Don't shake your head; you know it's true when you really think about it. I've always been this way. Too strong-willed and overly confident in my lackluster abilities. If only I'd been more like you, perhaps things would have gone differently. But I'm not you, and I never will be, so I foolishly thought I could beat Enigma. That I could earn that crown and ascend to greater heights.

I thought I could rule the world...

This is secret number two and where my story turns into one massive cliché that you and I would no doubt laugh about if it'd happened to anyone else.

I met a boy, Nix.

And that boy betrayed me.

Now, no one will ever know the real end to my story, and the fame I literally traded my life for will go up in a puff of smoke. What am I now to you? To mama and papa? To Aunt Arla? Am I the girl who gave up? The girl who lied? The girl who wasn't strong enough? The girl who let a man get to her and ruin her life?

Can I tell you the truth, cousin? Just you, and no one else?

I'm all of those things.

I won't tell you secret number three. I thought this would help, writing it all down, but it's not. Nothing helps. Nothing will. I should tear this up and destroy it myself, but I won't. I won't because in the off chance you do read this, Nix, there's still something I need you to know. Something important.

I didn't tell anyone about Enigma, you aren't allowed to. Only those of us on campus know. I didn't tell anyone about my guy either, because everyone knows falling for a man through an app is pathetic. There's no paper trail you can access. No proof you can find.

There's nothing. It's all turned to wind.

Like I have now.

Don't try and find out more, you won't be able to anyway. He's good at covering his tracks. Good at hiding. I'm sorry for being vague, but this is as much of the truth as I can safely share with you. I'm sorry I wasn't strong enough.

I'm sorry I can't be there for the day you achieve your dreams.

I love you, cousin, and I know you, maybe better than anyone. So I'll leave you with this.

Don't try to fix this.

Stay away from Foxglove Grove. I should have taken your advice that day when you said it wasn't the right fit for us. I'll regret not listening for…well. I guess my life has come to an end already, hasn't it? If there's something after, though, I can promise you, I'll be regretting it still then.

I'm sorry.

I'm sorry.

You don't have to forgive me.

Love,

Branwen Cherith.

CHAPTER 1:

He couldn't do it.

Nix squeezed his eyes shut and pumped faster, praying for the end to hurry up and come already. He'd been unable to face the camera—even with the mask on to help conceal his identity—but turning his back to it had only helped ease his nerves so much.

It was the knowing it was there...

Watching him...

That others, *strangers*, were on the other side of it staring while he—

Well. Maybe not multiple, but there was at least one. One person who'd sent him this invitation—Favor, as it was called—with the instructions to touch himself to release. That person was there, the username taunting him when he'd entered the chat room and set his camera up, but he hadn't been able to check to see if any others had come to see the show.

His show.

Good Light, how had Branwen done *this*?

He bit his bottom lip hard enough there was an accompanying tang of blood and let out a low growl of frustration. He could do this. He had to do this.

For her.

Thinking about his cousin right now wasn't helping him get off any quicker, and he dashed those thoughts from his mind. In his left hand, his dick was still full and leaking, but no matter how turned on he was, he just couldn't seem to shake the trepidation enough to reach the finish line. Which wouldn't do, because if he didn't follow the rules and come on camera...

Nix was currently in his childhood bedroom, alone in the house since his parents were still staying with Branwen's three hours away. He was a rather vocal lover, so he'd thought being on his own would help him accomplish this task, since he could be as loud as he needed. Unfortunately, though he was alone, he wasn't *alone*, and that fact kept getting to him, worming its way past the jolts of pleasure brought on by his lube-slicked palm.

He'd set the camera on his desk and had started the live feed over ten minutes ago. Though he'd bitched out and turned away before he could see the chatroom open to viewers aside from the one who'd invited him. That person was still there, right? Was probably the only one?

How popular was this app?

With another sound of frustration, he dropped his forehead to the mattress, the move lifting his ass higher in the air. He'd spread his thighs and put himself on full display for the viewer, jerking himself off with his dick aimed low so they could see as much of him as possible even from this angle.

He'd done as much research into the app as he could, but there wasn't much information out there that was accessable to the open public. The app had been created for the rich and elite students of Foxglove Grove University, a prestigious school Nix had only ever been to once when he'd been touring to try and find the right fit for him.

Foxglove hadn't been it.

Not that it mattered any more, since that's where he'd find himself at the start of the upcoming semester anyway.

From what he'd gathered, Enigma was a fancy hookup app meant to have their members jumping through hoops to prove how deviant and depraved they could be. Only those who attended or had attended the school were allowed to join, and there was a farce of anonymity and discretion.

Farce, because there was no way to keep one's identity a secret if they were going out screwing people they'd met through the app. But whatever. The app also operated on a tiered system. The lower ones meant nothing, but he'd skipped right past those while hacking his way into the program.

After the funeral, Nix had found the email with the QR code in his cousin's multi-slate. He'd also found the app downloaded to her device, though it'd been locked. Since then, he'd managed to hack into the system, but only a few of her chat logs were accessible and nothing else, the rest of it under biometric locking mechanisms he couldn't break through.

Now that she was dead, no one could.

The QR code had still worked, surprisingly enough. Apparently, whoever managed the app didn't bother checking to see if their members were still alive or not. It wasn't as simple as downloading the app to his own device, however. In her letter to him, Branwen had mentioned something about crowns. He'd figured out that part of her message easily enough.

Everyone had a profile photo, something that was meant to be obscure—not an actual picture of your face or anything that could reveal your identity. Though the first two levels operated the same as any other hookup app, anonymity was still the number one rule.

It made Nix wonder how many random people his cousin had slept with, or exchanged sexual favors with like he was doing right now, without ever having seen their face before.

This was already a lot for him; he didn't think he could fuck someone without knowing what they looked like beforehand. Clearly, Branwen hadn't felt the same way, since over the tiny profile photo of an ivory mask, there was a small golden crown.

She'd wanted it and she'd gotten it.

So why had she killed herself in the end anyway?

A boy. A boy who'd betrayed her. A boy who had something to do with this secret world and these dirty dealings.

Nix had downloaded the app and created an account. He'd been able to hack the system and manipulate it into believing he'd already successfully beaten the first two tiers and was currently a part of the third one, which was known as Bishop. But that's where things had gotten...complicated.

Moving up the first two tiers was simple. To go from Pawn to Knight, a person simply needed to invite twenty people using their own personal QR code. Nix had tricked it into believing he'd done this. Then from Knight to Bishop, ten official Favors needed to be completed.

Favors were given by the top three highest tiers, and Knights were allowed into a specific forum where they could click on suggested favors from higher members and decide whether or not to do them. Nix had simply left a program running that sorted through all of the favors and selected the ones that were the easiest. A photograph of his ass in a public setting. A picture of his dick fully erect. Ridiculous, but ultimately harmless.

He'd checked off ten Favors within three days that way, and had risen the ranks to Bishop. But that was where things got tricky.

There was no forum for Bishops to shop around in. Rooks and Kings, the two tiers above, did the shopping. They had open access to all of the Bishops' profiles, including the material used for their first ten favors which were stored on their accounts.

It had taken almost four days for someone to finally contact Nix with an offer, and by that point, he probably would have been willing to do anything. When he'd first read the message, he'd even been relieved that it was nothing too extreme.

Now that he was in the midst of it however...

This was only one of five. He'd need to complete five in order to reach the second highest tier, and even then he'd still be one below the one he needed to be in.

The one Branwen had fought so hard to enter.

King.

People in the King tier didn't interact with those beneath the Rooks or Bishops. For the latter, it was only to offer Favors. Nix was hopeful there'd be more between them and the Rooks.

He needed to get closer so he could actually learn who these people were. Learn what they did and what the real purpose of this damn app was.

He couldn't do that if he didn't gather his courage and stop fucking around.

It was an orgasm, damn it.

It wasn't like he'd been asked to saw his own arm off or anything.

Nix rocked his hips back and forth and tried to focus on the slick sounds of his own precome mixing with the lube. He just needed to come. He just needed—

The multi-slate and his computer dinged at the same time, alerting him that a comment had been left in the chat, and he froze. Nix had decided to film with his computer and keep his body-borne device on him so he could shut the camera off as soon as he was finished. But knowing he was already going to be struggling with this, he'd been sure to mute the chat beforehand…

Hadn't he?

There was a second ding and he jerked, realizing with a start how absolutely stupid and pathetic he probably looked to whoever was watching. Lifting his head, he forced himself to peer down at the small rectangular screen attached to the top of his wrist and read the messages.

Maestro: You're empty, Songbird.

Songbird? Nix's brow furrowed. Was it a dig? He'd made his username Nightingale, but it was impossible to tell if this messenger was teasing him or not. At least there was still only the two of them present in the chat. No one else was watching this awkward exchange but him and the user who'd offered the Favor. He read the second comment.

Maestro: Are you skittish, or is this part of the act? This says you're a Bishop. Aren't you trying to become a Rook?

Nix swallowed the sudden lump in his throat and told himself there was no way whoever this was had figured out he'd cheated and skipped the first two tiers. He was fooled, he had to be. There were no hidden meanings in that statement. He thought Nix was in the Bishop tier because that was as high up as he could go on his own.

The chat dinged a third time.

Maestro: I don't like being ignored, Songbird. Want my Favor? You better fill that tight ass in the next sixty seconds or I'll ban your account.

He sucked in a sharp breath. That couldn't happen. If he was banned he'd lose all progress! There was no telling if he'd even be able to hack his way back in a second time without getting caught.

Nix couldn't risk that. He needed to make it into the King chatlog.

For Branwen.

No other messages came, but Nix knew the messenger hadn't abandoned him just yet. There was no explaining how, but he could practically feel the fiery lick of the gaze of whoever was commenting to him.

A commenter who'd also just offered him a coveted Favor...

How much time had passed since he'd sent that message?

Shit.

Nix dropped back down all the way, pressing his face into the cool star-studded comforter he'd picked out when he'd been fourteen and reached behind him. The moment he found his puckered hole, he pushed a finger through, gritting his teeth against the resistance. It wasn't his first time doing anal play, but in his haste not to lose this chance, he hadn't thought to lube his hand, and, though he was experienced, the last time he'd had sex was at least a year ago.

And it hadn't been any good.

He wiggled that single digit down past the first knuckle, letting out a harried breath as soon as it was inside, and then eased it back out slowly. He was so focused on the task he almost didn't register the sound of another ding, already corkscrewing his finger back in, this time successfully past the second knuckle, when he did.

Nix stilled again, unsure of what to do. His left hand was still working his dick, and the right was now bent behind him. If he wanted to read the message, he'd need to remove his finger, but if he did that, would the messenger get angry?

If that person made good on their threat and booted Nix from the app...

He was going to have to get up and check his computer, it was the only other option.

With a deep inhale to attempt to steady his racing heart, Nix lifted himself onto his knees and turned on the bed, careful to keep his finger lodged inside of himself. He wobbled a bit from the odd angle the second his bare feet touched the cold hardwood floor and leaned toward the computer to read the messenger bar to the right. The move brought his masked face closer to the camera, but he didn't allow himself to dwell on that.

The white half mask only covered his face from the top of his nose to his forehead, a dash of gold glitter embellishing the top.

Branwen's mask, which he'd found in her school backpack.

Maestro: You can do better than that.

Nix blinked at the comment and whoever Maestro was, they saw his reaction and replied again.

Maestro: My instructions were clear. I told you to fill yourself. Is this a joke to you, Songbird? Is a single finger really all you can take? This might not be the right place for you if that's the case.

Nix gulped and straightened. "Can I have a minute to grab something?"

The question was out of his mouth before he could help it, shocking him almost as much as it must have shocked his viewer because it took longer for him to respond to that than it had the other times.

Nix convinced himself he was only playing it safe by asking, by leaning into this mirage. Enigma was a sex app, after all, filled with forums and chatrooms carefully organized by kink. He'd scrolled through a few of them earlier, too much of a chicken to stop on any, but there were loads filled with BDSM and the like.

Maestro: Sixty seconds. Starting now.

He shot into motion, dropping both of his hands so he could reach under the desk and pull out one of his smaller suitcases his old roommate had shipped back from the university last week. When he'd initially left a month ago, it'd been with the intention of returning, but now...Now he had a new plan. A new goal.

Making it into the King chat was paramount to achieving it.

Nix almost sighed in relief when he finally found the small navy blue bag at the bottom of his suitcase, whipping it out and unzipping it in full view of the camera, completely forgetting it was even there in his haste. The pearly white dildo sprung free from the bag and he smiled in victory.

In a flash he was back on the bed, sprawled out on his back this time with his legs spread wide, his erect dick bobbing with his movements. He wasted a few precious seconds applying a hefty sum of lube to the toy before he brought it to his entrance.

Where he paused.

Again.

If a single finger had been too much, there was no way he'd be able to comfortably take the dildo, right? Not without some preparation. It was about an inch wide, so not that bad, but he hadn't used it in almost as long as it'd been since the last time he'd slept with someone...

The messenger app dinged, and somehow, his gut sank even before he turned his wrist and read it.

Maestro: No pain no gain. Prove to me you want it.

If he had the time to think about how ridiculous this all was, he'd probably laugh. He'd come home for a funeral, and yet here he was now, lying on his bed, dick wet and swollen, ass about to be filled with silicone, listening to the instructions of some faceless pervert on the other side of his computer screen.

Nix had never been all that interested in pain, in any capacity, but if that's what it would take to unlock Branwen's secrets…

…Did the band-aid method work on all things?

Time to find out.

With one hard shove, Nix forced the toy past that tight ring of muscle and cried out in agony at the intense sear of pain. He dropped back onto the bed, staring up at the ceiling as tears began to fill his eyes, stubbornly refusing to pull that intrusive rod out no matter how badly his body begged him to.

He breathed through it, waiting for his body to adjust.

He should have known his audience was too impatient for that.

When it dinged he almost pretended not to hear, but then lifted his right arm above his face to read it.

Maestro: You're bleeding.

"You *like* that," the accusation burst out of him before he could help it, the incredulity in his tone impossible to miss. But what kind of sicko got off on seeing a stranger bleed?

It was yet another reminder about the danger he was truly in. On the surface, this might just look like a sex app, but Nix wasn't a moron. No one went through these extreme lengths to cover up *nothing*.

Branwen wouldn't kill herself over nothing either.

Maestro: Should I come over there and give you a hand, Songbird?

"You don't know where I am," he hated that he sounded afraid and unsure but…This could literally be anyone.

Maestro: I could find you.

"I…" He licked his lips and urged his voice to steady when he said, "Demon Passing. The Night of the Nightshade. How about you find me then?"

It was risky, showing all his cards this early, before he'd even made it into the King chat, but missing this opportunity would be foolish. He was already here, on his back, taking a rubber cock for this Maestro person. Might as well go all in.

There was a moment where everything seemed to still as he waited for a response, but then—

Maestro: Fuck yourself hard and come screaming my name. Then, I might consider hunting you at the party.

The Night of the Nightshade was the most secretive event for Enigma, taking place only once a year. And one of the very few confirmed times every high-standing member met in person. He'd only been made aware of it because Bishops were given an invitation to try and prove their worth by making it into the King tier before then.

Whoever had pushed Branwen to the edge, they would be there.

"Deal." Nix didn't second guess his decision, dropping his arm so he could reach for his dick again.

Even though it still stung, he slid the dildo all the way out to its crown and then drove it back in, pounding his own ass in beat with the pumps of his fist on his glistening cock. He worked himself into a frenzy, grunts turning to sharp moans of pleasure as the pain dissipated and turned into skyrocketing bliss.

Fire licked across his skin and he broke out in a sheen of sweat, his heels bracing on the edge of the bed as he drew closer and closer to release. He kept his gaze downcast the whole time, watching himself in his hand to avoid looking up at the camera.

"I'm going to come! Maestro! I'm going to—" He managed to say it just in time, thick, creamy ropes of come spurting from his slit before he'd even fully finished speaking. He continued to ride the toy through it, ringing himself dry in the process until he was certain there was nothing left for him to give.

In a gasping heap, he fell on his back, his arms dropping at either side of his head. The dildo was still buried deep, but he didn't have the strength to reach down and remove it, focused instead on calming his breathing.

Nix had no clue how long he stayed like that, lying in his own mess, but when he finally peeled himself up, wincing when he sat on the end of the toy, the light indicating the chat was active was off on his computer.

He scrambled to his feet, legs giving out so that he crashed to his knees in front of his desk, the sting barely registering as he panicked and searched the chat.

Maestro was gone.

And he hadn't left any other comments after the last one.

Had...Had that not been good for him? Had Nix done something wrong? Had he blown his chance?

Tears brought on by frustration threatened to form, but before any of them could fall, his private messenger lit up.

Maestro: See you soon, Songbird.

It wasn't over. He was going to offer Nix another Favor. He squeezed his eyes shut, the mixture of anxiety and relief warring within him. He wanted this, needed it, but there was no telling what Maestro would ask of him next or even when that would be.

What if Nix was still a Bishop in three weeks when he entered Foxglove Grove?

Knowing there was nothing more he could do at this stage, he forced himself to shut the computer off and then stood to go clean up.

At least he was one Favor down. Only four more to go.

He was closer.

Become a Rook.

And then hunt a King.

CHAPTER 2:

The stares were nothing new. He hardly even noticed them anymore as he lounged in the high-back leather chair and closed the app on his multi-slate. Being watched sort of came with the territory, that was a big part of the reason he preferred lurking in the shadows more often than not.

But tonight wasn't about personal comfort. There was one reason and one reason only that he'd dragged himself all the way up Munin Mountain to Club Essential, why he'd chosen the third floor and seated himself at the very center of it, pretending not to hear all the hushed whispers coming from every corner.

Lake Zyair was here to be seen.

Having spent the past year on another planet, it was little wonder that every member in the place was staring at him. Rumor about the newly configured line of ascension would have spread like wildfire, and most of the club members were no doubt curious which side of the coin it was all going to land on.

He was the younger of two choices now, true, but he was also the best choice. The closest in line. Really, there shouldn't even be a debate over who was going to get the throne, but his uncle had caused a fuss and used Lake's absence against him—Of course, leaving out the part about how Lake hadn't been the one who'd wanted to leave in the first place.

However, he'd learned a lot while he'd been away on Vitality. Had no regrets.

"And so returns the wayward prince," the familiar voice, smooth and deeper than his own, came from the left a second before West appeared. His childhood best friend winked at him and dropped down into the chair next to his. He clinked the glass in his hand against the one Lake had left on the circular end table between them and then swallowed the contents in one gulp.

"I haven't been titled," Lake reminded, the word *yet* hovering in the air between them, unspoken, but clear.

Returning home early had been an annoyance, but getting to be with the two people who were more like brothers than friends to him? That made it all worth it. It felt pathetic and like bullshit, like a weakness to have missed anyone, let alone two people, but the three of them had been thick as thieves ever since they'd been little and were closer than blood.

West chuckled, then lifted his smoky gray gaze and set it over Lake's shoulder. "You're late."

Yejun, the final member of their group, dropped down with less class in the seat on Lake's other side. He leaned over Lake unapologetically and swiped his untouched glass, then sat back and sipped at the amber contents lightly before replying, "I was busy."

"Getting your dick wet, no doubt," West snorted. He slapped Lake's arm with the back of his hand. "You won't believe how much ass this guy has gotten while you've been away."

Away.

As if Lake had merely been on vacation.

To give himself a moment to bank down the spark of annoyance, Lake allowed his gaze to finally wander across the expanse of the room. It'd been a little over a year since he'd last stepped foot in Club Essential, but the bouncers had recognized him at the doors, his scan code had still worked, and every person there knew exactly who he was without having to be told.

A public announcement may not have been made—yet—but everyone knew what his return to the planet truly meant.

A changing of power.

A change grand enough to have Imperial Lake Zyair, fifth in line for the throne, giving up on his new life on the planet

Vitality. He'd spent the past thirteen months there, developing friendships and connections with the Vital Imperial family, even going so far as to become an official member of Kelevra Diar's Retinue.

Kelevra, Imperial *Prince* of Vitality. A title that would soon be attached to Lake's name as well. The friendship had been fruitful for the both of them, allowing them to create a political alliance between their two planets that otherwise wouldn't have been possible. In truth, he'd intended to stay another year at least, but then the deaths had happened, and the infiltration, and Lake had been given no other choice but to come home.

There were exclusive clubs on Kelevra's planet as well, but nothing like this. They had something similar in the sense that the Imperial family was forced to run the planet along with another party, but for them, that was the Brumal Mafia. For Tulniri, it was Club Essential.

The main hub of the club was built directly into the side of Munin Mountain, a sprawling natural stone structure covered in greenery. There were five levels in total, with the third level considered the leisure space. This area was where members could sit and relax, drink, or laugh with a friend. Share photographs of their last bloody kill or videos of their latest great fuck. The possibilities were endless, really. Lake had heard every story there was to tell in this very room growing up, ever since he'd been initiated at the age of thirteen.

It was expensive to maintain the yearly club membership fees, so faces came and went, but legacies such as himself and his friends were brought in. They didn't need to jump through the same hoops as the rest.

That sort of stature came with its own caveats, however.

From the views of the floor-to-ceiling glass walls, the capital city could be seen sparkling below, a fine layer of fog only helping to reflect the glittering lights. He knew from experience that if he moved to the window and peered down and out, he'd see the school.

"Are you all set for senior year?" Yejun asked, seemingly

reading his mind. When Lake glanced over at him, though, he merely stared back, patiently waiting for a reply.

Club Essential was considered a secretive society, not a secret one, since everyone on the planet knew how deeply rooted the club was in everything around them, from politics to clothing brands. Some members were obvious, like the Imperials and the dean of Foxglove Grove, though none of them would ever speak publicly of the club or admit to being a part of it. Still, due to the secret nature of it all, when one thought of an intricate, underground society, they most likely pictured someone like Yejun Sang.

At six feet three inches, he towered over most of the crowd. His hair was inky black and shone like pure silk. He never left the house without it styled, though the styles themselves varied depending on his mood.

When they'd been younger, he'd been the runt of the three of them. In elementary school, he'd even needed West's help against bullies on the playground. Now he was the tallest, though only by an inch, and with their reputations well known throughout, it was more likely he'd be the one doing the bullying.

Yejun grinned at Lake's obvious perusal of him, his full, cherry-red bottom lip stretching, showing off the snake bite piercings there, the jewelry the same shade as his hair and just as shiny. He had another black bar above his right eyebrow and a row of hoops on both ears. It wasn't his stature or his piercings that tended to stop people in their tracks, however. It wasn't even the mess of dark ink tattooed all over his arms and his neck.

Yejun Sang was gorgeous.

And the fucker knew it.

His face was what caught everyone's attention, tricked them into overlooking the rest of him. To give him a chance. He was the most charming of the three of them for that very reason, and he wasn't above using that charm to his advantage.

"Missed me, did you," he teased now, blowing Lake a kiss for good measure that had West instantly groaning and rolling his eyes.

Lake and Yejun hadn't ever hooked up past an exploratory kiss here and there in high school. Oh, and the time or two they'd exchanged hand jobs. But that was about it. They'd realized early on that sharing fuck buddies between them was much more enjoyable than potentially rocking the friendship.

What they had, what the three of them had, was stronger than anything. Even sex.

Which was saying a lot, considering how much sex played into the Club and its dealings.

"Man, don't feed his ego, seriously." West stood with a flourish and stabbed a finger toward their friend. "I wasn't kidding before. He really has slept with half the student body."

"If you'd stayed away a bit longer as planned," Yejun pretended to pout, "I would have succeeded in bagging them all before graduation. With you here?" He clicked his tongue. "You'll steal all the attention. At least you'll only take the men."

This time, it was Lake's turn to roll his eyes. "I'm not here for that."

"Well, sure," he agreed. "But it's not really like you have a choice?"

Right.

Eight years ago, they'd created the Enigma app with the secret intention of helping the Club.

This year, as seniors, they were finally going to be able to use it the way it was always meant to be used.

Others had already, of course. Those who'd come before them, but this was the first year in five that there were three legacy members up for ascension. Graduating from Foxglove Grove didn't just mean prestige, a foot in the door on the planet, and parts of the galaxy. It also meant gaining traction within the Club itself.

It meant a chance for a seat on the Order.

"We don't just have one task," West grumbled, clearly not happy about it. "We've got two."

"Don't tell me you forgot?" Yejun directed at Lake and

straightened in his chair, losing the playfulness he'd been purposefully laying on thick in an attempt to lighten the mood. He'd always hated being on this level of the club, preferring the penthouse or the lowest level where the private rooms and dancehall were located. "You do remember what we have to do this year, right? What our tasks are?"

"And that it has to be completed before Demon Passing," West added, sounding every bit as concerned.

The three of them hadn't really gotten the chance to talk privately since Lake had arrived last week, since he'd spent most of his time at the palace learning about the situation and giving reports on his time on Vitality. But the lack of faith here…

"Seriously?" He scowled at them.

"We're the Demons of Foxglove Grove," West said. "That comes with a certain—"

Lake held up a single hand and his friend instantly quieted, though it was clear by the way his gaze hardened he wasn't happy about it. Sometimes, the two of them butt heads about things. He'd been hopeful that would have changed since he'd been away for so long, but he should have realized old habits died hard.

West wanted to tell him off for pulling rank; that much was obvious, but he kept himself in check, either due to their friendship or the fact they were being so carefully monitored, and they well knew it. Every single member in this room would kill to run off to West's daddy and tattle about whatever detail they believed was worth it.

"I've been on the app since I got back," Lake told them. "It's good."

"Now that you're back, you can help with the screening process. Carry your weight," Yejun suggested with another grin.

"Weren't you just complaining about him taking all the prey?" West pointed out.

"There's plenty of ass to go around."

"We only need one," Lake stated, proving that he did, in fact, remember their task.

The rules were simple. To carry on the great legacy of Essential, every three years, the highest-ranking senior members of the prestigious Foxglove Grove would cultivate and offer up a sacrifice to the club.

This year, that honor fell to Lake, West, and Yejun.

"Essential is tied into everything on this damn planet," he continued, lowering his voice, gaze sweeping around them to ensure everyone was watching from a safe and respectable distance and couldn't eavesdrop. "Which means if I want that title, I have to first prove myself to the Order."

"Those stuffy old assholes wouldn't know a good time if it bit them on the ass and tried to plow inside," Yejun griped.

"Everything has to go perfectly," Lake insisted. "We can't afford any errors."

"The app should have been useful in helping you narrow things down."

Originally, they'd designed the app to be accessible only to students currently enrolled in the university, but over the years, the rules on that matter had been pushed and pushed until the waters had been muddied.

Now, anyone who'd graduated within the past twenty years, as well as anyone who worked with the school in any type of fashion—be it as a professor or merely on the board—could create an account. As far as Lake knew, there weren't many old-timers who'd taken that offer, but there were some. The Club itself offered more than enough entertainment in that department, which had helped, but still. The anonymous setup of the profiles had been great in the beginning, yet complicated things now that they had to actively screen out the older members who wouldn't make the cut.

The three of them had various tastes but similar types. Before, when the plan had been for Lake to remain off-planet for a while longer, it'd only been West and Yejun who'd had to worry about sharing the sacrifice between them. Lake's arrival meant one more opinion when it came to selecting someone from the masses.

At least there was comfort in knowing their tiered system held strong, even with all the other changes that had been forced by the Order. Not many ever made it to the higher levels, which helped narrow it down for them, as intended.

A lot of thought had been put into that system, and Lake and West were already pissed enough about how their rules had been altered and messed with to fit the needs of the Club outside of its initial purpose.

On the outside, it probably came off as pointless fun. Another way for the rich and elite to classify themselves. In reality, there were much darker and greater intentions behind the five tier system.

Pawn. Knight. Bishop. Rook. King.

To download the app, let alone create an account, one needed an invitation with an active QR code. The first two tiers were mere smoke screens, designed to trick less desirable users into believing Enigma was nothing more than another hookup app. Past that, things got interesting.

"We've got less than fifty Bishops," Yejun rattled off the numbers effortlessly. "Twenty-three Rooks. There are eleven Kings, including us."

"What are you thinking?" West asked. "Pick from the Bishops? It would simplify things."

Lake shook his head. "Too generic."

Yejun snorted. "When was the last time you checked their chatrooms? The freaks who congregate there are many things, but generic...I'm not sure it's fair to label them as such."

Lake quirked a thin brow. "Since when were we about playing things fairly?"

"So the Rooks then?" West hummed, considering it. "Twenty-three is more than enough for us to pick a good candidate."

"I don't want good," he said. "I want the best."

His friend frowned. "You want to sacrifice the best candidate for enrollment? Isn't that a waste?"

"We'll need followers," Yejun agreed with West. "The

students who've managed to find their way into the Rook and King chatrooms are clearly the most like-minded. They're already well suited for Essential just for that alone. The Order would agree. It's a guaranteed instant acceptance of our choosing. Is it worth throwing that away on an outdated ritual?"

Lake rapped his fingers against the leather armrest. "I've considered that. I have a plan."

"What plan?"

"Later." He stood with a flourish and adjusted the button of his vest, charcoal black with gold embellishments similar to the ones his friends wore. "Let's focus on one thing at a time."

West wasn't pleased with that answer. "We're in this together, remember?"

"Of course we are." Lake slipped his hands into his pockets and tipped his head. "If there's something you want to say to me, say it."

"Hey now," Yejun stepped between them with a forced laugh. "Let's not do this here, hmm? The Roost is ready for us to move in. Why don't we regroup there later? Foxglove reopens in a few weeks. It'll be best if we're already situated beforehand so we can get a head start on things."

Right, because now that they had a list of names, it was time for them to start making their way down it.

An image of a blond in a white mask gasping on sheets with ridiculous stars decorating them invaded his mind, and Lake willed his twitching cock to settle down before he got distracted.

Lake held West's annoyed gaze, the corner of his mouth lifting mostly because he knew that would only add fuel to his friend's internal fire. "By all means. It's not like I want to be smothered in that palace for another night when there are other options."

Sure enough, West's eyes narrowed. "Whatever."

Yejun tsked as West stormed off without another word, some gazes tracking him as he made his way across the thin black carpeted floor. "Don't take his surliness to heart," he said.

"He missed you, and he just doesn't know how to articulate that properly. He's always been shit with his emotions."

True.

But since Lake wasn't much better, he opted not to bother acknowledging that. Instead, he clapped Yejun on the back and motioned for him to lead the way, checking his multi-slate as they went.

He'd been there for a half hour.

That should be long enough to satisfy the Order and gain him Favor. And if not…

Fuck them.

Lake was back on Tulniri now, and he'd come with a plan.

"From here on out," he told Yejun as they passed at least a dozen members of Essential, "if we want something, we take it."

"What are you saying?" Yejun reached the door first and pushed it open, holding it with a shoulder for Lake, a wicked smirk on his face. "We're the Demons of Foxglove Grove. If we want something, it's already ours."

Lake chuckled.

"So," he asked once they'd started down the long, narrow hall toward the elevators, "got something in mind? What is it you want, Imperial-soon-to-be-only-in-line-for-the-throne?"

This time the devilish expression came from Lake.

"Everything," he admitted, staring at his murky reflection displayed across the golden surface of the closed elevator doors. "I want everything."

CHAPTER 3:

"How's it feel, Songbird?" the husky voice, now familiar to him after weeks of listening, came through the speaker of his computer where Nix had left it on the sink counter.

He was in the bathroom, inside the shower stall, with the curtain pulled back so the camera could catch all of him as he slicked soap suds down his torso and across his chest. It wasn't anywhere near as awkward as it had been that first time, his nerves better adjusted to being viewed by the stranger behind the screen.

Maestro had contacted him three more times since, once a week for the past three, always impossibly late at night. It was random days, and it'd gotten to the point where Nix would inadvertently lay awake in bed well into the early hours, anticipation and disappointment keeping him up in turns. He'd convinced himself it was because their situation was preferable. He needed to complete five Favors in order to move onto the next tier?

Might as well be with the same person.

Someone he'd developed some level of comfort with, as twisted as that sounded.

Maestro's Favors ranged in style and flare, but they were nothing crazy, nothing that involved bringing anyone else into things, which Nix appreciated. He'd also locked the chatroom, so it was only the two of them whenever they met like this, and insisted they switch to comms so Nix's hands would be free to do what he needed to please him.

Nix had no complaints. He'd been curious about Maestro's voice, hoping that alone would help him figure out the other man's age.

He sounded young, and even though that wasn't an accurate way to judge, Nix had chosen to believe it was the truth for his own peace of mind. At the end of the day, even if finding release was no longer a struggle for him, this was still what it was.

He was still masturbating in front of a stranger.

"It feels good," he replied, words echoing slightly in the shower stall. He'd remained home alone these past weeks, so there was still no fear of being overheard by his parents. They wouldn't be back until the day before he was set to leave, which suited him just fine at the moment.

He'd rather them not stumble on this and ask questions he couldn't answer. It'd been difficult enough to convince them transferring to Branwen's school was in his best interests instead of against. They thought he was merely grieving and making a rash decision.

They weren't entirely wrong, but even knowing that didn't change his mind.

His hand slid slowly, fingers trailing into the wiry hairs that led to his already aching dick, but a tutting sound came through the speakers, instantly giving him pause.

"Not yet," Maestro chided. "Tell me what the body wash you're using smells like."

"Orange and ginger."

A chuckle crackled from the computer. "Don't sound so eager, Songbird."

"Can't help it," he admitted, eyes slipping shut so he could block out reality a little better. In his head, he'd painted a million and one pictures of Maestro. Sometimes he was tall. Sometimes he had broad shoulders. Sometimes it was eyes as dark as night. Other times they were as blue as the sky in the middle of summer. But he was always around the same age.

Nix didn't really care that he was most likely way off base

looks-wise, but age…

The last thing he needed was to arrive at school next week and discover that one of his old and balding professors was the man who'd brought him to orgasm several times over. It was a risk he knew he was taking, one he couldn't get around, but for now, so long as he was able, he was going to allow himself to pretend.

Two more Favors. This one, and then one more and he'd have made it. He'd be crowned a King.

"What are you thinking about?" Maestro asked.

"You."

There was a pause and then, "Sometimes you say things and I wonder if it's all part of the act, or if you truly mean them."

Nix frowned. "This isn't an act."

"Right. Tell yourself whatever you need to, Songbird. But do it later. I think we've talked you up enough, don't you? Touch yourself for me. No—" his tone sharpened when Nix reached for his dick again, "—not there. You know where I want those long fingers of yours."

Nix nibbled on his bottom lip and turned around, presenting his rear to the camera before he leaned forward and pressed his forehead against the slick light gray tiles. His right hand wandered back, fingers tracing his crack before he found the right spot. At the first feel of his pointer prodding at his rim, he groaned.

"You have pretty hands," Maestro said. "Have I ever told you that before?"

He shook his head as he worked that finger inside and stared down at his weeping dick. He desperately wanted to stroke himself but knew doing so would earn him a scolding, so he refrained.

They'd settled into a silent agreement of sorts over the weeks. Nix did everything he could to please Maestro, and in return, Maestro took extra care to ease Nix into things. That's why they'd talked so much beforehand. The other guy didn't give a fuck what his body wash smelled like; he just knew Nix was still nervous in the beginning.

It was kind of sweet...Almost enough to trick him into the illusion that this was fully consensual and he wanted to be here.

Almost.

"Insert another finger, Songbird." The sound of a zipper going, followed by a sharp inhale filled the room.

He was touching himself.

He was touching himself to Nix.

Why was that so hot?

Another bead of precome spilled from his slit, plopping onto the shower floor between his feet, and Nix let out a whine even as he slipped in another finger. The stretch felt amazing, with no sting at all. Considering he'd done this even on the nights when Maestro hadn't contacted him, that wasn't surprising.

Before, he'd only managed to masturbate every now and again since he'd been living in the college dorms with a roommate. Since meeting Maestro, however, Nix hadn't gone more than a day.

He needed to earn that crown so he could put an end to this before he became some kind of sex junky.

Nix pulled his hand free and then shoved in three fingers at once, almost missing the dark laugh that came a moment later.

"Getting greedy already, Songbird?"

"Please." He wasn't sure he was speaking loud enough for the other man to hear, but it was taking all of his concentration not to reach for his dick right now.

"Please? Begging now, too?"

"You like it when I beg," he lifted his voice for that, somehow managing.

"That sounds like an accusation," Maestro said, but he didn't appear to be upset by it. "I also like how quick on the uptake you are. Should you be rewarded? Want to get off?"

"Good Light," Nix nodded, the steam from the shower and the way his balls were already drawn tight making the room spin slightly from the motion. "Yes. Please."

"Turn around for me, Songbird. I want to see the look on your face when you come on my order."

Nix didn't have to be told twice, twisting back around, those fingers burying in as deep as he could make them. His free hand went to his dick, giving one solid pump that had his hips thrusting forward and his skull hitting the wall with a hard whack he barely felt through his lust.

"Roll your thumb over your crown," Maestro instructed, humming in approval when Nix followed the command. "There you go. Do you need to be penetrated for a good orgasm?"

The question caught him off guard, and for a second, Nix faltered.

"I won't be angry with the answer, Songbird."

He licked his lips. "No. No, I don't need anal play to come."

"Is it preferred?"

"Are you asking if I'm usually a bottom?"

"I think our first time together gave that away already, don't you?"

Nix's cheeks stained pink, but with any luck, the other man would just think it was a flush caused by the shower. The water was still spraying over him, running down his chest, and vaguely, he wondered what he looked like. What did Maestro see?

Why did he feel like the answer to that was too much?

"Grab your balls," Maestro said suddenly. "Do it how you usually would. I want to see."

Nix pulled his fingers free from his hole and cupped himself, his left hand dragging down his length at the same time. He started pumping his fist as he lightly squeezed his balls, eyes closing again.

"Are you thinking of me, Songbird?"

"Yes." He was too far gone to feel embarrassed, his hips rocking forward to meet his hand as he picked up the pace. Maestro would probably go hard. He seemed like a rough lover.

"Wish I was there with you right now?"

Nix nodded and bit his bottom lip as a fresh gush of precome leaked from his tip at the thought.

"What would you want from me?" Maestro asked, a little breathier than before, reminding Nix that he was also jerking off wherever he was. "My mouth? Hmm? What about my fingers?"

"Your cock," Nix blurted, and it was so tempting to reach back and reinsert his fingers. He hadn't been lying before, but now that the thought had been implanted in his mind, it was impossible not to want it. Not to feel empty and needy. "I bet you're big."

Maestro snorted. "Gathered that from my voice, did you?"

Nix didn't answer, too busy picturing it. If Maestro were really here, he'd probably spin him around and fuck him against the wall, wouldn't he? He wouldn't be gentle or easy about it either. He might even make it hurt on purpose.

Later, once the high of arousal had left him, Nix would probably be mortified by these thoughts. In the past, pain had never been enjoyable to him. He'd never wanted to be taken by anyone, roughly or otherwise. Even when he had participated in sex, his lovers had been sweet with him, kind and caring. Thoughtful.

Maestro might ease him into things, but he was part of the King tier, which meant he'd done all sorts of deviant things to rise in rank.

Unlike Nix, who'd cheated by hacking the system.

"Why are you frowning, Songbird?" Maestro's somewhat displeased voice pulled him out of that rabbit hole.

Nix blinked open his eyes and landed them on the camera.

"You shouldn't be frowning while thinking about my cock," the man continued. "Unless you're worried you won't be able to handle it?"

"I..." He swallowed and grew silent, unsure how to answer that.

"Don't waste energy worrying about the inevitable. When it comes time for it, I'll spear through you the same way that silicone toy did our first time."

His hands stilled on his body, though his dick remained hard and leaky. "Wh-what?"

"You sound scared, Songbird."

Yeah, because he was.

Sort of.

Another part of him—a messed up part that had bought into this fantasy far too strongly—felt…excited.

There'd always been the chance he'd encounter Maestro on campus, even if the other man wasn't a professor. That they'd meet by chance and he'd recognize the sound of his voice or be recognized himself. Nix was still masked, but aside from the upper half of his face, Maestro had literally seen all of him.

But there was also the chance none of that would happen. That Nix would be ignored if they stumbled into one another. Enigma was meant to be anonymous and neither of them had agreed to meet in real life…

Sure, he'd just been imagining the other man would like it rough, but there was a big difference between a safe fantasy and being told point-blank what Maestro intended to do if they did run into one another on campus.

"Unfortunately, you've caught my interest. I like you, Songbird. Don't you like me?"

"I…" He wanted to say he didn't know him. Could he? Would that kind of honesty cost him his chances of moving up? He was so close…He couldn't throw it all away now by accidentally saying the wrong thing.

This was confusing though. In their past three meetings, Maestro had kept it casual. Hot and intense, but casual. This conversation felt the opposite of that.

"You will," Maestro finished for him, sounding more confident than Nix felt like he'd ever been about anything in his entire life. "I'm close. That frightened expression of yours seems to do it for me. Keep stroking. I didn't tell you to stop."

Nix hesitated.

"If I come before you, you won't get my Favor," he threatened. "You won't get to try your luck elsewhere either. I'll kick you from Enigma faster than you can blink. You come for me or you come for no one. Understood?"

The possessiveness had his dick straining and Nix found himself thrusting into his fist all over again, his motions sloppier than before. He pushed the fear away, focusing instead on the pleasure building and the sharp intakes of breath coming through the speakers that clued him in to the fact Maestro hadn't been kidding.

Would they come together?

"First chance I get, I'm going to bend you over my knee and make you sob, Songbird," Maestro warned. "Better hope I don't catch you in the middle of the cafeteria, otherwise we might end up with one hell of an audience."

"What?" Nix shook his head, but he didn't stop pumping.

"Not a fan of that idea? You're going to have to get over that. I've got plans, you see."

"I don't like...I'm not into exhibitionism." He left out the part about how he'd yet to agree to doing anything with Maestro in person.

"Don't worry, there are only two people in the world I'll share anything with, and neither of them are big on crowds either. At least," he seemed to reconsider his words, "they weren't before. Perhaps things have changed."

"I don't know what you're talking about," Nix admitted.

"If you hide behind this screen forever, you'll never get fucked by my cock," he said. "Imagine how good it'll feel when I tear through you. When I pound that sweet ass of yours so hard you scream. I'll pump you so full of my come, you'll feel it dripping out of you all day—"

Nix cried out as the orgasm hit him, strong enough he had to lean all the way back against the wall to prevent himself from crashing to his knees. His hole clenched down on nothing all the while, his dick shooting ropey streams across the shower stall and out into the bathroom.

Since when did dirty talk elicit such a strong reaction within him?

He came down slowly, his ears picking up on the sounds of the shower still going, and the soft snick of a zipper going back up. It was the latter that finally had him forcing himself to refocus, pushing off the wall only to wobble on his feet for a moment.

"Careful, Songbird," Maestro drawled, and when Nix lifted his head he sucked in a breath when he saw he'd somehow managed to shoot come all over his computer screen. "Wouldn't want you to hurt yourself before we have our chance."

"Chance?" he repeated dumbly.

"Bring the mask with you to Foxglove," he gave one last order and then signed off.

Leaving Nix shaking in the chilling shower spray with a mess to clean up and a cloud of uncertainty hanging over his head.

CHAPTER 4:

Foxglove Grove University was a grand school tucked on the outskirts of the capital city, directly beneath the massive rise of Munin Mountain. Technically, this wasn't Nix's first time visiting the campus, though he'd opted not to enroll the summer he'd attended the tour with his cousin.

He walked the familiar path that led through the heart of the main area now, his feet clicking lightly on polished black and gray cobblestone, eyes tracking his surroundings as he tried to place it all in his memory. Things hadn't changed, but since he'd already known the school wasn't for him, his mind had wandered early on in the tour.

Branwen hadn't felt the same. The entire flight back home, she'd gone on and on about how fantastic the school was. How it was like a tiny town all on its own. A world separated from the rest.

She hadn't been wrong.

On either side of him, buildings with large glass windows and iron embellishments towered, many allowing a view into classrooms and study areas. Students milled within, the golden lighting from the lamps illuminating them as they went about their business. The sky above was dark and gray, a light rain pattering down, bringing with it a chill cold enough to have Nix caving his shoulders inward.

The man at his side chatted on happily, seemingly unaffected by the weather as he led Nix through the main areas.

"This is the medicines library," Grady, Nix's new

roommate and self-proclaimed tour guide, tossed out an arm to the left, practically whacking into Nix in the process. "What did you say your major was again?"

"Computer science." Most of Nix's credits had fortunately transferred over. There were a couple of general education classes that hadn't made the cut, but so long as his core classes counted, he wouldn't lose time, at least.

"Right," Grady snapped his fingers and carried them on their way. "You won't be needing that library then. Best just to avoid it altogether. Some of the med students are dicks. High stress majors will do that to people. Speaking of, computer science is rather competitive at the moment. Why would you choose to transfer universities in your final year? Seems like social suicide."

Nix flinched but his new roomie didn't notice.

"Have you thought about joining any clubs?" Grady asked next.

Nix slipped his hands into the front pockets of his jacket and debated whether or not to show the app on his multi-slate. It may be too soon. At the end of the day, Enigma was a hookup app to the majority of the students, and while sex was a fairly open topic on their planet, the university also boasted a mixed student body. There were many who came from other planets, and even galaxies, to attend Foxglove Grove. Some of them would no doubt arrive from cultures and societies where talk of pleasure and sexual acts were taboo. He couldn't announce to Grady he was into that sort of thing within an hour of their very first meeting.

He'd have to wait, find the right time or look for some sort of in. From the research he'd done, Nix had discovered that at least a third of the student population had an account on Enigma, but that didn't mean they were all active or that Grady was one of them.

If Grady found the whole hookup culture dumb or distasteful, Nix would be shooting himself in the foot right out the gate. Ideally, he'd like to do this without involving anyone else, but logically, he understood there was no guarantee. If he needed Grady's help for some reason in the future, it was best not to burn that bridge beforehand.

Besides, it wasn't like Nix was an expert on sex apps. Before now, he'd never even used a dating app, let alone one meant specifically for purely sexual encounters.

His mind wandered to last week. He hadn't heard from Maestro since. It was a bit of a bummer since he'd been hopeful he could make it to the final tier before his arrival to school. Even after that odd conversation with the other man, Nix had still thought there was a chance it was all part of the game.

He'd been wrong though, hadn't he? His gaze wandered around the area, taking in all of the students milling about even though it was the first day.

Who was Maestro?

Was he one of them? Was he watching even now?

Nix almost laughed at himself. It wasn't like the guy knew what he looked like. It'd been all talk. There was no reason to worry about actually running into him. The only thing he should be afraid of was not being able to get that final Favor.

If he didn't hear from Maestro soon, he was going to have to try entering the forums again. Maybe he'd get lucky a second time and attract another king. It would be awkward all over again, having to be sexual in front of yet another stranger, but he could do it.

He'd have to.

Nix shook his head, not wanting to go there.

"—avoid the Demons if you're smart," Grady said, the tail-end of whatever advice he'd been giving shooting through Nix's distracted state.

"What?" He came to an abrupt stop, and his roommate turned with a furrowed brow.

"The Demons?" Grady must be repeating. "Better known as the Demons of Foxglove Grove." His eyes narrowed slightly. "You weren't listening at all, were you."

"Are they really called that?" Bit on the nose if you asked

Nix.

"Don't let anyone else see you make that face," Grady warned, stepping closer as though to shield Nix from any prying gazes from other students.

They weren't alone on the path, but due to the sprinkle of rain, there weren't many others standing around them.

"The Demons are treated more like gods here," he continued, voice lowering into practically a whisper. "And this year's group is the worst. They're childhood friends who came from prestigious families. They practically own the school *and* the town."

Nix cocked his head. "You sound scared of them."

"Yeah, because I'm smart. You've got top marks," he poked him in the center of the chest, "you should be, too. They're super popular, but nothing good ever comes from drawing their attention."

"So, they've got a lot of friends." Were those the people Nix was looking for? Should he speak to them about Branwen? He needed to interact with the people she'd been close with, and if these Demons knew everyone, maybe they'd have an idea what social circles she'd hung out in.

"Uh, no," Grandy corrected, heaving a breath of frustration when this time Nix was the one to frown. "They don't have friends. Look, I don't know how things went at your last school, but here, there's a hierarchy. The Demons? They're top of the food chain. And the rest of us? We're just here to make them look good to the planet and the universe."

Foxglove Grove was the second most prominent school in the galaxy, coming in only behind Vail University, which was located on the planet Vitality. Many students traveled galactically to enroll in either, though the history at Foxglove was older and richer. In comparison to its thousand years of existence, Vail was a baby.

Maybe that's why it was doing better. Those in charge of Vail were able to present fresh perspectives on how to run things, whereas Foxglove was still too rooted in tradition and heritage.

Case in point, these Demons having run of the place simply because of their bloodlines.

Grady seemed to finally notice they were standing in the rain and reached into the pocket of his yellow raincoat and pulled out an umbrella in the same color. "You should invest in one. It rains a lot here."

"Right." He'd had that in his pocket this entire time?! Nix would have said something, but then his roommate opened it and stepped closer so they could share and he decided to bite his tongue. "Thanks."

"No problem." Grady was already distracted again, glancing every which way as though trying to decide where to lead him next. There was a crossroads in the path up ahead, and if they went straight, they'd be heading closer to the impressive mountain. "Are you hungry?"

He started to veer them right, and Nix followed with a shrug.

"We've got a convenience store and two cafeterias on campus," Grady said. "The smaller one is free for all, but Café Soul is only for upperclassmen."

"Which one are we going to now?"

"The smaller one," he told him. "We just call it the cafeteria. If you say that's where you're going, everyone will know what you mean."

"Why? Is the other one the only one with a name?"

"Pretty much."

"Aren't we upperclassmen?" They were both seniors.

"Yeah, but take it from me. Avoid Café Soul if you can. That's where the Demons and all their groupies hang out."

Nix blew out a breath. "This is all sounding very cliché rich kid." He hesitated before asking, "Did they do something to you?"

"Me?" He shook his head vehemently. "No."

Nix wasn't satisfied with that response. With the way he was talking about them, it was clear Grady's animosity toward the Demons was personal. "A friend of yours then?"

His new roommate turned toward him too quickly, knocking his foot against the edge of the path. He tripped, careening backward, the umbrella going with him.

Nix tried to grab onto him, but it all happened too quickly, as if it were a scene from a bad movie.

Grady stumbled a few steps, the umbrella whacking backward as his arms floundered.

Smacking right into a tall blond's face.

"Light," Grady righted himself and started to turn, "I'm so sorr—" the apology died on his tongue with a strangled gurgle that had Nix frowning.

The blond still had his head turned away, a red line on his left cheek from where one of the tips of the umbrella had clearly scraped across his skin. He wasn't carrying anything to protect himself from the light drizzle, the shoulders of his black blazer sprinkled in water droplets.

Behind him, two other guys watched with curiosity, the easy ways in which they held themselves doing nothing to mask the fact they were actually poised and ready to strike at any given moment.

One had a buzz cut, the fuzz of his hair dyed a snow-white shade that didn't match his dark brown eyebrows. He had on a black bomber jacket with white sleeves, which was worn over his standard-issue uniform. The school's crest, depicted in a circular pin, was stuck off-center on his leather belt, which hung low on his hips.

The other one had longer hair that looked like spilled ink, especially right now with it slightly damp from the rain, strands sticking to the rise of sharp cheek bones. It wasn't that long, just long enough for him to pull it back into a small bun at the back of his head, and was probably the least distracting thing about him. Tattoos marked the exposed skin of his hands and his neck, the rest covered by his uniform and leather jacket. He had more facial jewelry in than Nix had the time to count.

They were both eyeing Grady down as if they pitied him,

the slight upward curve of their cruel lips the only indicator that was also a lie.

Nix could recognize predators when he saw them. Bullies were nothing new to him, though he himself had never had to deal with that sort of thing at any extreme type of level. It was so obvious looking at these three now that they'd be good at that sort of thing.

Good at tearing others down.

Sure enough, Grady caved in on himself as though trying to make himself smaller and took a deliberate step back toward Nix. His head bowed, gaze set on the wet cobblestones as if making eye contact would cause him to spontaneously combust or something.

"Lake," Grady stuttered when he spoke to the blond, wringing his hands in front of himself. "I'm so-sorry. It's my fault. I wasn't watching where I was going. Please accept my apology."

The ensuing silence was deafening.

"I…" Grady swallowed and tried again. "Really. I'm sorry. Are you okay? Should we go to the nurses?"

The one with the buzz cut snorted and covered his mouth to hide the smirk. When he noticed Nix had caught him, he tipped his chin. "What are you looking at?"

It was so tempting to call them assholes to their faces, but Nix refrained. He was here for Branwen. If he got off on the wrong foot on day one, it would make things so much more difficult for him than it needed to be. In order to find answers, he needed to be able to talk to people, and something told him if he rubbed these guys the wrong way, most of the student body would react the same way Grady was now.

In fear.

"Let's go." He grabbed Grady's elbow and tried to move them around the three guys.

He should have known it wouldn't be that simple.

The one with the tattoos stepped in their way and let out a low whistle. "Come on now. Don't be like that. We're not the ones in the wrong here, are we?"

"He already said he was sorry," Nix stated, losing some of his patience. He swallowed the rest of his irritation down and straightened his spine. "It was an accident."

"Nix," Grady said his name quietly, pulling his arm free and giving him a small shake of his head.

"You should listen to your friend, *Nixie*," the guy with the buzz cut suggested a second before his eyes narrowed. "Wait. I don't think I've seen you before."

The one with piercings gave him a slow once over. "Nope. He's new."

Suddenly, Lake was standing in front of him, hand capturing Nix's jaw to force his gaze up. There was only a couple of inches difference between them, but when their gazes locked, it felt like he was being peered down upon by a giant.

The sheer intensity of it cut off anything he would have said, and the most he even managed to struggle was to wrap his fingers around Lake's wrist. And that was it.

For a charged moment, no one spoke and Nix felt himself locked in, caught up in the green of the other man's eyes. Almost like freshly sprouted grass. Or the leaves of a tree kissed by the sun. Or—

He stopped himself.

What the actual fuck?

Nix yanked Lake's hand away and took a step back, forcing himself to glare even though all of his instincts were screaming at him to follow Grady's lead and tuck his tail. He'd never been the type to cower, though, and he didn't intend to start now.

"What's your problem?" he asked, voice clipped. He was grateful he'd managed to keep it steady and not give his frayed nerves away. If he focused on it, he could still feel the lingering sensation of those warm fingers at his chin...

He'd never felt chemistry like this before, instantaneous and raw. Why the hell did it have to be with this guy, of all people?

Lake continued to stare at him wordlessly for a while, and

then he tipped his head, signaling his friends. It appeared as though he was going to leave it there, but after only a couple of steps he paused. "Did you remember to bring it?"

Nix felt the entire world tip on its axis at his voice.

The same voice he'd listened to during his most intimate moments.

At his shocked expression, Lake chuckled darkly, the sound lacking any thread of kindness.

"See you soon, Songbird." He didn't turn back or add anything else, merely started down the path with his friends on his heels.

There was no way...

Nix must look foolish, standing there with his mouth open, staring at the retreating backs of the Demons of Foxglove. But he couldn't help it. Couldn't even bring himself to care what the other students—some of whom had somehow noticed the commotion outside and were standing by various windows in surrounding buildings watching—thought of him.

Only one person had ever called him that before, but there was no way...

What were the odds that Lake, of all people, was Maestro?

CHAPTER 5:

Maestro: The Roost. 5 PM.

Nix reread the message for the hundredth time and then dropped his arm and stared at the impressive building in front of him. He'd learned about the Roost during his tour yesterday with Grady, but they hadn't gone near it, especially since after their encounter with the Demons, Grady had put a swift end to their trip and retreated back to their dorm room.

He hadn't liked that Nix seemed to know Lake, even after Nix had explained they didn't really know each other. Now he had to worry about his suspicious roommate on top of everything else, and he couldn't even be mad about it. It wasn't like there'd been a way of this working where he could have avoided interacting with Maestro through the app. Nix had needed those Favors.

Still needed one.

Which was why, despite all of his instincts screaming at him to turn heel and run in the other direction, he was here. Standing outside the Roost, better known as the dorm of the Demons.

Not that it could be considered a dorm in any sense of the word.

Admittedly, he was a little bit awed by the architecture of the place and was using that as an excuse to linger outside, putting off the inevitable down to the last second. It was a believable thing to be distracted over, at least.

The Roost was built at the base of Munin Mountain, a

river flowing from somewhere further away, trailing beneath the front porch. It was at least three stories high, with tall glass windows set in metal frames. The second level had a wraparound balcony, and a tower of sorts was in the back, partially connected to the mountain's rock. Moss and ivy grew around the structure, and tiny red flowers with glowing centers flickered like miniature flames, sprouting seemingly at random.

Nix tipped his head all the way back and took a step to the left, catching sight of the edge of a massive building much higher and mostly out of view. The Essential Club. It couldn't be a coincidence that both it and the Roost were housed on the same mountain.

Everyone on the planet knew about the Club Essential, even Nix who'd grown up on the other side of the world. Though it was a hush-hush society, their hands were in every aspect of the planet's functioning. Government, agriculture, commerce, entertainment...You name it, there was no doubt a club member was involved in some way, shape, or form.

He glanced between the corner of the metal structure high in the sky and the intricate building before him.

What were the odds these two things weren't connected?

They were clearly members of the club, that went without saying. Lake Zyair was an Imperial who had a real chance at the throne, after all. It'd be impossible for him not to be a part of Essential.

Yesterday, after running into them and realizing who Lake was, Nix had spent some time carefully combing over all of the public information about the three he could get his hands on. There was a ton of it, but it was hard to tell how much was fact and how much was smokescreen. People with money could make up stories and hide the truth as easily as snapping their fingers.

From what Nix was able to glean as a definitive fact, Lake's parents had died when he was younger, and he'd moved into the Corleone residence. He, West, and Yejun had been together throughout their entire childhoods, up until a little over a year ago when Lake had suddenly enrolled in Vail University on the planet Vitality. His return most likely had something to do with the fact the Emperor and her Royal Consort had just passed suddenly.

Grady hadn't been kidding when he'd called the Demons kings yesterday, either. It wasn't just on campus. From what Nix could find, it appeared as though Lake and his friends were revered—and feared—throughout the capital.

And Nix was the idiot who'd accidentally gotten involved.

Shit.

The sky was already gray, a light pattering of rain falling down, and he knew his time was up. A wooden bridge led from the walkway to the porch, and Nix started over it, gripping the handle of his yellow umbrella tightly. Only a single light was left on, hanging over the front door. He tried to peer through all the glass siding, but all he could make out were various furniture shapes and darkness.

He lifted his fist to knock, but there was a click and then the door swung inwards on its own. Creepy. But not enough to scare him off.

Yet.

Stepping beneath the threshold, Nix gave himself a moment to adjust to the poor lighting, trying to map the large space but unable to make out much of anything. Then he placed his umbrella by the door and took another tentative step forward.

The flick of a lighter across the room had him jumping slightly, eyes catching sight of the bottom half of a face as whoever it was stuck a cigarette between their lips. They snapped the lighter shut almost as quickly as they'd lit it, but Nix could make out their outline now.

"Lake?" He cleared his throat and moved closer, careful so as not to trip or walk into anything.

The man was sitting, the ember of his cigarette acting like a beacon for Nix.

"Can we turn a light on?" he dared ask, growing more

and more uncomfortable with each passing breath. He'd been worried about this meeting already, but now, met with darkness and a mysterious figure who'd yet to speak, he was starting to really wonder if he was a moron for coming.

If not for that one Favor and the intense curiosity he felt toward Maestro, he certainly wouldn't have.

"I'm disappointed, Songbird," Maestro's voice came from the left, and Nix startled a second before strong hands captured him from behind.

He was shoved forward, yelping when his knees banged into the edge of a table. There wasn't time for him to curse though, his body forced over a flat surface. He tried to fight back, but the shock of it all cost him, and a moment later, the lights flashed on all at once, blinding him.

"I was able to recognize you instantly." Maestro—Lake—stepped into view. He was standing behind a long leather couch that didn't have any armrests. His knit black uniform shirt was unbuttoned all the way down to mid-chest, and when he propped his hands on the back of the couch, it caused the material to open further.

His expression was cold, inscrutable. He was attractive, probably the most attractive individual Nix had ever seen, but it was impossible to miss the hint of arrogance and the flicker of malice that seemed to waft off of him.

As far as looks went, he was better than Nix had even imagined.

As for everything else…

He shivered.

With the lights on, he was able to make out how big this area of the house truly was. Out the windows nearest, rockface and plant life could be seen. The sound of trickling water from somewhere nearby filled the otherwise silent room, and the smell of cedar and moss mixed with a strong cologne tickled at his nostrils.

Nix had his head pressed against the slick surface of a coffee table that rested only a foot or so off the ground. Whoever had pinned him had a knee planted firmly on his back. He tore his gaze off of Lake and up, needing to see who it was sitting in the chair.

West Corleone stared back at him, still absently smoking the cigarette as if his large presence wasn't already threatening enough.

That must mean the one holding him down was Yejun Sang. The third Demon of Foxglove Grove. It was tempting to greet him just to be a smart ass, but Nix's survival instincts, fortunately, were in full operation and kept him quiet.

"You sure this is him?" Yejun asked, tugging Nix up by the collar of his shirt, ignoring when that forced the material in front to tighten over his throat. "He doesn't look like much."

Nix ground his teeth when he was shoved back down.

"I don't know," Lake drawled, and there was a hint of something in his tone that had Nix's entire being going on high alert. "Let me double-check." His eyes met Nix's. "Strip."

He sucked in a breath, sure he'd misheard. "What?"

Lake flicked a wrist at Yejun. "Help him."

"Wait, no, don't!" Nix clawed at the edge of the table to try and get away, but Yejun's hands hooked into his pants and tore them down his legs along with his boxers. He cried out when he was grabbed by the back of his shirt and pulled onto his knees, whipping his elbow behind him.

He connected with Yejun's jaw, spinning to kick out while he had the chance. He'd managed to make it off the table and onto his feet before West was suddenly on him.

West lifted him and spun his body as though Nix weighed nothing, slamming him chest first back down against the solid table lengthwise. He covered him, waiting for Yejun to take over before he moved to capture Nix's wrist. As soon as he'd removed his multi-slate, he dropped back into the leather chair he'd been sitting in and pulled a laptop off the wooden block that acted as an end table.

Nix's face burned as his shirt was torn off of him and he was left completely naked. They'd even taken his socks and shoes.

Yejun straddled his back to keep him down, leaning over to see his face. He whistled. "Embarrassed already? How does someone like you think you'd make it with Enigma? You can't even handle this?" He reached back and slapped Nix's bare ass hard enough for him to jerk.

"Get off of me!" Nix floundered, even knowing there was no way he was a match for even one of them, let alone three. He wasn't small by any means either, but these guys...He was starting to see why they were called Demons. "This is illegal!"

West chuckled and Yejun winked down at him.

Lake started around the couch, catching Nix's attention, and he froze all over again.

"What are you doing?" Nix demanded the second Lake disappeared from view, only for Yejun to shush him.

"We ask the questions here..." He paused and turned to Lake. "What did you say his name was again?"

"Phoenix Monroe," West answered for him, reading off his ID on his device as he broke into it.

"What?" Yejun snorted. "What a stupid name."

"It's Nix," he corrected, only for the man to dig his knee in harder.

"Yeah, that's not much better. That why you did it? Mommy and daddy gave you this stupid name and you foolishly thought it meant you had more than one life?"

Nix frowned. Was he mocking him because of his name, really? Phoenixes died and were reborn, sure, but no one would actually believe being named after one would pass on that trait. It seemed like an unnecessary and almost childish jab until it hit him what was really going on here.

He gasped when strong hands pushed against his inner thighs, spreading his legs wide so that they hung off the sides of the table. Nix bucked, but Yejun let out a hoot as though it were a fun game they were playing, and Lake, who was now leaning over Nix's private parts, merely hummed.

"It's him," he told his friends.

"Of course you'd recognize him by asshole," West stated.

"Or is it his cock and balls?" Yejun shifted, planting a palm down on Nix to keep him in place even when he climbed off and turned to take a look himself.

"Please." Nix buried his head in his arms. "Please stop."

"He doesn't like an audience," Lake said.

"Where's the audience?" Yejun asked, only to make a sound of understanding a second later. "Oh. You mean us. This is nothing. Wait until the Order gets their hands on you. That'll be something."

"If he's the one we're looking for," Lake corrected.

"What do you mean?" Yejun frowned. "You said—"

West swore, interrupting. "It's not him."

There was a moment of silence and then Yejun asked, "What do you mean? How could it *not* be him?"

"He skipped over all of the tiers." Lake moved from between Nix's thighs and over to where West was sitting, dropping an arm over the back so he could stare down at the screen. He frowned at whatever he saw there.

"He did," West agreed. "But he's not our guy."

"Bullshit." Yejun sprung up, forgetting all about containing Nix in his burst of annoyance.

Nix took the opportunity, scrambling up and stumbling back off the table. He didn't make it far, however, only a few retreating steps before Lake lifted his head and caught him with a warning gaze that instantly had him stilling like a deer in headlights.

"Stay right there, Songbird," Lake commanded in that same low, silky tone he'd always used as Maestro.

It licked over Nix's skin in the way it was no doubt meant to, and he found himself paralyzed and enthralled all at the same time.

"Wow, got him trained already?" Yejun asked, snapping Nix out of it enough to send him a glare. "Or not."

"He is a hacker," West told them, clicking away at his keyboard as he did, "but not the one we're looking for."

"How do you know?" Yejun insisted.

"His signature is different."

"So, Songbird hacked into the app but had nothing to do with the break-in at the club?" Yejun held up his hands when this time Lake was the one narrowing his eyes at him. "Sorry, *Nix*. Damn."

"Break-ins?" Nix asked. When all three of them looked his way, he said, "I had nothing to do with that."

"He's got skills," West said then. "According to this, he managed to hack my programming in four days and seventeen hours." He sent Nix an impressed glance. "What's your major?"

"Um, computer science."

"And you clocked Yejun pretty good just now with that elbow."

"Dude, really?" Yejun said, affronted.

"You're a senior, yeah?" West nodded to himself before Nix could answer. "We'll have classes together for sure. You're skilled enough to have tested into Professor Adair's Advanced Algorithms Thursday slot."

"I…did." Nix cleared his throat. "This is very weird, and also," he motioned down at himself, not bothering to hide his junk since he'd been standing there naked all this while already anyway, "what the fuck?"

"Oh, don't mind him," Yejun clapped West on the shoulder. "He just wants to have sex with your brain right now, that's all."

"It's hot," West agreed, as though that sentence made any kind of sense. Which it did not.

Nix turned to Lake. "Please, what is going on?"

"There've been a few security breaches at the Club House the past few months," Lake surprisingly explained. "We've been tasked by the people in charge to find the hacker responsible."

The Club House? They must be referring to that big building on the side of the mountain where Club Essential had its home base.

"And you thought that could be me?" He blinked. "I only

just got here yesterday."

"Whoever tried to break in is virtually untraceable, but we determined they'd used the Enigma app. You were clearly new to it and uncomfortable being sexual in front of someone else—not a trait of someone who'd been a user long enough to climb up to the Bishop tier. You also said things that led me to believe you could be trying to get closer to me."

"Yeah," Nix snapped. "Because I needed your Favors in order to rise higher."

"And," Yejun crossed his arms, "why exactly is that? No offense, but you're kind of a prude, Firebird."

"He's right." West stopped whatever he was doing on the computer. "Why'd you want in so badly? It's definitely not to fuck."

Nix winced at how blunt that was.

"You're going to want to answer," Lake suggested. "Otherwise you won't like what happens next."

"I get the feeling," he stupidly said, "I'll feel that way no matter what."

"Told you he was smart," West grinned.

Yeah, Nix had totally been right about Foxglove Grove being a hellhole better left alone.

CHAPTER 6:

If at any point in his life, someone had told him there'd come a time when he'd be naked in the middle of a massive living room, being leered at by three of the richest men on the planet, he would have laughed in their face.

Honestly, it was tempting to laugh still over how absolutely ridiculous this all was, but the fear and that never-ending swirl of curiosity that always haunted him kept him from doing so.

Nix needed to come up with a plan, but his brain was struggling and he was starting to get chilly. He quickly sorted through the information he had, though it wasn't much. They were looking for someone who'd gone against the super-elite club they were all a part of and had mistaken him for that person.

Okay.

Now they knew Nix was not in fact who they were looking for.

Good.

But West had confirmed what Lake had already suspected, and they knew Nix had still hacked into their systems. Obviously, there was more to the app, just as he'd supposed from the start. Somehow, the app and the club were linked. Therefore, even if it wasn't anything as serious as trying to break into the club itself, messing with the app was still pretty bad. Right?

Of course.

They wanted to know why, and it'd certainly be easy enough to explain, to tell them all about Branwen and his secret mission to find out who had pushed her to the edge. Only…What if it'd been them?

If Lake was a King on the app, it was safe to assume the other two were as well. All Nix had to go on was his cousin had been speaking with a King before her death.

If he tipped his hand now, he may never get answers.

Lake was too observant, though. If Nix fully lied, he'd catch on and then…Well. That part was less clear, but considering he'd already allowed Yejun to forcefully strip Nix *and* inspect his ass, whatever came next couldn't be good.

So, as close to the truth as he could manage without giving himself away. He could do that.

Hopefully.

"I did it for fun," he said, swallowing when it was clear none of them believed that. "Seriously. I knew I was transferring here, and when I heard about the app, I was curious."

"And you just decided to hack in and play around… because?" Yejun asked.

"I'm a senior this year," Nix replied. "I didn't think I'd have time for the other tiers, and I wasn't planning on staying on it long term."

"No?" Lake's eyes narrowed.

"No."

"Then why do it at all?"

"I told you," he repeated. "For fun." This wasn't going to work. He needed to give them more. He dropped his gaze and crossed his arms, allowing himself to look meek on purpose. "My cousin died recently. They left me a note."

"A note?" West tilted his head, and Nix could tell this part he was starting to buy into.

"Yeah," he nodded. "I've been a straight-A student all my life. I don't have many friends back home. Most of my time was spent studying."

"That's why you're so good with computers."

"Probably. I've been learning since I was ten so." He shrugged. "Anyway, my cousin told me they wanted me to be different this year. To...try and break out of my shell or whatever. Since it was their dying wish…" He let his words trail off. "It's stupid."

"That part isn't," West said, "but messing with my programming? That was next-level idiotic." He seemed to be considering something for a moment before he snapped the laptop shut with a loud click and put it back on the end table. "I can think of a few ways you can make it up to me though."

"Excuse me?" Lake straightened behind his chair and slid his hands into his front pockets. The silent warning he sent down at his friend was somehow deafening.

"What? You don't expect me to just let him get away with it, do you?"

"Please," Nix felt panic sink its claws back into him, "I didn't mean anything by it. Really."

"I believe you," West reassured, but before he could feel any sort of relief in that, added, "But it doesn't mean shit to me. Actions have consequences, Nixie. Demons don't forgive. You want to walk out of here and let bygones be bygones? You're going to have to pay the price for your deception."

Nix cast a pleading look to Lake.

Lake was clearly the one in charge here. If he told his friend to forget it—

"All right," Lake said, and Nix felt the floor drop out from under him. "I set the terms."

West seemed like he wanted to argue but then agreed with a single shoulder shrug.

"One final Favor," Lake held his gaze, "isn't that right, Songbird? That's all you have left to earn that crown you wanted so badly."

"You're not really thinking about giving it to him?" Yejun asked incredulously, then laughed when he took in Lake's expression. "Well damn." He tipped his head at Nix, eyes dropping to his dick. "I mean, he's got a hot body, sure, but is it worth all that?"

Despite his earlier thoughts, Nix moved his hands in front of his junk, earning a chuckle and another wink from Yejun.

"You do the Favor," Lake continued. "You enter the King tier. And you stay there for the rest of the year. Understood?"

Right, because Nix had lied about wanting to achieve it just for shits and giggles. He couldn't understand what possible reason Lake could have for wanting to order him to stay on the app, but that wasn't the main issue right now.

Did he lie and say he wanted nothing more to do with them or their app? Or did he play into this and potentially tip his cards? They'd obviously be able to tell he wanted it if he agreed too easily, but…If he missed this chance and Lake changed his mind and kicked him out after all he'd never get answers.

Become a King.

Hunt one down.

Avenge Branwen.

He was so close to the next step. Was he really going to give it all up because of a silly thing like pride?

"What—" he paused and licked his suddenly dry lips, "What's the Favor?"

Lake moved so he was fully behind West and then clapped both hands down on his shoulders. "Suck his dick."

Oh.

"Don't look so disappointed, Nixie," West drawled, already reaching to undo his fly, as though Nix had already agreed and this was a done deal. "I promise it'll be *fun*."

He flinched. He'd been hopeful that Lake would make him do something with him. Even in front of the others, he probably could have handled that, but to do something so intimate with a stranger…

How was Lake any better, he scolded himself. Nix hadn't even known he was Maestro all this time. Everyone in this room was a stranger, whether he liked it or not.

And, whether he liked it or not, he was going to have to do this.

"I do this," he directed the question to Lake, "and we're even?"

"If you're asking if you're forgiven," he corrected, "sure. There's nothing that ties you to the hacks into Club Essential. The app is just a pet project of ours. Something to pass the time with."

"You're not a threat," Yejun translated for him, "is what he's saying." He moved closer, holding up both his hands in a sign of surrender a second time when that had Nix instantly retreating. "Relax, Firebird, I'm just getting comfortable so I can enjoy the show."

He sneered before he could help it.

"Is that a problem for you?" Lake asked.

"We share everything," West told Nix, slipping his pants down to his ankles to expose his semi-hard cock. He grabbed onto himself and began stroking, smirking when that had Nix's eyes going wide. "Ever sucked a fat one before, Nixie?"

Lie or tell the truth?

He looked to Lake who was watching him far too closely for his liking.

"Yes," he admitted.

"Perfect," West motioned him closer with his other hand, "then get over here and show me what you got before I decide to ask for something more than a blowjob. Feel fortunate that I'm the only one here who didn't take a peek at that sweet ass of yours. Maybe that's the only reason I'm willing to settle."

Nix couldn't believe he was about to do this. He moved slowly around the coffee table, movements jerky and awkward, but if any of them noticed, they collectively chose to go easy on him by not pointing it out.

Easy on him.

Yeah right.

Even still, there were only so many steps between them, and once he got there, Nix hesitated.

"Don't be such a little bitch." West reached out and latched onto Nix's wrist, yanking him down onto his knees between his spread thighs.

All the while, Lake stood behind him, towering over his friend, staring down at Nix with unblinking green eyes. Yejun was also watching, but it was different—and not only because he already had his dick in his hand was stroking himself.

There was an intensity to Lake, a darkness that warned things could go from bad to worse if Nix chose not to cooperate. It was the fear of finding out how that could be that finally spurred him into motion.

West's cock was thick with a slight curve. He was big, but Nix could almost wrap his hand around it. It felt hot to the touch, already slick from the precome West had rubbed over himself, and when Nix gave a tentative pump, his balls twitched.

Not wanting to push his luck, he only stalled for a few seconds before Nix shifted into a more comfortable position on his knees and then leaned in, opening his mouth to welcome the silky crown. Tentatively, he licked at it, flicking his tongue over West's slit. A burst of salty musk hit him and he closed his eyes, telling himself to block out everything else and pretend.

Pretend he wasn't the only naked person in the room.

Pretend he wanted this.

Pretend—

He gasped when fingers dove through his hair and he was forced down, the entire length of West's cock spearing through his mouth in one go. He pushed against West's thighs, inhaling deeply the second he was lifted off, and then lowered himself, setting a gentler pace in the hopes the man would take the hint.

Wishful thinking.

"This is a punishment, Nixie," West growled a moment before his grip on Nix's head tightened, "remember?"

That was all the warning he got.

There'd only ever been two other people Nix had experienced this with in the past, and neither of them had been assholes about it. They'd allowed him to set the pace, let him get used to the taste and feel of them, figure out the best way to go about fitting their girth in his mouth.

It'd been a joint experience, pleasurable for all involved.

Absolutely nothing like this.

Nothing about this was mutual, even if he'd initially consented.

Tears and saliva streamed down his face as West's strong hands gripped his skull and fucked into his mouth. His thick cock hit the back of Nix's throat, causing him to gag, but that only seemed to spur the demonic man on further.

West humped his face like it was his own personal sex toy, careless about the fact Nix needed oxygen. He buried himself deep with every inward stroke and took his sweet time pulling back out, always stopping with the fat tip resting on Nix's tongue.

He struggled to breathe around it, but that cock continually blocked his airways, and it wasn't long before Nix grew lightheaded and felt himself swaying. His lips hurt from being stretched, and his throat wasn't too far behind. Every time he felt West slam against his passage he winced.

"You're going to bruise him," Yejun said from where he was still sprawled out on the couch at their sides. Despite his comment, he continued to wring himself in time to West's thrusts, his flushed cock straining toward Nix as though wanting a turn.

He wouldn't have to take him next, right?

The thought had Nix's gaze shooting back up to Lake, but their leader's expression was blank. For the life of him, he couldn't get a read on what he could possibly thinking. Nix tried to speak, gurgling around West's cock, but it was no use.

For his efforts, West dropped his head back and moaned, fingers digging even harder into the back of Nix's skull as he spread his thighs wider and yanked Nix forward. Once he was buried again, he held him there, making another sound of pleasure when Nix started to panic, his struggles increasing as he desperately tried to shove himself away from the other man.

His vision started to wink out as his lungs burned. He slapped at his thighs, begging him to release him, only to be ignored.

Was this seriously how he was going to die?

Suffocation by cock?

Humiliated and used and—

West grunted and suddenly came, hot come shooting down Nix's abused throat fast enough he choked on it. "Swallow it all, babe," the demon warned. "Unless you want to go another round?"

Nix's eyes widened and he tried to shake his head, swallowing as he was told. He kept doing so even when West finally stopped unloading. Even when he started sliding his cock free. Nix's tongue sought him out as he'd retreated, licking forward to lap at his rosy crown one final time.

"Holy shit." Yejun came next, still aimed Nix's way. He covered him in spunk, laughing when Nix jolted when a string of it hit him on the side of the face.

Before he knew what was happening, West was tossing him aside and standing. He tucked himself back into his pants and readjusted, Yejun doing the same. In no time at all, the only proof left that anything had happened between them at all was naked Nix, on the floor, white globs of their release sticking to his skin.

"Thanks, Nixie." West leaned down and patted him derisively on the cheek, laughing when Nix slapped him away.

"Guess we'll be seeing you in the King chat," Yejun said, moving to leave with West when the other man walked around the couch and headed toward a set of winding stairs on the other side of the room.

Nix stared after them, an odd feeling of rejection and degradation flashing through him, causing more tears to prickle at the corner of his eyes.

"Clean yourself off and get out of here," Lake said, reminding Nix that he was still there.

When he turned to look at him, however, he'd already been dismissed.

Lake followed after his friends without so much as a

second glance back.

CHAPTER 7:

Demitrious Corleone was a world-class dick. On the outside, he may appear to be the polished, well-mannered Royal and CEO of Core Technologies, altruistic and good-tempered.

What a fucking farce.

West downed his third drink in the past twenty minutes, knowing it wouldn't matter. His father wouldn't notice.

Not with Imperial Lake Zyair in the room.

At the end of the day, that was the worst part. The most unforgiving in West's eyes. It wasn't that Demitrious had driven a wedge between father and son, it was that, from the start, he'd attempted to do the same between West and Lake. As much as he wished he could claim it hadn't worked, West had to admit there was a string of resentment there that hadn't been present in their friendship before.

But he refused to act on it. Refused to allow his father to take anything else from him, especially not something as important as his friends.

Which was why he bit his tongue all through dinner, acting like he wasn't affected by the way his father praised Lake and all but ignored him.

They were at The Spark, Lake's favorite restaurant in the city, for their monthly family meal. Yejun had been invited, though he wasn't always—probably because this was the first dinner since Lake had returned from Vitality. They'd made it through fairly well, all things considered, and things were starting to wind down, so they could get the hell out of there soon enough.

The entire private room had been booked despite the fact that there were only four of them, and the relatively empty long table stood out. It was a waste all around—a needless display of wealth and privilege.

West wasn't against using his family name to get ahead, and Light knew he maxed out his credit cards almost as frequently as Yejun, but that didn't mean he was the type to flaunt his coin. Aside from his bike, most of his physical possessions of any real worth could fit into a backpack.

His father was the opposite. If there was a version of something dipped in gold and studded in rare gems, he wanted it. Didn't matter if it made no logical sense or was gaudy as fuck. The flashier the better in Demitrious's mind. It was the one and only reason he opened up the family home three times a year and hosted the Club. So that everyone could wander through the decadent halls of Corleone Manor and see for themselves just how truly above them the master of the house was.

"How are things coming with the task?" Demitrious asked then, his tone casual. It was a false projection, an act he put on perfectly, right down to the relaxed way he plucked his wine glass off the table and lightly sipped at the dark emerald contents. "With you back home, Lake, I'm confident you'll be able to solve this problem of ours before it's too late."

West ground his teeth and glanced away, one of his hands forming a tight fist in his lap beneath the table. It was too hard to tell if his father was doing it purposefully. Was it meant as an underhanded dig? A way of saying, "Son, you're not good enough, and we both know it," or was West merely too sensitive to it all now? Reading between lines that weren't there?

At his side, Yejun bumped his elbow against his arm and gave him a comforting look, silently telling him not to listen to the bullshit.

If Yejun had taken it as an insult against West, that had to mean it really was one, right?

Good Light.

This was exhausting. Always second-guessing himself. Always wondering how he could do better, please the older man at the head of the table more...

And for what?

West didn't even like the guy.

He was a shit father and an even shittier person, no matter what the rest of the world believed.

Demitrious was an esteemed member of the Order and had given them a task almost as soon as Lake had returned to planet. As seniors at Foxglove, that was to be expected. It was tradition that Legacy members undergo one final test of sorts, a proving of their worth in their final year. Sometimes, they were given the entirety of it to complete their assigned task. Other times, there was a different time limit, usually revolving around one of the school's acknowledged holidays.

For them, they'd been told to find the hacker threat by Demons Passing.

Which was in two fucking months.

"We're making progress," Lake lied easily, that frosty demeanor of his coming in handy against people like West's father. He was seated at the side of the table on Demitrious's right, while West was at his left.

Demitrious respected a cool head. It was one of the many reasons he'd given for being disappointed he'd ended up with West as his son and not Lake. West could still recall the elation painted across his father's face the night he'd discovered that the Zyairs, Lake's parents, had died in an accident.

He'd rushed to the hospital and had been the first to arrive, even before the rest of Lake's relatives. By the time Lake's uncle had made an appearance, Demitrious had already convinced Lake to come live with him. He'd acted as an unofficial adoptive father ever since.

The son he'd always wanted, a fact he'd never hesitated to rub in West's face.

West downed another drink and slammed his glass onto

the smooth cherry surface of the table with a little more force than necessary. It had the unfortunate result of gaining his father's attention for the first time in what had to have been an hour.

Demitrious glared at him pointedly, but before West could give in to the flash of anger coiled in his gut and snap back some snide remark, Lake spoke again.

"I have a plan," Lake said. "I'll be discussing it with the others tonight."

"Oh?" Demitrious smiled and swiveled his body back toward him. "Tell me more."

"We'll be bringing someone else in," he began, still speaking in that even and clipped voice. It was impressive since not many could maintain that air of superiority in the face of West's father. Though, Demitrious no doubt considered it as Lake thinking they were on even playing fields.

How wrong he was.

Lake didn't think himself equal to anyone, sometimes not even West or Yejun. Those were the rare occasions where West allowed himself to be angry with his friend and act on that anger. Fortunately for the both of them, those moments were few and far between.

They'd made a promise to each other as kids, the three of them, and Lake may be many things, but he never broke a promise.

That didn't mean he always clued West and Yejun into things.

Like this, for instance. Someone else?

Who the hell was he talking about?

"Someone who will be incredibly beneficial in helping us root out the threat," Lake continued, and Demitrious nodded his head, hanging off of every word.

Or, at least, making it seem that way.

West couldn't tell this time.

"A member?" Demitrious asked.

"No," Lake replied, but before he could be warned against

taking that kind of action, added, "Not yet, anyway. He will be, come the Night of the Nightshade."

"You've chosen a sacrifice?" West accused, ruining all his hard work for the evening by breaking his silence. "Without us?"

"Hey." Yejun grabbed his wrist, but West shook him off, not having any of that despite knowing his friend was merely looking out for him.

"Lake is an Imperial," Demitrious reminded curtly. "You will show him proper respect when in my presence. This is not the schoolyard, boy."

"He's got every right to be annoyed," Lake interrupted, careful not to let the irritation slip into his tone, even though West noticed the way his spine had straightened slightly. "Selecting a sacrifice is the duty of every Legacy up for review, not just me."

West inhaled slowly and dug his fingernails into his palms, focusing on calming his jangled nerves. Lake and Yejun weren't the enemies here. They cared about him, truly. They were on his side. Attacking them was the same as attacking himself, and West was no masochist. His father was the mismatched piece here. He was the thing that didn't fit.

"We did all choose together, though," Lake added, and West quirked a single dark brow, waiting for the explanation to come. His friend popped the last morsel on his plate into his mouth and chewed slowly, before saying, "We met with them the other day at the Roost. You confirmed there and then that he was to your taste, remember?"

Yejun covered what would have been a chuckle with a cough and reached for his drink.

West's lips twitched, the smirk forming against his better judgment, but damn it all. That was a good one.

"Well then, since you all seem pleased with the collective choice," Demitrious said, rising from the table, "I'll wish you luck, boys. Just remember, a lot more is at stake here. The Legacies of the past were all jokes compared to you three. Make me proud." He set his harsh gaze on West. "Or else."

They stood as well, bowing their heads wordlessly as he took his leave, waiting on the count of ten before straightening after he left.

Yejun let out a breath and dropped back down into his chair dramatically. "Well damn. I thought he'd never stop talking. Remind me why I had to tag along tonight again?"

"Because he asked for you," Lake stated, easing back down into the wooden chair on his side of the table. Now that they were alone, he selected a few more things from the trays filled with more food than a small army could eat.

"He just wanted to remind us about Demon Passing," West said. "Dick."

"Once we graduate and Lake takes the throne, we won't have to tiptoe around him anymore," Yejun reassured, clapping him on the back and shaking him slightly. "Which is why we *have* to succeed." He glanced to Lake and held his eye. "Which leads me to this plan of yours."

"You don't agree?" Lake cut the ferh steak and slipped a bite past his lips, all while maintaining eye contact. "You seemed fond of Nix the other night."

"Did I?"

"You came," West reminded with a shrug, only to have Yejun snort.

"I can come from just about anything." He sat back in his chair and crossed his arms. "I don't like it. Even if he's not the one we were after, the guy still managed to mess with West's programming. It's bad enough you allowed him to become a King, but this? The sacrifice—"

"Should be useful," Lake interrupted. "Nix has the potential to be."

West pursed his lips, considering it. "You want to use him as bait."

Lake snapped his fingers. "Bingo."

"And," Yejun drawled, "how exactly do you plan on going about that?"

"We know very little about this hacker," West began.

"Which one?"

"The one the Club wants us to find," he clarified. "We know he wants to expose Essential's less than stellar dealings to the world, and we know he's open to recruitment if it means achieving his goal."

West felt kind of shitty for having to bring up the elephant in the room, especially when Yejun immediately looked away and grew distant. He'd suffered from their recent betrayal the most and had yet to fully recover. But facts were facts, and they were on a time limit.

"We took out his pawn," Lake said, pretending not to notice Yejun's reaction the same way West was. "He'll be in the market for another."

"How can you be so sure?" Yejun asked quietly.

"Because clearly getting close enough to break into our systems isn't something he's capable of doing himself."

"He was found trying to break into the main servers within minutes by security," West agreed. "He's got skills to even make it that far, but they're nothing in the grand scheme of things. He's a threat, but not a big one."

"That's why we've been trusted with this." Lake dabbed at his mouth with a napkin.

"It's bullshit that we have," Yejun stated. "Other Legacies had easy tasks. This? We've got nothing to go on but supposition and luck."

"Like you even know what that word means," West teased, hoping to lighten the mood.

But of course, he only managed to have the opposite effect.

"I'm not a moron," Yejun snapped. "Just because I'm not an emotionless robot like you two whack jobs doesn't mean I'm stupid."

"Whoa," he held up his hands. "Sorry. Bad joke."

"This whole thing is a bad joke," Yejun swore and shot to his feet, his chair clattering to the ground. "You know the only reason we're going through this is so Lake's uncle can get off on it."

Hendrix Barden, also a member of the Order, was sixth in line for the throne, one place after Lake. He'd made his opinion on Lake being too young publicly known before the bodies of the Emperor and Royal Consort had even gone cold. It wasn't a hard conclusion to come to that this was all a part of his plan to prove Lake and the rest of them weren't strong enough to take positions within the Club, let alone the government.

"Have you tried talking to Beck?" West asked, referring to Lake's cousin and, unfortunately, Hendrix's son. West had always been a fan of Beck, the two of them having bonded over the fact both of their dads were trash.

"I will tomorrow when I see him on campus," Lake said. "Though I doubt he knows anything."

Right, because just like how Demitrious left West out of all things important, Hendrix did the same with Beck.

"Whatever," Yejun stated. "Barden can do whatever the hell he likes. He'll never beat us. Lake is next in line whether he likes it or not. Still, just in case…Bring the Firebird in, what do I care. But," he set his hands on his hips, "how can you be certain it'll work?"

"I can't," Lake said.

"So, if the hacker doesn't take the bait, we've just wasted our time, that it?"

"Do you have a better idea, June? I'm all ears."

"Fuck off, Lake. You weren't here. You don't know—" He stopped himself, running a hand through his hair to slick back the strands that had slipped loose from the small bun he'd put it up in. "You don't know."

"No," he conceded. "I don't. I'm sorry."

"Yeah." Yejun clicked his tongue, the anger leaching out of him all at once.

"Did we do it right?" West asked then, wagging a finger between him and Lake. "The whole apology thing? Us emotionless robots have been training for this moment for days."

Yejun tried to fight it but ended up laughing. "Man, shut

up."

"So it's settled then?" Lake asked, bringing them back to the topic at hand. "Nix will be our sacrifice."

"Don't expect me to be monogamous for him," Yejun warned. "I've got a list of names I still have every intention of making my way through this semester."

"Wouldn't dream of asking that of you," Lake deadpanned.

"Whether or not Yejun gets to stick his dick into more than one warm hole isn't the problem here," West interrupted, rapping his knuckles against the table. "It's how you plan on convincing Nixie to agree in the first place. After the other night? There's no way."

"He probably hates us," Yejun nodded. "I would if three strangers forcefully stripped me and forced me to suck one of them off."

Lake gave him a droll stare.

"All right," he admitted, "fine. I wouldn't. That sounds like a good time to me, but I acknowledge that my sexual preferences are not your average ones. Nix was terrified and humiliated. My guess? He'll sooner stab us with a blunt knife than allow any one of us to touch him again."

"The sacrifice has to be ours," West reminded Lake, "in all the ways it matters. The Club won't acknowledge him otherwise. And Nixie? He's not so big on public displays of affection."

Still, a thrill shot through West, straight to his groin, at the thought of getting another taste of the other guy. Nix was entirely his type, from the lithe, yet well-defined form, to his sexy little brain. The defiance Nix had somehow mustered despite the obvious fear he'd been feeling. West had always been a sucker for a smarty with a hot bod.

The thing was, he was Lake's type too.

"We're used to sharing things," he found himself saying, "but this is different."

"How so?" Lake stared him down, but West could tell he knew exactly what he was trying to say.

"You've had more time with him than we have," Yejun

jumped on. "You sure you're going to be okay with passing him around?"

"Since when has that ever been an issue?" he insisted. "What's mine is yours."

West nodded. "And what's yours is mine, yeah. But still."

Lake rolled his eyes. "What? You guys want some kind of reassurance?"

"It wouldn't hurt," Yejun grinned, showing that he was mostly teasing.

West wasn't.

Maybe it was residual resentment from their meeting with his father just now, maybe it was something else. Either way, he let himself push the issue even knowing it made him kind of a dick to do so.

"I watched him fuck himself on camera a few times," Lake said. "It doesn't mean anything."

"Prove it." West didn't back down.

After a brief stare-off, Lake heaved a sigh of annoyance. "Fine. I won't screw him until you two have a turn, deal?"

"Define, screw?" Yejun leaned forward, laughing when Lake glared. "All right, all right. That's good for me." He turned to West. "You?"

"Everything else is on the table," Lake quickly reiterated before West could answer. "The only thing I'm agreeing to is not penetrating his hole with my dick until you've both done the deed. Got it?"

"Poor Firebird," Yejun made an expression like he actually meant it even though he didn't. "He's going to have an awful time at Foxglove, isn't he."

"Or the best time ever," West corrected, challenging Lake with that statement. "I'm a phenomenal lay. If I take the lead here, we'll have him eating out of the palm of our hands in no time."

"No," Lake snapped.

"See, that," Yejun pointed at him, "that possessive look in your eye? That's what we're worried about."

"I'm not being possessive."

"Not being self-aware is more like."

"Are you two taking the deal or what?"

Sensing Lake was at his breaking point and this was as far as they were going to get, West grunted. "Yeah, brother. Yeah, we'll take the deal."

"So," Yejun asked. "Who's breaking the news to Nix that he's got new owners?"

"I will," Lake said.

"Better tell him quick," West replied. "The clock is ticking. We'll need to have a backup plan in place in case this doesn't work out the way you want it to."

It was a long shot if you asked West, but then, no risk no gain.

Judging by the way Lake had reacted the other night, it was safe to assume gaining Nix Monroe was more than worth it.

West could cause a stink and point out the obvious, how Lake was clearly trying to be underhanded here and was merely using the hacker as an excuse to tie Nix to him but…

What was Lake's was West's.

And Nix? Getting to feel that warm, wet mouth locked around his cock again?

Yeah.

He could live with that.

CHAPTER 8:

Nix wasn't sure what he'd been expecting.

He wasn't naïve. It wasn't like he'd imagined riding in on some white horse, solving the mystery like a master detective from those children's stories his dad had read to him as a kid and being revered by his family for his efforts. He'd never tricked himself into thinking it would be easy, and he'd never lied to himself about what this was at its core.

He wasn't here for justice.

He was here for vengeance.

Which was why it was so surreal to be sitting in the cafeteria, seated across from Grady, a tray of the same quality food he could have had at his previous school on the table before him. The chatter he picked up on here and there was all the usual as well, the same college bullshit. This person cheated on so and so. This one started dating blah blah. Did Sarfa fail the pop quiz today? What kind of asshole professor gives a pop quiz on the second day of school?

With each passing sentence, Nix felt the weight on his shoulders grow heavier and heavier.

He wasn't sure what he'd been expecting.

Fancy clothing and shiny pins with the university crest on them, yes.

Check.

A separation of the student body based off the usual classism and vapidness.

Check.

To have to get his hands dirty in his search for the truth. Obviously.

Check.

"Did you see West this morning by the fountain?" a girl whispered as she passed behind Nix with her friends. "He got a new tattoo over the summer!"

"Were you able to read what it said?" another excitedly replied. "I was too slow."

"I was too busy looking at Yejun," one of the guys with them laughed as they seated themselves at a nearby table. "Did his shoulders get broader? Is that even possible?"

"I saw him at his mom's exhibit a month ago," the first girl said. "I waved and he waved back!"

Nix felt that weight shift, settling lower until it was a heavy stone in his gut instead. His hand hovered over his tray, the fork clasped so tightly in his hand that his knuckles were starting to cramp and turn white.

He wasn't sure what he'd been expecting.

But being forced onto his knees in front of the university's most famous students hadn't been on the list.

Neither had blowing one of them.

Or the humiliation of it all.

The disgust, aimed at them and himself.

At the way he hadn't been able to get it out of his head ever since. Over forty-nine hours ago, he'd had West Corleone's cock in his mouth. He'd had Yejun's come on his face.

Lake's gaze on his body…

Had he noticed? The other two had been too distracted with themselves, there was a very good chance they hadn't paid Nix proper attention, but Lake…Lake had stared as if his eyes had the ability to peel through the layers of Nix's skin straight to the marrow of his bones.

What were the odds he hadn't caught sight of Nix's dick, hard and dripping between his thighs?

"Hey," Grady's voice cut through Nix's shame and he blinked, lifting his head to his roommate. "Are you okay? You suddenly turned pale." He glanced down at the barely picked at tray of food. "Is this not to your liking? Should we get something else?"

"No," Nix shook his head, grateful when his voice came out steady and strong, the opposite of how he currently felt. He tried a smile, only partially managing to make it believable. "I'm fine, thanks though."

"You sure? You—" Grady's sentence was cut off by a sudden burst of conversation around them. The din grew in excitement and he and Nix both searched the room for the source.

It didn't take long to figure out what had set them off. Nix saw it just before he heard the group that had been talking at the other table exclaim loudly, "It's the Demons!"

Lake led the way, like some horribly cliché teen movie, pausing just within the open doorframe of the cafeteria. His gaze swept over the masses, enigmatic expression firmly in place. The second his eyes locked on Nix, he started forward, the other two close on his heels.

Nix held his breath, certain this was a mistake or another one of the fucked up nightmares he'd had the past couple of nights. The Demons were the main cast, though there usually wasn't an audience and he typically could tell right away it was a dream.

Just to be sure, he dug his nails into his palm beneath the table, wincing at the sharp burst of pain.

Yejun winked at people as they passed while West played around on his multi-slate, following the other two without needing to watch where he was going. Whenever he came even close to walking into something, the nearest student would simply move it out of the way for him.

Lake had kept his word. Nix had checked his status on the app the moment he'd escaped from their house of terror. His account had a shiny little crown icon over the top, and he had access to the King chatrooms.

The problem?

They were wholly uneventful.

It was almost laughable, and Nix had been torn between dealing with the range of emotions he felt over what he'd been forced to do in the Roost, and how all of his efforts might have been in vain. He was no closer to discovering which King Branwen had been talking with. No closer to even knowing if anyone on campus was friends with her.

That group of students had been so eager to discuss what the Demons had been up to over the summer. Why wasn't anyone mentioning the girl who'd killed herself? Had he simply not heard any of the comments yet, or was it as he was starting to fear?

Did no one here…care?

Nix hadn't been as in touch with her as he should have been. The past few years, he'd been so busy with his studies and he'd just assumed it was the same for her. They touched base during major holidays and through the occasional text message, but he wasn't as involved in her life as he'd been when they'd been highschoolers. He was positive that she'd had friends, because she'd mentioned them in passing once or twice, he was absolutely certain of it. But…He couldn't recall if she'd ever given him their names.

Couldn't recall if she'd ever openly dated anyone on campus. Hell, she'd been using this app same as everyone else, and she'd made it to the top. How many of the student body had she been sexually involved with in order to achieve that goal? Yes, the app was anonymous, but only to an extent. Case in point, Nix's final Favor had been in person, sans masks, hadn't it?

Those same unmasked men who were coming up on him now.

Those three Kings.

The only three he'd identified so far.

Could one of them be the person he was after? All three?

Had Nix inadvertently blown the man responsible for his cousin's death?

Lake reached him and passed, dropping down into the

seat on his right before Nix could feel any sort of relief or misunderstand his motive. He was no longer looking at him, instead kept his gaze straight ahead while his friends settled in around them.

West made himself comfortable next to Grady, while Yejun took the spot on Nix's left.

"What's up, Firebird?" Yejun plucked a goji berry off of his tray and popped it into his mouth.

"Better question," West propped his elbows on the table and leaned forward, ignoring the way Grady tilted his body to avoid any sort of contact, "what the hell is that?" He pointed to the slab of meat that was still untouched on the tray.

"You want it?" Nix asked boldly, refusing to cower in front of them. He'd already done enough of that in his head. Had given them that power of him for free. He shoved the tray forward with a single finger. "It's fry loaf. Try it."

Instead of rising to the bait, West picked up the fork and stabbed into the meat, bringing a large chunk to his mouth. The second the morsal hit his tongue he coughed and wheezed, leaning to spit it out.

Into Grady's drink cup.

"Sorry," he said to Grady, not sounding apologetic in the least, "sorry. I'll get you a new one." He made no moves to do so. Instead clearing his throat loudly before sending Nix an incredulous look, "How could you eat that?"

"He didn't," Yejun laughed, draping an arm over the back of Nix's chair. "He tricked you into doing it."

West quirked a brow, silently asking Nix if that were true.

"Consider it as the two of you now being even," Lake suggested before Nix could decide which way to play things. He tilted his head wordlessly at Nix when he sent him a stare.

"What are you doing here?" Nix asked once it became apparent none of them were going to willingly offer up that information.

"Eating lunch," Yejun said.

"This is the small cafeteria."

"Ah," West grinned at him, "did your homework on us, did you? Why's that, Nixie? Were you hoping to avoid us?" He clicked his tongue. "Sorry to burst your bubble, boyfriend, but no can do. You're stuck with us for the foreseeable future."

Gasps rose up around them, but Nix was more distracted by the sound of his heart coming to a complete standstill in his chest. "What?"

Had just called him...? No, right? And if so, it was in jest. He was teasing him.

"Are you done?" Nix firmed up his voice and straightened in his seat.

"With?" Lake asked.

"Making fun of me."

"Who's making fun of you?" Yejun moved his arm so it was around Nix's neck instead and pulled him in, bringing his mouth right up to the curve of his ear. "Point them out to me. I'll kill them for you."

"Stop." He shoved him away with a scowl and swiveled toward Lake, dropping his voice to a low hush in the hopes no one else would be able to hear him. "Seriously, why are you doing this? Are you trying to humiliate me in front of the entire school now too, is that it?"

"You say that as though I've ever intended to humiliate you," Lake drawled, and for a moment it actually appeared as though he believed that, then it seemed to occur to him. "Oh. If you're referring to the other night, Songbird, then there's been a misunderstanding."

"There has not been."

"There has. That wasn't meant to humiliate you, Nix."

"No? Then what was it?" He wasn't buying it.

"An initiation."

"You could have chosen any Fav—" Nix was cut off when Yejun slapped a hand over his mouth.

"Everyone in here might already know that we're the Kings," Yejun whispered to him tightly, "but that doesn't mean you're allowed to verbally confirm it. Especially not like this, while throwing a tantrum like a toddler. You wanted it, didn't you? We granted your wish." He let Nix go with a snort. "Is that anyway to thank us?"

Nix glanced around, catching the interested stares. Not a single person in the room wasn't watching with abated breath, hoping to catch some sliver of juicy gossip they could spread around the rest of the campus and possibly the entire damn city.

It wasn't a stretch to assume the Demons were all in the King tier, considering their positions. Could that be the reason some students even bothered trying to achieve that tier in the first place? For the chance to be noticed by one of them? The chance to get closer to a Demon?

Was that why Branwen had done it?

No. No way. Even though they'd grown distance, Nix still knew his cousin. These guys? They weren't her type. Never had been. Never would be—

He sobered instantly.

Because no.

Now they really wouldn't ever be.

No one would.

The dead couldn't have a type.

Lake captured Nix's chin between two fingers, searching his eyes even when Nix glared. "What happened just now?"

"Nothing." He brushed him off.

"That wasn't nothing."

"Oh? You mean in the same way you supposedly weren't trying to humiliate me?"

"Do I really need to explain myself again?" Lake sighed, but at least he dropped the other thing.

Nix so wasn't going to speak to any of them about his cousin, not when they could very well be involved. He needed to believe it was a different King he was after though. Needed to for more than once reason, least of which being he wasn't confident enough in his abilities to think he could go up against people like them.

His family stayed out of politics. The rumor was it had

something to do with his great great great grandmother, who was once a member of Club Essential. She disagreed with a decision made once, went up against the wrong person, and their bloodline was almost wiped out.

Or so the story went. There was no way of knowing if that was true or not, but Nix had no interest in getting involved with the club or any form of government anyway. He was no essential member of society, so it wasn't like the club would take him anyway. One had to have something offer, something to contribute to the planet and those running it in order to earn that right.

"Fine, then tell me truthfully, why are you here?" he finally asked, anxious now that his mind had recalled why being around Lake and the others was such a bad idea.

"It's not obvious?" West took one of the berries off the tray and ate it, happier with his choice this time around.

"Enlighten me."

"Sassy," Yejun chuckled. "I like it."

"And we like you." West pointed at Nix, stabbing his finger in the air almost like he was delivering a threat.

In a way, he sort of was.

Nix blinked at him. "Huh?"

He was a decent lover, but he'd never been praised for his blowjob skills, and certainly not to the extent he'd have any grandiose misgivings that he could magically make a man fall for him just by giving one.

"Nix, we should get going." Grady stood with his tray, eyes downcast like they'd been the other day when he'd hit Lake with his umbrella. Despite how much he clearly hated the Demons, it was obvious he was also just as afraid of them as everyone else. "You wanted me to show you around the stadium and I have class in under an hour."

"We'll give him the tour," West said.

Nix opened his mouth to disagree, but Lake's hand dropped over his thigh and squeezed warningly. His protest died on his tongue.

Grady waited a moment anyway, but then sighed and nodded his head once before turning on his heels and walking away.

"I have to get to class," Nix lied as soon as they were alone at the table.

"No you don't," Lake called him on it in a cool tone. "You only have two classes on Tuesday, and you're done with them. Your next one isn't until…" He trailed off and motioned to West who was busy finishing off the fruit.

West typed on his multi-slate and then said, "Three tomorrow afternoon."

"Did you…hack my schedule?" Nix frowned at the three of them. "Why?"

"Ever heard of parrots?" West asked. "They're not native to our planet, but supposedly they're these annoying birds that like to repeat every sentence they hear." His gaze hardened. "I don't like it."

Yejun tapped his fingers against the table between them, chuckling. "Relax, man. One scary Demon is already more than enough, and Lake is already filling that role, right, Firebird?"

Well…He wasn't wrong…

He must have taken his silence as confirmation because he held out both arms as though to say told you so, laughing again when West huffed at him.

"Why were you curious about the stadium?" Lake asked him then, and Nix shook his head.

"I wasn't," he said. "And I don't need a tour."

"You sure?" Yejun pointed to Lake. "Not even if the captain of the waif team is offering you one?"

Nix, admittedly, hadn't known that. "You're the captain of the waif team?"

"He could go pro if he wants to," West replied before Lake had the chance. "That would have been the backup plan."

"Backup plan," Nix played into his hand, even knowing that was what he was doing, "for what?"

"We have a proposition for you, Songbird," Lake told him

quietly. "Would you like to hear it?"

He considered his options and asked, "And if I say no, not interested?"

"We pester you until you are," West said.

"Pester me how?" Nix knew he didn't want the answer, but the question came out anyway, his eyes locked with West's gray gaze. It was frightening and a little intense, though nothing near as dire as the one Lake could settle on people. There was a warmth there, a heat that he'd noticed the other night when he'd been sucking—

Nope.

Not going there.

Of course, West caught it though, obviously knowing where his mind had wandered, and the corner of his mouth tipped up. "I think you already have that figured out, Nixie."

"Are you really threatening me with sexual assault? Here? With all of these people present?" Nix demanded.

"Come on," Yejun reached up and started rolling the curve of Nix's ear between two fingers, "You were smart enough to ask that quietly just now, which means you're smart enough to know that even if we were to pick you up, place you on this table, and fuck you right here in front of this whole audience, no one would stop us."

He shuddered.

"What? No witty comeback this time?" Yejun tugged lightly on his ear lobe. "Don't disappoint me already, Firebird."

"Nix," he replied, speaking around the lump now forming in his throat. "My name is Nix."

"Your name is whatever we want it to be," West corrected. "You're whatever we want you to be."

There was no way out of this. They wouldn't let him get up and leave, which meant the least he had to do was hear them out. Maybe then they'd be satisfied enough to let him go. He'd figure out a way to turn down whatever it was they wanted to offer him after. Retreat first in order to fight another day, so to speak.

"Fine. What's the proposition?" He hated the way his voice

shook slightly at the end...and the way his balls tightened.

So what if they were sexy? Who fucking cared when they were literal monsters who took advantage of people?

"It's fairly simple," Yejun began.

"Yeah?" Nix didn't believe that for a second. "What is it then?"

"I already told you." West motioned to him and said slowly, as though speaking to a child, "Boy. Friend."

His brow furrowed. "What?"

"You're going to be ours, Songbird," Lake stated, losing his patience finally. "No, actually," he corrected, "you already are."

"Bullshit," Nix breathed out the word even though in his mind he screamed it.

"That's not the one," West said. "Not bull. Shit. It's boy. Friend. Say it with me."

"Hell no." He tried to stand but that hand on his thigh held him down. "Let go."

"Not until you agree," Lake replied.

"I'm not going to date you," he snapped. "Especially not all three of you."

"Whoa, did I hear that right?" the girl from earlier asked her friend, not even remembering to be quiet this time, and Nix inwardly swore.

Lake saw his reaction and gave a partial smirk, the type that would go unnoticed if not for the fact Nix was sitting so close to him. He leaned in until Nix could feel his breath against his jaw and whispered, "This is taking longer than I wanted, and now we have an even more attentive audience. You can agree and we can leave to discuss terms like gentlemen, or I make good on my promise."

It was hard to concentrate with him so near, but Nix somehow managed to catch onto that last part. "Promise?"

"I said I'd bend you over my knee and make you sob," Lake said silkily. "Remember, Songbird?"

He sucked in a breath.

"You do." Lake leaned back. "That's good. This should go

fairly quickly from here on, shouldn't it?"

"I..." He was trapped. "You suck."

"That's not the answer I'm looking for. Care to try again, or should I—" Lake wrapped his hand around Nix's elbow and made as though to pull him toward him.

"No," Nix threw up his arms and shook his head, "no. That won't be necessary."

"Change of tune, Nixie?" West asked, popping the last piece of fruit into his mouth, which he chewed excruciatingly slowly on purpose.

Give in and retreat now.

Fight another day.

"Okay," he said tightly. "I'll do it."

"Do what?"

"Whatever it is you actually want me to do." He turned to Lake, wanting to be clear that he in no way believed, even for a second, that this was about wanting to date him. "Whatever that really is, I'll do it."

"Good choice, Songbird," Lake praised.

And then he kissed him.

CHAPTER 9:

"I think you broke him," Yejun teased less than ten minutes later when the four of them stepped out of the cafeteria and into the cool midafternoon air. The sky was unusually bright, with not many clouds dotting the light blue canvas and no signs of rain.

Which felt odd, considering Nix's mood called for it.

His fingers brushed against his lips, slightly bruised from the rough kiss Lake had just imposed on him. He could still hear the gasps and chatter from the other students when it had happened, and a quick glance over his shoulder showed many of them had followed to the glass doors and the windows and were not so subtly staring out at them.

"He's not a fan of public displays of affection," Lake said matter-of-factly, not so much as a whisp of remorse in his tone.

Nix's eyes narrowed and he dropped his hand, fisting it at his side. "You know that, and yet—"

"It's all part of the game, Nixie." West flicked him under the chin and then stepped backward down the stone stairs. "I've got to run."

"Me too." Yejun practically hopped down after him, spinning once he'd made it to the stone path so he was facing Lake and Nix. "You've got this?"

Lake merely waved a hand off to the side, dismissing them. Yejun laughed, but West's jaw tightened and he shook his head before the two of them left. If the reaction affected him at all, Lake didn't show it. Casually, he slipped his hands into the pockets of his black slacks and then tipped his head in the opposite direction, indicating Nix should follow.

"I'm not a dog," Nix stated. "And if you expect me to do something, you're going to have to use your damn words first."

He didn't so much as blink. "You're so obedient when you're Nightingale."

"None of that was real."

Lake's mood darkened. Nix wasn't sure how he picked up on that considering the man's expression never wavered, but he knew the instant the change happened.

And he instantly regretted being the cause.

"Why did you do it?" Nix asked, desperately catching onto the first thing he could think of to change the subject and possibly return Lake to the robot version of himself. It was creepy, sure, but safer. The last time Lake had gotten annoyed with him...

He'd let West choke Nix on his cock.

Nix didn't want or need a repeat.

"We can't talk about it out here," Lake said. He didn't wait for Nix or explain where they were going. He didn't even listen and ask him to follow, trusting instead that he would out of what had to be sheer arrogance.

Arrogance that wasn't misplaced since Nix fell into step behind him like the good little puppy he'd just claimed not to be.

This was all for Branwen though. He could do anything for her, even lower himself like this. Even make out with the head of the Demons in the middle of a crowded cafeteria. Hell, worse, if it came down to it.

Though, he was pretty sure he'd draw the line at what Yejun had suggested. Nix was never going to be comfortable with public sex. Kissing though?

"Is that going to be a regular occurrence if I go through with this?" Nix wanted to be mentally prepared for things like that. "And what was that about dating all three of you? Were you guys serious?"

"You made it sound like you were smart enough to realize there was more to it," Lake drawled, leading them to the nearest parking lot. "West may have hacked into your private file, but that only gives us facts. Where you were born, where you attended school prior to transferring to Foxglove, things like that. He might think differently, but I believe it's impossible to fully know someone just through the use of a computer."

Nix opted not to point out that they'd broken several privacy laws if what he was saying was true. Not only because it would be hypocritical of him—he'd started it by infiltrating the Enigma app, after all—but also because it'd become abundantly clear already that people like the Demons weren't held to the same legal standards as the rest of them.

On the other side of Tulniri where he'd grown up, Nix was so far removed from the political happenings that he hadn't realized things were this extreme. His only life goals had been to graduate top of his class and gain employment. He'd wanted to apply to Trav Developments, the number one gaming company in the Dual galaxy, and that had been his main focus. He'd still like to achieve that goal, but that dream had taken a backseat in lieu of getting answers for Branwen.

"It's easy to lie in person," Lake continued, "but much easier to do through the safety of a computer screen, don't you agree?"

"Sure." That was most likely what had happened to his cousin. Whoever she'd been speaking with through the app had lied and tricked her into trusting them. Then, once she'd been on the hook, they'd done *something* to shatter that trust.

But what?

And why?

Lake moved faster than Nix could have anticipated even if he hadn't been caught up in his own musing, but one second they were walking, and the next, he had Nix backed up against the side of a silver hovercar. His arm was up by his shoulder, blocking him in, and his green eyes darkened as he stared Nix down as though in anger.

Though…anger for what?

He hadn't done anything…

"This isn't a game," Lake said and Nix bristled.

"West is the one who called it that," he pointed out. "So if you're pissed because of phrasing, take it up with him."

"Have you always been this bold?" He searched his face. "You weren't like this on the app. You were timid there. Sensual almost. Obedient. Is this the real you, Phoenix?"

Nix shoved his arm away, pretending not to know that Lake allowed him to do so. "Regular people aren't computers. They're multifaceted. I can be like this with you now and still have been the same person who was with you in those chatrooms."

"Regular people?" His eyes narrowed. "You're insulting me."

"You think I'm the one who's acting different?" He jabbed a finger at the center of Lake's chest. "Take a look in the mirror. You weren't exactly kind there, but you were nicer than this. More understanding."

"Understanding? Me?"

"Yes, you!" Nix faltered. "Unless…it was someone else using your username?"

"No one else is allowed to access any username but their own. Especially not at the King level. I'd hand you my multi-slate and let you try to open my account to prove it, but we're already behind schedule."

"And whose fault is that?"

"Yours for confusing me."

He pulled back. "How have I confused you?" Why did it suddenly feel like Lake kept stealing his lines?

"Get in the car, Songbird."

The door behind him beeped, and he spun around, watching as Lake rounded the car and yanked open the driver's side door. When he made no move to do the same, the Demon gave him a harsh look.

"Get in the car," he repeated.

Nix weighed his options. They were far enough away from the cafeteria that there was little threat of Lake using an audience against him now, but what would happen if he did refuse and walk away? What then?

He'd been on campus for half a week, had been working on building an account on Enigma for a month, and what did he have to show for it?

Nothing.

Nothing but a fake crown atop a black and white image of him in a mask.

"How many Kings are there?" the question was out before he could second guess himself.

If Lake found it odd, however, he didn't show it. "Seven, including you."

"That's all?"

"The screening process was intense," he cocked his head, "not that you would know."

"I had my reasons."

"Right," Lake said. "You wanted to change your life. That's what I'm offering. Get in the car."

"It's not an offer if you force someone to do what you want."

"It's still an offer," he corrected. "You're the one who gets to decide what happens next, Nix. Do you come willingly, or do you force my hand?"

What happens next...Hadn't he just been thinking that same thing?

Seven Kings, including himself?

That accounted the three Demons and left three unknown on the board.

"Who are the other Kings?"

"That's confidential," Lake replied, "and you haven't signed the NDA yet."

Is that where they were going?

"You'll explain it all, right?" Nix set his hand on the handle but didn't open the car door. "This isn't just some trap to get me alone again?"

"I don't need to trick you to get you alone, Songbird," Lake said confidently. "All I have to do is ask you to come and you will."

He snorted. "That so?"

"Yeah," Lake nodded. "That's exactly how it is. Deny it all you want. We both know you can't keep up the lie forever."

"The lie?"

"That you don't want me." He set his arms over the roof of the car and let loose some of that hidden chaos Nix had only caught glimpses of in the sound of his voice through the speakers of his computer. "You want me just as much as you did when I was a faceless stranger on the other side of your monitor. Maybe even more."

"Cocky?" Nix's voice came out too breathless for either of them to believe he wasn't affected, but he stood his ground anyway.

"I'm attractive. That's a fact."

Nix kept his mouth shut, because what was there to say to that?

"It's also a fact that you're going to be mine, Songbird."

"That so?"

"Yes."

"Why would I—"

"Because," Lake cut him off. "I'm going to give you what you want in return."

Nix felt his chest seize and barely kept his composure. "And what is it that you think I want?"

"You were thriving at your old university," he said. "You didn't come all the way here for our curriculum. You came here for a King."

Was that all he knew? Nix tried to search his eyes to see if there were any hidden meanings behind those green orbs, but he couldn't find anything. In the short time they'd known one another, he'd already learned that Lake only ever showed the face that he wanted you to see, nothing more and nothing less.

Could Nix trust a person like that?

Had Branwen?

"Okay," he admitted, bending the truth since being honest and admitting he'd actually come to hunt one down was out of the question. "So what if I did come for one?"

"I'll do you better," Lake replied. "I'll give you three."

This again. "And all I have to do is pretend to be your boyfriend, that it? Fake date you and your two best friends?"

"What makes you think it'll be fake?"

Nix gave him a bland look. "Come on. I know I'm not ugly, but I'm hardly anything special either. First day of school and the three hottest guys on campus are magically interested in little old me? I don't buy that. This isn't a fairytale."

"It's good that you're aware," Lake said. "Because I'm no prince."

"That's not something I'm in the market for."

"No," he agreed. "You don't seem like the type who often needs saving, no matter how timid you are in the bedroom."

Nix rolled his eyes, but Lake wasn't finished.

"Get in the car," he ordered. "Or I'll come over there and put you in it myself."

"It means that much to you?" Nix couldn't figure him out, and not for a lack of trying. Despite what he'd said about this not being a fairytale, the whole thing felt too surreal to be reality. "You need me to fill this role, whatever it is, that badly?"

"Yeah," Lake confirmed. "And if you're as smart as I think you are, it'll mean that much to you too, once you learn the stakes."

He'd stalled enough. This was only ever going to end one way and they both knew it from the start. The fact that Lake had allowed him to play it out for this long was already telling in and of itself, and Nix tucked that information aside to be picked apart later.

For now…

With one tug, he yanked open the car door.

And got inside.

CHAPTER 10:

Lake hit the gas and rounded the corner tight enough it sent Nix careening in the passenger seat next to him. The corner of his mouth twitched, but since the Songbird was glaring his way, he resettled his features quickly.

Emotion was a dangerous thing. When you offered someone a glimpse at how you felt, you were giving them the chance to uncover your truths.

Lake didn't want anyone riffling through his feelings. Didn't want them messing around in his head, trying to discover things they shouldn't. When they'd been younger, it'd been an oddity of his, something the other kids tried to make fun of him for on the playground before realizing his identity. Usually, that last part came only after West had given them a fat lip for their insolence.

It was hard to imagine there'd once been a time when the two of them never fought with each other, when they weren't constantly butting heads like they did now. If he could go back in time and choose a different path, turn down Demetrious's offer to move in with them, he would. He'd known all about the inferiority complex West had with his father, but he'd foolishly believed he could help if he was there.

Lake had only made it worse.

That was why he'd offered Nix up to West the other night when his friend had shown an interest. Originally, he'd called Nix there to test his theory and confirm he was in fact Nightingale from the app. Stripping him had been a tactic meant more to show him who was in charge; things weren't supposed to get sexual.

But West had clearly wanted him, and Yejun too...And Lake had thought maybe letting them get a taste could be received as some sort of truce. Yejun understood why he'd left for Vitality, but West...

His best friend was still hurt and feeling neglected. Abandoned. If the man currently glaring daggers at his side could help mend the bridge between them? Lake would use Nix as often as it took to achieve that goal, and it wasn't the only one the Songbird could come in handy for either.

"The hacker we're looking for is clever," he began, still speeding down the winding road toward their destination.

Back on Vitality, he'd had to be cautious; he couldn't afford to get pulled over by the cops, even if the ticket would be immediately waived the second they saw who was driving. Word could always get back to Tulniri he wasn't acting on his best behavior, and his place in the line of succession could be compromised. Now that he was free to do as he pleased, Lake let loose. He'd missed the speed and the thrill. The risk. It used to be that taking a drive was the only thing that could clear his head when things got too tangled in his mind.

"From what I gathered at the Roost, you aren't talking about the app. This hacker, he's after Club Essential?" Nix asked, gripping the handle above him tightly in one hand.

"That's one theory," Lake said. "Another is that he's after us."

"Us being?"

"My friends and I."

"The Demons." He hummed in understanding. "Why?"

"Do you pay attention to the news, Songbird?"

"Not really. But if you're asking if I'm aware of your situation with the throne, yeah. I don't think there's a person alive on this planet who isn't." He paused and then. "I'm sorry for your loss."

"Don't be." Lake had barely spoken to the Emperor and

Royal Consort, better known as his aunt and her lover. They'd never been close, even when his parents had been alive, and while the Emperor had shipped him off to Vitality with the excuse that it was to create ties between their two worlds, another part of him had always suspected there'd been more to it than that.

She'd always known that he was a threat.

She hadn't been wrong.

"I'm aware of other things, too," Nix told him then. "Like, for instance, that this car can go the regular speed limit."

"Know a lot about cars, do you?"

"Yes, actually," he surprised him by saying.

The problem with hacking into his personal files was that they'd only been able to uncover information about his studies and living situation. There'd been a basic family tree of his immediate family, but aside from that, the only glimpse at hobbies Nix may have had came from his Inspire social media account.

Which was filled with random photos of plants and steaming mugs of hot beverages. There hadn't even been a single selfie. Not one.

At the end of the day, there was more about Nix Monroe that they didn't know than things they did. But Lake wasn't stupid enough to tell him that. He needed Nix to sign these documents, not because he wouldn't proceed with his plans if he didn't—Lake would—but because it made the others more comfortable knowing there was a layer of legality between them and what they were doing.

"This is a JF-897," Nix said. "There were only five shipped to the planet, so to call it expensive would be a massive understatement."

"Do you like it?" Lake could already tell the answer to that, but he wanted to hear it anyway.

"Not even a little." He sneered at the controls. "It's so pretentious."

Lake chuckled. "I'll let West know you don't approve."

Nix sent him a look that was a mixture of wariness and confusion.

"He bought it for me as a welcome home gift," he explained, laughing when that caused Nix to pale. "I'm curious, are you afraid of him because he almost choked you on his dick, or are you—"

"Like you mentioned already," he interrupted. "I'm not an idiot. I know you guys are scary. I knew it before I even stepped foot into the Roost that night."

"But you came anyway."

"Yeah." Nix turned to stare out the window as trees whipped by.

"Do you regret it?"

"What do you think?"

Lake considered. "You're hiding something. Only someone confident or desperate would willingly walk headfirst into danger. You've done it more than once by my count. I would have said it was the latter without hesitation before but now…"

He'd expected Nix to cower away from them when they'd entered the cafeteria earlier—and he sort of had, but not near the extent that Lake had presumed. And even though he'd been anxious and on edge, that hadn't stopped him from talking back. During their private chats on the app, Nix had been soft and warm, but in reality, he was a jagged mystery.

"I don't like when there's something I can't see through," he confessed. "I don't like that there are things about you I don't know. West would say that's half the fun, but—"

"The two of you are very different," Nix surmised. "So, what? Is this the part where you threaten to hurt me if I don't tell you all of my secrets?"

"You don't even sound scared of that possibility."

"You aren't the only one who has things to do, Lake."

They exited the forest area that surrounded the campus and shot out onto the crowded city streets. The number of other cars forced Lake to slow down, but he didn't mind. They were close enough to the office building now, and it wouldn't be much longer before they reached it.

"Finding this hacker is important to the club," Lake said, opting to get them back on track. "That's why they've ordered us to find him."

"If it's really that important," Nix argued, "then why would they trust you guys? Why wouldn't they put together a team or something? Everyone knows the club is packed with members from every organization and career. Surely there are people in law enforcement who could handle this instead?"

Lake hesitated. He could tell him now since there was no way he was letting Nix walk away without signing the documents. Nix hadn't been serious when he'd mentioned threats just now, had merely been poking fun at Lake, but he'd learn quickly that Lake wasn't above resorting to that form of persuasion.

"There are these things called Legacies," he began. "They're members born a part of Essential by blood or familial positioning. My parents were both members before their deaths. Yejun's parents are members. West's father…you get the point. Legacies are sworn in at the age of thirteen, but we aren't considered for official roles until we've graduated from Foxglove."

"Foxglove specifically?" Nix frowned.

"Yes. All Legacies have to graduate from our university. As seniors, we're given a task which we must complete. Usually it's something simple, mere semantics, where we prove our loyalty to the club and its values."

"Being told you have to flush out a hacker who seems to pose a legitimate threat doesn't seem all that simple," Nix drawled, and Lake nodded, waiting for him to come to his own conclusions. It didn't take long. "This has something to do with your bid for the throne, doesn't it? Either someone is trying to block your way, or the club wants a stronger confirmation from you that you won't turn on them the moment you've got the crown."

It couldn't be the latter since the Emperor was an

esteemed member of Club Essential and had been since its creation—hell, that's where the name had come from even—but he'd exposed enough secrets already. The fact of the matter was, Lake didn't trust Nix. He wanted him in an inexplicable way he'd never experienced before, but it was too obvious the other man was hiding something. That couldn't be ignored.

No matter. Whatever that secret may be, Lake would unravel it.

"As far as operating the planet," Nix surprised him by adding, "you're pretty much as essential to it all as they come. That is, *if* you can keep your place as the next in line. This being a targeted attack does seem like the most likely option."

"If someone is using this method to try and keep me from the throne," Lake pulled into a medium-sized parking lot and circled the twelve-story building, "that means finding this hacker is the only way to thwart them."

Nix waited until they'd parked at the back of the building before admitting, "I'm still not sure what any of this has to do with me or having to date you."

Lake shut the car off and unbuckled, turning in his seat to better face him. "What if I told you there was no connection and we just want to fuck you?"

They'd been infiltrated before while he'd been away, and the repercussions...well, they were still ongoing. That was yet another reason to keep Nix close instead of pushing him away. If his secret happened to somehow coincide with the hacker or the last student who'd betrayed them, then Lake would uncover the truth and make him pay for his deception.

When he thought about how broken Yejun still was...

"I'd call you a liar," Nix replied. "If this was just about sex, you could have taken it the other night easily enough."

"Rape, you mean."

"Going to try and tell me that you're above that?"

Lake wasn't fond of the tone he was taking, but he kept his cool. "There's no need to rape someone who's already interested." He shifted closer, hand shooting out to capture Nix's chin when he attempted to turn away. "Admit it, Songbird. You'd climb on and ride my cock right now if it meant getting what you wanted in return."

Nix frowned at him, and it was there in his eyes, a flash of something that proved all of Lake's assumptions correct.

"I don't know why you wanted to enter the King tier so badly." He was going to find out though. "But it's obvious that was only part of your goal."

"I already explained that," Nix insisted. "My cousin—"

"Died. Yes. So sad."

He slapped Lake's hand away with enough force it actually worked. "Don't you dare talk about her like that."

Ah, so it was a she. Was she even really his cousin? An ex-lover, perhaps? That would explain the crazed desperation and the almost ridiculous lengths he'd been going to. Maybe this really was about opening up his horizons.

"Is it sexual exploration?" Lake murmured to himself. "Is that what you're really after?"

Nix glanced away, his cheeks heating, but that wasn't enough to either confirm or disprove his hypothesis.

"If it is, this deal really will benefit the both of us," Lake said. "Come. We can't talk out here about private matters such as this."

"Where are we?" Nix sent a suspicious look out the front window toward the building.

"It's an office space we've used since we were younger," he told him, seeing no reason not to. "It's where the Enigma App was created and developed. Only the three of us and our staff have access, so we can go over everything comfortably inside."

"Does everyone know you're behind the app?"

"Yes." It hadn't started out that way, but in the years since, Lake was pretty sure it was a well-known fact amongst the student body. Everyone at the club knew, obviously.

"Why did you create it?"

"Why do you think, Songbird?"

"I think you've never needed a hookup app to get laid."

"Very true."

"I'm not the only one hiding things," Nix pointed out, but that was seemingly the end of the discussion, as he quieted afterward and didn't ask any other questions.

He also didn't make any moves to get out of the car.

Was Lake going to have to drag Nix in kicking and screaming or—

"Okay." He undid his belt and had one foot out the door in an instant, pausing only to send Lake a questioning glance when he didn't immediately follow suit. "Coming?"

He chuckled before he could help it. Nothing was ever as it seemed when it came to the Songbird.

That was half the problem.

CHAPTER 11:

The building was just your everyday average office building. There was a small lobby with an elevator just beyond it. Nix was quiet the whole ride up, noting that Lake had pressed the second highest floor, but not trusting himself to ask about what was at the very top.

Truthfully, he was nervous. Part of him was convinced this was another trap, that the whole boyfriend angle had been a mere ruse to lure him here so that Lake could…He didn't know what, but nothing good. People like the Demons of Foxglove, the type that grew up wanting for nothing, used to always getting their way, wouldn't understand things like boundaries.

Wouldn't understand Nix even if he told them no.

The other night was proof of that, and if he'd been smarter, as smart as Lake assumed, he would have ended this whole thing there and then and gotten out.

But it was too late to get out now.

As soon as the elevator doors opened, Lake grabbed Nix's wrist and pulled him out and down the hall. He wasn't gentle about it, practically hauling him into a room at the end.

"What was that for?" Nix demanded as soon as Lake released him. He rubbed at the tender flesh, scowling at Lake's back as the other man headed straight for a large oak desk to the left.

The office was a decent size, nothing too flashy. Much like the rest of the building he'd seen so far, there wasn't anything unusual or spectacular about it. A large window took up most of the wall across from the door, the panes of glass giving him a view of the bustling city. It'd started to rain since they'd entered, droplets pinging lightly around them.

The desk had a built-in holo-strip for the computer monitor and a stack of paper books organized neatly on the side. A single leather couch tucked against the far corner and a wooden shelving unit were the only other pieces of furniture. There was nothing identifying to be found; the place could have been the workspace of literally anyone.

"Is this more your style?" Nix found himself asking, mostly just to fill the quiet while Lake pulled open a desk drawer and rifled through it. He took in the beige walls and the thin forest-green carpet beneath his feet.

"As opposed to?" Lake said.

"The Roost." Their home on campus was all high beams and glass and nature. It'd felt like it had a life of its own. Had felt…He stopped himself from thinking the word special, but it hovered on the outskirts of his mind anyway.

"Both the Roost and this place came as they were," Lake told him, coming back around the desk with a file and a pen in his hands. "They're passed down. The Demons of Foxglove Grove always live in the Roost for all four years of their life at the university, and this office space used to belong to Yejun's older sister. She gifted it to him when he told her about our app project. We were kids at the time and didn't bother changing the décor."

"And now?"

"Now?" Lake humored him by considering, and it was obvious that's all he was doing. Allowing Nix a reprieve, some time to work himself up to things, the same way he had with every one of their sexual encounters through Enigma. "It just doesn't matter now, I guess. We don't spend much time here."

"Was Yejun's sister a King too?" If there were only Seven Kings total… "What happens when they graduate? Or something happens to them?"

Lake tipped his head. "Something? Something like what?"

Nix shrugged like it was no big deal and forced himself to say casually, "I don't know. Like they get into an accident or die. Anything is possible."

He was silent for a moment. "I'm trying to assess if that was meant as a veiled threat, but I don't believe it was."

"It wasn't."

Lake nodded. "No, Yejun's sister wasn't a King because she'd already graduated by the time we created the Enigma app. My cousin was, but he graduated last year, and while club members are all allowed to use the app, only those currently attending Foxglove are allowed to climb the ranks to King level."

"Why?" No, that wasn't the right question. "So, once they graduate, they're removed or dropped down a tier?"

"If they choose to stay on it," he said. "They'll be placed back in Rook."

Which meant the person Nix was looking for might no longer even be in the King tier. Shit. If that was the case, what then? What the hell was he supposed to do if he'd gone through all of this already only to hit another dead end?

"The app was always meant for university students," Lake continued when Nix didn't immediately add anything else. "Since you're about to sign this NDA, I'll let you in on the truth of the matter."

That caught his attention. "What?"

Lake grunted. "You didn't really think we'd gone through all that trouble just to get laid, did you? You sounded like you knew that already."

"I mean…Yeah, until I realized you were only thirteen when you made it."

"Were you a horny kid, Songbird?"

"Don't be disgusting."

"That's my point exactly. We created the app because there was need for it for the club, not for ourselves. Everyone knew we were going to become Demons eventually."

"And people would willingly throw themselves at you once you were." Nix waved at him. "Yeah, yeah. I get it."

"I wouldn't mind, you know?"

Nix frowned. "Mind what?"

"If you brought some of this haughtiness to the bedroom." Lake took a single step closer. "*Some*, Songbird."

He cleared his throat, trying to ignore how that small mention had his body heating in anticipation. "We were talking about the app."

Lake chuckled at him but didn't push him further. "The app was set up much like the club, with layers. Many of which are smokescreens, meant to hide the true nature or purpose of Enigma as a whole."

"I'm not interested in your club," Nix stated.

"No," he surprisingly agreed. "If you were, we wouldn't be standing here now. Threats to the club are wiped out immediately, no exceptions. But the club and the app aren't one in the same, more like…the app is a stepping stone of sorts."

"Is it a screen or a stone? Pick one."

"You're getting impatient."

"And you're getting redundant." It wasn't impatience that Nix was feeling, but it was much better for Lake to think that than to know the truth.

Hopelessness was starting to settle in, along with a heavy mixture of doubt. He'd foolishly thought this would be simple—join the app, become a King, find out who'd messed with Branwen. Only, now he was learning how wrong he'd been and how complicated all of this was.

He'd come here to find a King, true, but the plan had never been for him to become entangled with one, and since Lake was here spewing all these secrets willingly, it was obvious that's exactly what the Imperial Prince intended for them to become.

Entangled.

But to what end?

And to whose benefit?

"*This*," Nix said then, calming himself some since losing it wouldn't get him anywhere, "is a smokescreen. What are you trying to get at, Lake?"

"Most of the students who download the app remain on the first two tiers their entire time using it." Lake opened the file he'd brought over as he spoke, flipping through the pages that were attached to it. "For them, it's a hookup app. A way to blow off some steam and mess around between classes. The Favors are in place to weed people like that out. You don't know since you didn't experience it yourself, but Favors can be anywhere from tame to diabolical."

"Give me an example," Nix hated that his curiosity was piqued, but it was.

"West once ordered a Knight to seduce the headmaster's son and publicly dump him afterward."

Nix made a face. "What? That's so childish."

"Yejun ordered two Bishops who both wanted to rise to Rook to fuck in the middle of the field during our waif home game last year."

"...Did they?"

"Yes. If you know where to look, you can still find the footage online."

"And they just....were allowed to do that?"

"Oh, of course not. The school has a reputation to uphold outside of Enigma. They were both expelled."

Nix stared at him for a moment and then accused, "Yejun knew that's what would happen, didn't he."

"No one held blasters to their heads, Songbird. They made their choice."

"They were pressured into it."

He shrugged. "That's not my problem."

"So," he caught on, "what you're saying is you'll have no problem pressuring me into things too."

"I thought my actions thus far had already proven that to you, but if I was mistaken, allow me to clarify." Lake held up the pen and only then did Nix notice the tip of it wasn't normal. "Yejun may not have forced those Bishops, but I won't hesitate to use force against you if I must."

Nix stared at the end of the pen—which wasn't a pen

really, since the tip was a tiny curved blade of sorts. The object itself was opaque, made of blown glass at first glance. It'd be pretty if it didn't look so deadly.

He almost laughed at that thought, because the same could be said about the man holding it.

"Should I prick your finger," Lake asked when Nix made no moves to take the pen from him. "Or will you behave and do it yourself?"

"You want me to cut myself for you?"

"Songbird, I want you to do a lot more than just bleed for me. And you will. But first," he waved the pen, "we get the paperwork out of the way."

"You want me to sign something before you've even fully explained the terms to me?" He shook his head. "Not a chance in hell."

"I can easily make this hell for you, Phoenix. Don't push me."

"My name is Nix," he corrected tersely, still eyeing the pen. "And I'm not signing it to something without reading the fine print first."

Lake sighed as if he were dealing with a small child and not a totally appropriate response to a ridiculous ask. "Students who manage to make it into the top two tiers of the app are considered for membership in Club Essential. Not many make it, mostly because not many bother."

"Since they're asked to do things that can result in their expulsion," Nix stated, "that makes sense."

"Exactly," he agreed crisply. "That's the whole point. The club is already extensive, we don't *need* new members. The reason for recruitment is simple. It's not out of necessity for numbers, it's necessary to maintain power."

Nix wasn't following, though he hated to admit that.

He didn't have to. Lake saw right through him.

"Club Essential is whispered about in the streets, in broad daylight and the dead of night. In offices and school rooms and even the grocery store. Our identities are hidden, but we're known to all. Our power, our wealth, our," he reached out and flicked a finger at the button of Nix's pants, "proclivities. We do nothing to hide those. Because we want the planet to know who owns them."

"Careful," Nix said, pushing Lake's hand away and retreating a step, "you're starting to sound a little too much like a storybook villain for my liking."

"This isn't a fairytale," Lake reminded, smirking. "This planet belongs to whoever sits on the seat of the emperor and the members of Essential. It's impossible to become emperor outside of the Imperial family. But Essential? People might not know how, but they do know there's a way to become a member of the club. Aspiration and desire. That's what truly keeps the world running. Knowing there's hope to achieve the unobtainable keeps people in line."

"They're less likely to fight against it because there's a one percent chance they could become a part of it?" Nix made a sound of contempt. "As you've already pointed out, I have no interest in the club, so I don't know what purpose there could be in telling me any of this."

"That's simple." Lake tucked the file beneath his arm, and then before Nix could ask what he was doing, his hands shot out. He captured his wrist a second time and stabbed the sharp tip of the pen down into his pointer finger.

Nix cursed and tried to pull away as blood dripped from the wound, but Lake held firm, waiting for the end of the pen to turn completely crimson before allowing him to distance himself. "What the actual hell?!"

He shoved his finger into his mouth and sucked, glaring at Lake. "You're insane if you think I'll sign anything after that!"

"And therein lies the purpose of my rant," Lake informed him coolly. He pulled the file out and turned it so it was facing Nix, then held out the pen. "You now know a secret of the club outsiders aren't allowed to know. So, your options have been simplified. Either you sign this agreement, or," he held his gaze and delivered the threat like he was offering to buy him a cup of coffee, "I stab you in the neck next."

Nix's breath caught in his throat and he froze.

"What's it going to be, Songbird?" Lake motioned to the file. "Your blood on paper or seeping into the carpet?"

He was serious. Even though his expression didn't waver, it was clear that Lake meant every word. It was also blatantly obvious Lake knew what Nix would choose. He'd set a trap after all, only it wasn't to get him to sign any documents.

"You're an asshole," the words slipped past his lips, filling the space between them. "I already agreed to go along with whatever you wanted in the cafeteria, and I willingly followed you all the way here. You aren't doing this because of the contract. You're making a point."

"It's a friendly warning," Lake corrected. "I'll discover the secret you're keeping from us in due time, but until then…I need you. But I don't trust you. Prior to this moment, you were still clinging to this image you'd formed in your head of who Maestro was. I'm Lake, Nix. I'm an Imperial in line for the throne, and I'll do anything, harm anyone, I have to in order to achieve my goals. Fall in line, Songbird, be who I need you to be, and—"

"I won't get hurt?" he sneered, only for Lake to laugh.

"No, no, you'll most certainly get hurt—in the bedroom and outside of the bedroom. Don't let Yejun's charms fool you; he's the most vicious of us."

"Pot calling the kettle black."

"I advise you not to get on his bad side," Lake added as though he hadn't spoken. "Take my advice or don't. For now," he held up the file again, "sign."

Nix hesitated. "Why me? If you could just as easily kill me right now, that means I'm nothing special. Why not ask someone else? More than half the student body would trade their right arm for a chance to be with you."

"You're the one I want."

"You can't mean that." It made even less sense to Nix than everything else about this fucked up situation did.

"Sign, Songbird."

They both knew he was going to. There was no other choice since he wasn't about to die here. With a growl, he snatched the pen out of Lake's hand and messily scrawled his name in thin red ink at the bottom of the page presented to him.

"There," he practically snarled once he was done, "happy?"

Calmly, Lake shut the file. "Place this on the desk."

"You're joking?"

He stared at him unblinkingly.

Nix inhaled slowly and then did as he was told. "All right. I did it. Now tell me exactly what it is I actually committed myself to." He stopped in front of the desk and tossed the file down onto it. "Because—"

He hadn't even heard Lake approaching, but in the next instant, Nix found himself bent over the desk, his cheek sticking to the file he'd just placed there. Lake's chest sealed over his back, his dark voice coming against the curve of his ear.

"You committed yourself to me, Songbird," Lake said, and the hint of excitement in his tone was impossible to miss. "Shall we begin?"

When he felt Lake bump his erection up against his ass, Nix's mind momentarily went blank.

CHAPTER 12:

"Wait." Nix scrambled to come up with a logical reason he could give to Lake not to do this, but there was nothing. What could he say to an Imperial? Someone who was used to getting what they wanted when they wanted it?

How had he ended up here?

"Is it starting to feel real, Songbird?" Lake asked, rolling his hips so that Nix persistently felt him while he spoke. "There's a vast difference between reality and the happenings behind the safety of a screen, isn't there? You got a taste the other night with West, but—"

"You're not West."

"No," he sounded pleased, "I'm not. Maestro or Lake, I'll let you choose which name you'll be screaming in a bit. Either way, it was me who told you this would happen. I'm merely keeping my promise."

"What does that contract say?" Nix struggled to keep his head clear enough to seek out answers while he still could.

"The NDA?"

"It wasn't just an NDA."

"True. The footnotes? You signed your soul away. We own you now."

"Until?"

Lake paused. "Until?"

"When does it end?"

"When we catch the hacker."

The pieces came together then. This wasn't about them

wanting him. Suddenly, all the little clues Lake had already dropped like breadcrumbs made sense. The hacker had tried to come for them and failed, but he must still be trying.

"I'm bait." Nix didn't like the twist of disappointment that revelation brought him. He'd known there was more to this, that in order for someone like Lake to go this far out of his way there had to be something serious. But still. It stung somewhat. "You're going to use me to lure out the hacker."

"He's interested in the Demons," Lake confirmed. "He tried to do what you did even, but he failed."

"He tried to become a King?"

"He wasn't as brave as you are," he brushed his fingers through Nix's hair, "and sent someone else to do the hard part for him. Our guess is he wasn't willing to reveal himself to complete those final steps the same way you were."

Right, because no matter how good of a hacker, the app only allowed you to fake your way through the system so far. There was no way to rig going from the Rook tier to King.

"You debased yourself so prettily that first night," Lake praised. "The second I saw you sitting on your bed, chewing on your bottom lip," he smoothed his thumb over Nix's mouth, "I almost came right there and then. You were so naïve, Songbird. I wanted to defile you. I want to defile you still. Corrupt you and make you scream until your voice is hoarse, and the only words you can remember how to say are 'I'm' and 'yours.'"

"That's…" Scarier than the threat of being stabbed in the jugular with a pen had been. "You sound obsessive. It's not cute. It's actually freaking me out."

"I'm not trying to be cute," Lake said. "Why would I? I already have you right where I want you. There's no need for masks between us any longer."

Nix got the uncomfortable feeling that he was seeing the real version of Lake. A version the other man kept buried beneath that icy exterior. "Something is seriously wrong with you."

"I think I've managed to hold myself back long enough. I

could have done this the moment we bumped into each other on campus and I recognized you."

"Are you asking me to *thank you* for not fucking me in the dirt?"

"In front of half the student body?" Lake added. "Yeah. Yeah, I am. But since I doubt you're going to, how about we get things started?"

He growled and tried to lift off of the desk, but was quickly overpowered.

"I warned you it would be like this," Lake shoved him down, holding him with a vicelike grip on his nape, "didn't I?" His free hand yanked Nix's pants, dragging the rough material to his knees along with his boxer briefs.

The first brush of cool air against his backside had Nix making another sound of protest. He planted his palms against the smooth surface of the desk and tried to force himself off it, but only managed to lift himself an inch before Lake had him back down, this time harder than before. He cried out when his cheek connected with the wood, the pain jarring.

"You should be grateful I brought you here. That I'm easing you into how things will be from now on," Lake continued, working his own belt free now. As soon as he had it off, he captured Nix's wrists and bound that at his narrow back.

"Stop!" Nix had never considered himself weak before, but against the Demons of Foxglove, he was finding he fit in that category. Lake orchestrated his body however he saw fit with very little effort so that he was bound and back over the desk with his bare ass in the air in no time at all.

"If West were here, he'd lube you with his spit," Lake said, and Nix froze. "If it were Yejun, you'd be lucky since he doesn't leave the house without packets of the stuff on his person. Me, though?"

A gust of hot air had the hairs on the back of Nix's neck rising.

"Tell me, Songbird, how did my best friend's cock taste, hmm?"

"You told me to do it!" The fear was very real, his heart pounding in his chest loud enough he was certain there was no way Lake could miss it.

"And now I'm telling you to do this," Lake replied. "So, what's the problem? You meet the two of them and suddenly my cock isn't good enough for you?"

"No!" Nix had to think. He couldn't allow panic to set in, otherwise he'd end up saying the wrong thing and making this worse for himself. This past week, he'd learned a lot about who Lake was, and forgiving? That wasn't a characteristic on the list. "That isn't it at all. Lake, *please*."

"What exactly are you begging me for?" he asked. "Do you even know?"

No, no he did not.

"Just..." Nix latched onto the first thing he could think of, "Go slow. Please."

Lake considered. "Ah, you want less pain, is that it?"

"I—"

"I'm going to get something across the room," he interrupted. "If you move so much as a centimeter while I'm gone, I'll tear you in half with my cock and use your blood as lubrication, got it?"

Nix gasped but nodded his head.

That earned him a little slap on the ass. "Good boy. Wait for me."

His heart continued to thump as he listened to Lake's retreating footsteps, followed shortly by the opening of a drawer by the bookshelf. It wasn't long before that hot presence returned to him, making the task of staying still not nearly as imposing as Lake had made it out to be.

A finger hooked into the belt securing his wrists and he was lifted off the desk and spun around. Before he could say anything, Lake dropped down and removed his shoes and the rest of his clothing until Nix was left in only his school uniform shirt.

"Hey!" he protested again when Lake suddenly tore the

thin material in two, sending buttons flying. "I need that!"

"Not right now you don't." He shoved the material all the way down until it was settled over the tied belt, restricting Nix even more and causing his chest to push forward slightly. "Stand right here." He moved him over a step and then pulled something from his pocket—clearly whatever he'd gotten from the drawer just now.

"What the hell?" Nix gasped a second time as he watched Lake pop a large white dildo down onto the desk, testing to be sure the suction cup base held.

Satisfied that it did, Lake grabbed Nix by the back of the neck all over again and forced him around until he was practically bent in half, the tip of the silicone cock pressed against his lips.

"You're going to want to get that nice and wet for yourself," Lake warned. "It's the only kind of lube I'll allow you."

"Wha—" He should have known better than to try and speak. Nix's head was immediately shoved down, and he was forced to open his mouth and welcome the toy or be hit in the teeth by it.

At least he didn't force him the same way West had. As soon as he was sure Nix had taken it, Lake loosened his hold, allowing him to set the pace however he saw fit.

The plastic tasted bland on his tongue as Nix rolled it around, trying to slick up as much as he could. He pooled saliva in his mouth and wondered if Lake had been insincere before. Perhaps West wasn't the one with the spit kink?

It was like Lake could read his thoughts, however, for as soon as it came to him, the demon at his back chuckled.

"I'm not West, Songbird. The longer you take, the more impatient I'll become."

He did the best he could to focus on wetting the toy, telling himself that it was for his own benefit, even if all of this was being controlled by the bastard at his back.

This whole day had been surreal, from the drive to the contract in blood to this. He wanted to fight back and argue, but knew it'd simply be a waste of his efforts. And Lake knew it as well.

Nix needed this strange partnership—or whatever it was—to work in order to find the person responsible for terrorizing Branwen. If he had to allow Lake to humiliate and abuse him for a bit? So what?

A fucked up voice in his head laughed at him and pointed out snidely that he wasn't exactly as innocent as he was playing.

Case in point, his dick was swollen and achy.

That didn't go unnoticed by Lake either.

"Already hard and all you've done was give head to a rubber cock?" he tutted and yanked Nix back up by his hair, smirking when that caused him to yelp. "When was the last time you fingered yourself?"

Nix blinked at him in confusion.

"Yejun hasn't gotten to you yet, and I know West hasn't made a move since the Roost," Lake reiterated. "Which means you've gone untouched by us for at least a few days. Our last Enigma session was almost two weeks ago. Did you touch yourself after that?"

Nix dropped his gaze, glaring when Lake propped a finger beneath his chin and lifted his head back up.

"You're blushing, Songbird," Lake teased. "You don't have to. I know you've been thinking about me when you get yourself off. If you're good for me for the rest of this, maybe I'll take pity on you and tell you a secret."

"What, forcing me suddenly no longer appealing?" Nix snapped and instantly regretted it. He braced himself, but retaliation never came.

"I'm still going to make you sob," Lake shrugged like it was nothing. Then in a flash, he had both hands under Nix's thighs and was lifting him.

With his hands bound, Nix could only brace his chest against Lake's as he was raised over the desk and positioned to Lake's liking. He'd only just processed what was going on a second before he was lowered and he felt the tip of the dildo breech his hole.

"Don't!" He cried out as he was dropped onto the length of the toy in one move, all eight inches of it invading him. When he tried to wiggle free, Lake readjusted his hold, pinning him down by the tops of his thighs so he was forced to sit on the desk with the entire toy stuck inside of him.

Nix groaned in a mixture of pleasure and pain, leaning away from Lake. The move only had the toy pressing against different spots, and he hissed at the stretch and the burn.

"Put your head on my shoulder," Lake ordered, quirking a brow when Nix didn't immediately move to follow his command. "This isn't just my office. Unless you want someone walking in on you getting fucked by a desk—"

"All right." Nix glared but leaned forward, awkwardly figuring out how to best rest his head on his shoulder with his arms still tied. He ended up planting his cheek against the spot between his shoulder and neck, facing the wall as he waited for whatever came next.

Lake's hands returned to the bottom of his thighs, settling right beneath the swell of his ass. He lifted Nix slowly at first, carefully pulling his body off of the toy inch by torturous inch. Once he had him hovering over it with only the crown still inserted, he repeated his earlier move, dropping him back down with enough force it was like a punch to the gut.

Nix swore, but Lake was already hauling him back up again steadily.

It didn't get easier when he was forced back down a third time.

Or a fourth.

Or a fifth.

He lost count after that, his sounds of discomfort turning to mewls of desperation, his thighs widening of their own accord to welcome Lake when he stepped in closer. Whenever he was lowered onto the dildo, Nix started gyrating his hips, trying to hit that sweet spot, only to be tormented by yet another unhurried dragging against his inner walls as he was lifted.

"Look how wet you are for me now, Songbird," Lake said, drawing his attention down between them.

Nix pulled back to do as he was told and sucked in a sharp breath, but it wasn't because of his own exposed dick.

Lake's cock was proudly out, jutting upward and slicked in his own juices. He could practically see the vein at the bottom throbbing, took in the flushed and angry red head—which was much wider than the toy Nix was currently sitting on.

Everything about it was bigger, in fact.

"Good Light," it was out of his mouth before he could help it, but that was really all he could say.

"As big as you imagined?" Lake joked, gripping himself in a hand to give a leisurely stroke that had a single bead of pearly precome leaking from the slit.

"Bigger," he admitted. "Too big." There was absolutely no way.

"You'll take it," Lake told him, unencumbered by Nix's obvious rejection. "The boys will help stretch you out first."

Nix opened his mouth, closed it, and tried again. "Are you insinuating…"

"That you'll take West and Yejun's cocks before mine?" Lake nodded. "Unless you're okay with not being able to walk for a few days. I did bring a tube of sun cream back from Vitality. Though…" His gaze dropped pointedly down Nix's body. "If I fuck you once, Songbird, we aren't stopping until I've had my fill, and I've been known to go for days. Not even sun cream will be able to fix you then, and unfortunately, we've got other things to do. Fucking you until you can no longer run from me will have to wait."

"That's—" Nix had figured out that they were all going to share him, they'd said as much, but this… "You just expect me to actually sleep with them both? To—"

"Spread your legs like you're doing right now and welcome them into that pretty hole of yours?" Lake said. "Yes. Yes, I do. And you will."

"What happened to not sharing me?"

Lake frowned, clearly not understanding.

"The last time, in the shower," Nix reminded. "You said either I come for you or—"

"Oh," understanding dawned on him, "that. Haven't you realized already? West and Yejun are closer to me than blood brothers. You come for them? It's as good as you coming for me."

Lake's eyes narrowed. "You come for anyone else, however…"

"That was the deal," Nix confirmed, even though they hadn't actually gone over terms and conditions like he'd wanted. It was fairly obvious though, and he sure as hell wasn't going to complain right now while in the process of being impaled by eight inches of rubber. "I have to be with you three to attract the hacker."

"Yeah, that's why," he snorted, but Nix didn't get the joke. Lake didn't give him the chance to ask either, moving in closer until that massive cock of his bumped up against Nix's. He wrapped his hand around them, managing to capture them both so his other arm could slip beneath Nix.

Nix quickly dropped his head back on Lake's shoulder, giving him most of his weight as the Demon started fucking him onto the toy again. It was shallower this time, with Lake only able to lift him a few inches off the dildo with one hand.

But he made up for it.

Lake rubbed their cocks together, smearing precome down their hard shafts as he gripped them. He wasn't slow or careful now, stroking them together to a tempo that only grew frenzied with each passing second.

The feel of the toy impaling him and keeping him stuck in place to the desk while his body was manipulated had Nix's balls tightening. His dick felt like it was going to burn off, the heat from Lake's cock like searing iron against him. The sounds of their bodies coming together, their precome mixing and the hinges of the desk creaking filled the room, drowned out only by their harsh panting.

Lake took from Nix the same way West had, even if everything about how was different, and Nix felt a moment of clarity where it really clicked for him what the three of them had meant.

They really, well, and truly *believed* that they owned him.

"Come for me, Songbird," Lake said. "Come for your king."

Nix opened his mouth to tell him to stop being ridiculous, but what ended up coming out was a moan as his body obeyed.

He orgasmed, twitching around the dildo as Lake left him on it to reach forward. His hands continued to work them against each other, fingers gathering Nix's come to use as more lube for himself as he did.

Lake pulled Nix off of him enough to lean him back, and then his mouth was at the side of Nix's neck, latching onto his pulse point. He gave one hard suck that had Nix's hips bucking and another gush shooting forward. That seemed to be all Lake needed to push him over the edge as well and he growled as he came.

"No more," Nix begged when a moment later he was forced all the way back until he was resting on his elbows on the desk. The pop of the toy's suction giving way had him grimacing, but the toy remained buried inside of him nonetheless.

Ignoring him, Lake dipped his fingers in the mess on Nix's chest, collecting a few thick globs of come before bringing his hand up to Nix's mouth.

When Nix tried to resist, he grabbed him by the neck and yanked him forward, shoving two digits in deep.

He rubbed his fingers against Nix's tongue, giving him a dark, warning look when Nix still wasn't reciprocating. Lake left his mouth and collected more, waiting this time with his hand held aloft.

"You're such an asshole," Nix grumbled, unable to help himself even as he willingly took those fingers back into his mouth and licked them clean the way he knew the Demon wanted.

Sure enough, Lake smiled, some of the edge leaving his gaze. "Who tastes better?"

Nix tilted his head. Surely...

"Me or West?"

That was a dangerous question, but it was obvious by the tightening grip on his nape that he wasn't going to be allowed time to try and find a safe answer.

"You." Nix figured it better to please the demon in front of him, right?

Lake nodded like that was what he'd expected to hear and then removed the toy, smirking like the bastard he was when Nix groaned as he was emptied. He undid the belt next, adjusting Nix's shirt.

"What about the come?" Nix asked with a scowl as Lake pulled the two halves together and redid the single button that had survived his terror earlier, covering the mess but in no way dealing with it. Sure, he'd fed him some of it, but not all, and pretty soon that was going to start to dry and itch. Not his idea of a good time.

"It stays on until we get back home."

"Seriously?"

Lake picked up the rest of Nix's clothes off the ground and tossed them at him. "Get dressed. Quickly. Unless you want to walk back to campus?"

For a moment, despite all the threats, Lake had seemed more like the man Nix had spoken with before coming to Foxglove.

He'd forgotten Maestro wasn't real.

Had lost himself to sensation.

It wouldn't happen again.

Nix pulled on his pants, angry at the way his ass smarted and how the rest of his body felt amazing in the afterglow.

Lake was also in the process of putting his clothes back on when his multi-slate rang. After a glance, he answered, "Yeah?"

"Where are you?" West's voice came through the tiny speaker on the side of the device. "The Order is asking for us."

"I'll be there shortly," Lake replied, then paused, eyes finding Nix's.

Nix frowned and mouthed *what*, not wanting to interrupt

their conversation.

"By the way," Lake drawled.

"Yeah?" The sound of a car door slamming came through the line. "Spit it out, what is it?"

"*Nixie* says I taste better than you." A single curse word managed to come through before Lake ended the call.

Nix stared at him, completely at a loss for words. He only reacted when Lake stepped toward him and pressed his thumb against the massive hickey he'd left at the side of his neck, and even then, all he could do was wince and pull away.

"Call me an asshole again, Songbird," Lake said. "I dare you."

CHAPTER 13:

"Why did you need to come here?" Grady suspiciously stared at Hunters Cross, the main art building on the east side of campus. It was a two-level structure with high ceilings they could see even from out on the pathway. "Are you taking an art elective?"

"No." Nix sighed. Last night, when he'd returned to their dorm, Grady had tried his best not to push about the event at lunch, but he'd only lasted ten or so minutes before making his discomfort known.

The first day was already an indicator of that enough, but he'd reminded Nix about his warning not to get involved with the Demons, and Nix hadn't known how to explain things, so... He'd mostly just mumbled he was figuring it all out and he was sorry Grady had been involved. The thing was, that wasn't even a lie.

Nix was still trying to figure it all out. He'd signed the NDA—or contract, or whatever it'd really been, since he'd never gotten any serious answers—but after the wild sex they'd had in the office, Lake had simply driven them both back to school and dropped Nix off in front of his dorm. They'd barely said two words on the drive over, despite all of the questions swirling in his mind. Mostly, he'd been too high-strung to sort through his thoughts enough to ask any of them.

That, and he'd been scratching at his chest, glowering at the dried come coating his skin and the way his ass still smarted from having the toy shoved into it with no preparation.

Before, rough and vulgar sex hadn't been his forte, but he'd realized that had started to change once he'd met Maestro. That thrill and dash of embarrassment he'd felt whenever the ping of his computer announced it was broadcasting and he was being watched had set something off in him that he hadn't been aware of prior.

This wasn't the time or the place for a sexual awakening, though. He wasn't here for self-discovery. He was here to—

His multi-slate dinged, and he twisted his wrist, wincing when he saw it wasn't a text but a message through the Enigma app.

Incubus: You're late.

Nix had received a message from the same sender in the middle of his last class with Grady, ordering him to Hunters Cross by two pm. The clock at the right corner of his device told him it was now one minute past.

The only person he'd ever interacted with on the app was Lake, but the tiny crown icon above the black circle with the skull in it indicated that whoever Incubus was, they were a King.

Which meant it was either one of the other Demons or one of the other three he'd yet to meet. Nix doubted he'd get so lucky, so…Either Yejun or West it was.

"Don't tell me," Grady said then, as though reading his mind. "You aren't meeting Yejun Sang here, are you? Come on, Nix. How many times do I have to warn you? Those guys are dangerous."

"I know." He really, really did. "But…"

"You don't have a choice." He caught on and swore, then sheepishly glanced at the building, suddenly looking at it as though it would magically morph into a beast and swallow them whole. "Do you…want me to go with you?"

That was really nice, and Nix felt guilty that he'd gotten Grady involved through association. From here on out, he'd try his best to keep his roommate and the Demons as separate as possible. It wasn't fair to Grady to make him uncomfortable, though, admittedly Nix was still a little more than a bit curious why he seemed to dislike and fear them as much as he did.

He'd yet to share that information, and Nix didn't have the right to pry. Maybe he'd never find out.

Sadly, he wasn't here to make friends either so…

"No," he smiled at Grady. "But thank you for offering. I'll be fine."

"I hope so." He lingered another moment before shaking his head and stepping back. "I'll be at the library. Call me if you need anything."

The library was one of the closer buildings, just down the street and to the right. Nix had no idea if he'd intended to head there beforehand, but it was another kindness that he was offering his help.

Why hadn't Branwen met more people like Grady instead of whichever King she'd gotten caught up with? Things would probably have been different for her if she had.

"Thanks," he repeated, waving when his roommate finally turned on his heels and headed away. With a deep inhale, he straightened his spine and wrapped his hand around the strap of his backpack before bounding up the stone steps toward the front door.

Hunters Cross was one of the larger workshop buildings on campus, offering several different art programs and four large studio spaces. There was also a private gallery in the back with a separate entrance leading to the city for when showings were put on. Inside, everything was done in whites and pale grays, a sharp contrast to the décor of the rest of the school, and Nix paused at the foot of a wide stairwell leading up to the second floor.

No sooner had he stopped than his multi-slate dinged again.

Incubus: 27A.

Clearly this King was watching him somehow. Nix glanced around, but none of the other students seemed to be paying him any interest. Were there cameras? He tried to find them on the ceiling but couldn't. Deciding not to waste any more time and potentially piss off whichever Demon was waiting for him, he gave up.

There was a large A with an arrow next to the stairs, so Nix traveled up. At the landing, the second floor branched off in four directions, and it took him another minute to find the right way. He passed over a dozen rooms before he found the right one, his hand hovering over the silver handle of a closed tan wooden door.

Would it be Yejun or West?

Shit.

He was nervous. Was it too much to wish that Lake would be there as well? He'd never been alone with the others before, and frankly, now that the NDA had been signed, he wasn't sure what to expect.

Would West want a repeat of the other night?

Would Yejun?

Had Nix signed over his body completely for them to use at their leisure, was there more to it? Lake had said this was about finding the hacker but...Truthfully, Nix still didn't really understand why he'd need to actually fool around with the three of them in order to accomplish that. Couldn't they fake it?

He'd have to ask.

There was a prick of self-loathing for not having already done so. For not pushing the issue the other day and demanding answers right then and there. For not pushing Lake away or trying harder to resist.

That physical connection between them was familiar though, comforting in a fucked up sort of way. Nix's entire universe seemed to be turned on its axis and he was struggling to understand the depths of what he'd gotten himself into, but when he was being touched by Lake, spoken to in that familiar voice that had talked him through all those Favors, he sickly felt more grounded.

He needed help. Lake was an asshole who was using him, and now that they'd met in person, there weren't any redeeming qualities to him that Nix could find, and yet...

No. He couldn't allow himself to fall into this trap. There needed to be a clear separation in his mind between his actions and his emotions. Somehow, he'd been strongarmed into playing this part for the Demons, but the way he felt about it, the way he ended up feeling about *them*, was entirely in his control.

His weird thrill toward Lake's sexual advances made sense, but there was no such past or connection to endear West or Yejun to Nix. He'd treat them as a means to an end, keep them at arm's length no matter what.

Mind made up, Nix forced his features to settle and then tugged open the heavy door, slipping into a large, open room painted bright white. It was a rare sunny day out, and sunlight spilled in through the far wall which had one huge window, casting shadows from the easels set about.

Some of them had partially finished works on display, but the room was empty save for one other person.

"Took you long enough, Firebird." Yejun was busy sketching something in charcoal on the other side of the room. There was a small table tucked into the corner with a holo-cube and the device was currently flickering through various photos of the same man posing—someone Nix didn't recognize.

Yejun was sitting on a stool with one leg crossed over the other, a medium-sized sketchpad set over his thigh. He didn't glance up from his work, waiting for Nix to come over on his own.

Not seeing how standing by the door would benefit him, Nix started walking, carefully weaving through the other easels as he did until he was standing a few feet away from the Demon.

"What?" Yejun asked, sketching a few more lines before finally lifting his head. His dark brown eyes found Nix's, his expression calm. The set of his shoulders and body language also gave off the sense he was relaxed, but Nix wasn't sure if he could trust it.

"You wanted to see me?" Nix's voice sounded almost too loud in the room and he shifted on his feet.

Yejun chuckled and then motioned to a nearby stool, positioned a bit ahead of his so that he could keep both the holocube and Nix in his line of sight. "Sit down. I'm not going to do anything weird to you."

"It's unclear if our definitions of weird are similar," Nix mumbled, but he took a seat, lowering his backpack to the ground. "Where's the rest of the class?"

"What do you mean?"

Nix waved at the other easels. "Did it end? Why are you the only one here?"

"Oh, those." Yejun returned to his drawing. "Those are all mine."

Huh? His confusion must have shown because Yejun laughed.

"This is my private studio room, Firebird. No one else is allowed in here without my permission." He pointed to the holocube. "I had this model in here earlier and took the photos I would need so I could send him away before your arrival."

Nix tensed. "Why?"

"Relax, I said I wasn't going to do anything to you. Damn. Your trust issues seem worse than mine."

"You have trust issues?"

"Got screwed over by a friend recently. Iris. Pretty name for such a poisonous person." Even though he was the one who'd brought it up, Yejun's mood soured instantly. He scowled and ripped the page he'd been working on from his sketch pad, crumpled it up, and tossed it carelessly over his shoulder. A second later, he drew lines on a fresh page, the crease between his brow lingering. "Lying bitch is lucky she's gone."

He felt himself go cold. "Like, she's dead?"

Was it him?

Was Yejun the King—

"What?" He sent him an incredulous look. "No, man. Of course not. She just transferred. Why would you—" Yejun caught himself. "Oh. Right. Sorry. That was tacky of me. You mentioned your cousin recently passed. That's got to suck."

Nix deflated some, confused over the odd mix of emotions in him. On the one hand, if it had been Yejun, he'd have found the culprit. On the other...Having experienced what it was like to be held down by both Lake and West, Nix had concluded that he hoped the King he was after *wasn't* one of the Demons. Not only because he'd signed that contract already and it was too late to go back and undo it, but also because he had no clue how he'd be able to take one of them down on his own.

Hell, he still didn't really have a plan in that regard anyway, no matter who the King ended up being.

"I'm sorry for your loss," Yejun surprised him with the sincerity in his tone. "I've never lost anyone close to me, but I imagine it's got to be a pretty shitty feeling."

"Yeah," Nix replied. "Kind of feels like I woke up one day and everything was different, but I can't quite put my finger on what's changed, and that drives me crazy." Logically, he knew the missing thing was Branwen, but because she wasn't a daily fixture in his life and hadn't been for some time, it was almost like his subconscious struggled to put two and two together.

Like, the grief and confusion were always there, but he couldn't always process that's what he was feeling when he first woke up in the morning. And then, as soon as it did hit him, the rage came quickly after.

"It's nowhere near the same thing," Yejun said, "but that friend who screwed me over? I sort of feel like that. It's better now, but when it first happened last year I was a nightmare to be around."

Was that why Lake had told him Yejun was vicious? Had he been taking out his emotions on others? Was that why he'd ordered those two Bishops to have public sex, knowing they'd get expelled and never rise in tier?

"What happened?" He probably shouldn't ask, but since Yejun had brought it up...Nix risked it.

For a moment, it appeared as though he wasn't going to answer, but then Yejun resituated the sketchpad on his leg and said, "She tricked me into thinking we were friends when, in reality, she was just like everyone else. She only wanted something from me. The second she got it? She had no problem tossing me to the wind."

"Did you meet on the app?" Nix knew he said his friend—not that they sounded like they'd actually been friends at all—hadn't died, but it couldn't hurt to second-check.

"No," he told him. "We met in class. Figure drawing is my main focus and I was retaking one of the basics last year because they had better models than the advanced classes. I'd pop in now and again and she and I got to talking one of those times. Seemed like we had a lot in common, so I hung around sometimes."

"I heard you were a playboy."

Yejun snorted. "Don't get it twisted, Firebird. She and I weren't fucking. I don't fuck my friends. Too messy. Anyway, I didn't call you here to share my feelings."

"Why did you want me to come?"

"Figured Lake, King of Stoicdom, didn't properly explain things to you yesterday," Yejun said, grinning when Nix quirked a brow at the jab. "What? Come on. He's not here and I won't tell. Stoic should really be that guy's middle name."

"You aren't wrong," Nix agreed.

"I'm typically not." Yejun winked at him.

Maybe this wouldn't be so bad. He was clearly the biggest flirt of the three, but he'd said he wouldn't do anything, and so far he was keeping his word. If he really had called Nix here to fill in the gaps for him, it was best he take advantage while he could.

"Lake had me sign an NDA or contract or whatever. I get that I'm supposed to help you draw out the hacker by pretending to be involved with you, but I'm still not really clear on the why or the how."

"The hacker we're after tried to use someone else to get to us," Yejun explained. "Luckily, we discovered their plans before they could infiltrate the Kings too deeply, but it put us on edge. We know it's the same person who attempted to get into the club's computers, and thanks to that little act, we've got a better understanding of what they're actually after."

"Which is?"

"Lake. They want to stop him from taking the throne. The person they used before worked their way up the tiers organically. We're not sure if they were on the same team from the beginning or if the hacker recruited them after the fact, but they were working together."

"What could they get from being a King that they couldn't elsewhere?" Nix didn't understand. Lake had told him that the app was really a secret recruitment tool for the club, sure, but… "Were they hoping they could make it into Club Essential?"

"I don't think so. They were collecting data on us, and our guess is the plan was to release it to the public all at once. Irrefutable evidence that we're deviants and Lake is unfit to take the throne."

"Okay," Nix pursed his lips, "but it's not like the planet isn't already aware of the stuff that goes on with Enigma."

"It's one thing to hear about college kids fucking around—literally. It's another to see it and have it flooded all over the news. If Lake's reputation is destroyed to that extent, he'll no longer be considered an essential piece on the board. It's the fact that he's in line for the throne that keeps him safe. If the entire planet demands he step down? Both the Council and the Order will vote him out. If he's not essential to the running of the government, there's no need for him to remain in the club."

"The Kings get up to a lot more than just sex with other students, don't they," Nix said. "You guys dare people to do dangerous things and then laugh when it ruins their lives."

Yejun didn't bother trying to deny it. "Sometimes we can be bullies, sure."

"If you know that's the sort of thing that could ruin your reputation, why risk it?"

"Because we can? Because it's fun?" He rolled his eyes. "Things work a certain way here, everyone knows that. Implicating us implicates the entire school, and very few people would be stupid enough to attempt that sort of thing. That's how you're made to disappear."

Nix tensed. "Have you...Killed people before?"

It was crazy to even consider, to think about them going around straight up murdering others and getting away with it. But it wasn't out of the realm of possibility, and it certainly wouldn't be the first case where Imperials and Royals and those in power committed those types of serious crimes with no repercussions.

"You really didn't come prepared, did you?" Yejun looked at him more closely. "Murder? Murder is easy for an Essential. I doubt the majority of the public would even bat an eye over something as small as that."

What could they be hiding that was *worse* than killing?!

"We're losing the plot," Yejun stated then. "Let's get back on course, yeah? My point was, right now, the only part of the club's darker proclivities that can be proven involve sex. The bottom level of the Clubhouse is literally a sex club, after all, and so long as you're invited by a member, just about anyone can enter there. So long as everyone just thinks this is about sex, it's no big deal."

"But you just said—"

"Okay," he sighed, "so maybe if there was a legitimate body count, people might be angry. Especially if that count included one or several well-known members of society. Then again, maybe no one would care. This hacker is trying to find dirt on us, any kind of dirt. If they gather enough of it, spin it the right way, release it at the right time, they might be able to make an impact. We aren't willing to risk that possibility."

"So," Nix drawled, "what you're saying is you've done worse than force someone to give you a blowjob, and you know that's wrong and want to cover it up?"

Yejun snorted. "Still bothered over that?"

"Over being force-fed dick? Yeah." He gave him a pointed stare. "You try and see how quickly you can get over it."

"You offering, Firebird?"

Nix faltered as Yejun leaned closer.

"Picture my lips wrapped around your dick already?" His

eyes trailed down the length of him suggestively. "I'm not opposed. Maybe once I'm done with this sketch, I could eat."

"Um," Nix cleared his throat. "No, thanks. That's not...No."

Yejun chortled. "Well, damn, Firebird, aren't you adorable. I can see why Lake chose you for this. You've got that whole naïve, innocent thing going for you. It's a good act."

"Who says it's an act?"

"Don't get mad, it wasn't an insult, but we both know it's got to be an act. A naïve person doesn't have hacking skills like yours, and they sure as shit wouldn't be bold enough to take on the Demons of Foxglove Grove all in the name of—What did you call it again? Fun, right?"

That was what he'd said. It'd been an excuse, but it seemed like the rest of them had believed it at least.

"Whoever your cousin was to you, she must have had some influence to get you to step this far out of your comfort zone," Yejun added.

"To be fair," Nix said, "this was further than I intended to go."

"That's true," he agreed.

"You all didn't really give me a choice. Especially not Lake."

"You were going to sign the contract no matter what," Yejun nodded. "At least you got something out of it."

Had...Had Lake told them about what they'd done?

"The app boasts anonymity for everyone except us. The whole campus knows we're the Kings. Pretty soon, they'll know you're one too. Under our protection, you can have anything you want. All you have to do is play the part convincingly until Demons Passing."

That was news to him. "Just until then?"

Yejun hummed. "That's our deadline for tracking down the hacker. West should have discreetly slipped your name to some of his boxing buddies by now. The chatty ones who can't keep a secret to save their lives. The whole school should know about you by the time we're done here. You want a job at Star Eye Holding, right?"

"Yeah...Don't tell me that was in my file?"

"West found your university admittance essay," Yejun confessed. "The guy is thorough."

"More like invasive," he grumbled.

"You'll be thanking him by the end of the year. It's not just the students who treat us differently here, it's the staff as well. You want into Star Eye Holding? Being associated with the three of us will guarantee your spot. You're getting to experience something no one else has ever gotten to before," he continued. "It's been a really long time since we've all fucked the same person, and it's never been a public spectacle before."

"What?" He shot off the stool before he could help it, but somehow managed not to make a break for the door. That wouldn't do him any good anyway.

Yejun frowned at him, until he realized why Nix was reacting so strongly. He held up both hands, his left smeared in black charcoal. "Whoa that's not at all what I meant. I'm not saying it won't happen, but typically the three of us aren't big on sharing with anyone outside of our circle. Wow, you really are against exhibitionism, aren't you?"

"We don't need to take it that far anyway." Nix remembered what he'd been planning on bringing up. "Isn't this all an act? The hacker only has to think that I'm involved with the three of you so he'll approach me."

"He doesn't have access to the app any longer since we got rid of his mole," Yejun said, "but that doesn't mean he doesn't have eyes elsewhere. Lake really should have done a better job explaining things to you." He brushed a loose strand of his hair out of the way, smearing charcoal across the rise of his cheek in the process. "It's not just the hacker we're trying to fool here. The club ordered us to find this person, which means we have to show them we're actively doing so."

"How exactly does the three of you dating the same person help sell that?" If anything, he was only more befuddled.

"Because Lake told the Order that you're an ace hacker who we've recruited to help us in the hunt," Yejun explained, "and we're paying you in sex."

"Excuse me?" His mouth dropped open. "Who in their right mind—"

"Club Essential would," Yejun guessed where he was going with that and replied. "The club recognizes more than just coin as currency. Sex? That's premium. You'd be surprised how much gets done on this planet through quickies in the boardroom."

Nix couldn't see how that was possible. Why?

"Think about this logically," Yejun suggested. "Strip away everything you associate with sex and think of it solely as a commodity. One that offers entertainment and a different sort of relief. When you're as wealthy as most of the members of the club, money doesn't hold the same appeal. Coin goes straight into our bank accounts. It's all digital. You can't see it, taste it, hear it moan or scream your name…It's lifeless. Members of the club, especially those at the top, need something to rekindle that spark.

"Sex is usually it. Plus, there's power in sex. Power exchange in knowing you can lord over the fact you pinned someone down, that you've spread their thighs. That you've been inside of them…" Yejun seemed to get distracted by his own thoughts then, staring off into the distance for a moment before he snapped himself out of it and laughed. "The point is, the Order one hundred percent believes you're helping us for the chance to ride our cocks. It all comes back to Star Eye Holding, see? You're fucking us for a chance at a better future. That's how they'll take it."

"And if they find out that's not true?"

He tilted his head, hand pausing with the charcoal over the page. "What part of it isn't?"

"I'm not doing this because I want to have sex with you three."

"Then," he batted his long dark lashes at him and set his chin on a closed fist, "whatever are you doing this for?"

Too late, Nix realized what he'd done. If he'd truly manipulated his way into the app for fun, there wouldn't be any other reason for him to agree to this other than because he wanted to sleep with them. But…It was too obvious that wasn't the case.

Shit.

"Caught you," Yejun grinned, and there was a flash of something in his eyes, there and gone, that had Nix's skin prickling.

"It's not…" What could he say to get out of this? "Maestro." Well.

Double shit if that was the best he could come up with.

Yejun seemed to consider it though and then, "You fall for him or something? Through a computer? Damn, Firebird."

"I didn't fall for him," Nix backtracked, wringing his hands. "But I did…I don't know. I was really freaked out that first time and he was…Gentle? Kind?"

Yejun made a choking sound that only partially sounded forced. "Gentle and kind? I have never heard those words spoken in association with Lake a day in my life, and I've known the guy since we were in diapers. Are you sure you got the right King?"

"I asked him that myself yesterday." This could work. It was awkward as hell, especially since there wasn't a chance it wouldn't make its way to Lake's ears, but at least Yejun didn't appear to be suspicious of him.

As if to further prove that, Yejun went back to drawing. "No chance. The app is built in such a way that no one else can access your account. Take yours for example. Now that you're a King, if you handed me your multi-slate and I tried, I wouldn't be able to log in. There's a hidden thumbprint and retina scanner."

"There's what?" Nix twisted his wrist and blinked down at his device, though the app wasn't open at the moment and his screen was black.

"Yeah," Yejun continued. "West is a genius, didn't you realize? It's programmed to secretly scan that information and copy and send it to his main server, all without the user knowing. That's why if you try opening the app now without looking at it, it won't work."

"His server?" That caught his attention.

"His shit is all in his room at the Roost," Yejun made a face. "I don't know. Don't ask me any questions about it, I'm not good with tech. That's all his department. And," he motioned to him with the charcoal stick, "yours now, too, I guess."

If West had all the information of every user stored on a computer in his bedroom…

Nix had to find a way to get to it. If he could, he'd be able to search through the accounts and find the King he was looking for.

This was good. Signing this contract. Getting involved with the three of them. This morning, he hadn't been so sure, but now…

Lake had been off planet last year, so it couldn't have been him.

Yejun still wasn't entirely in the clear, but it sounded like he'd been pretty busy with this friend of his. A friend who was still alive, unlike Branwen. He seemed like the open type, so there was a good chance Nix could discover more about him as they went and eventually check him off as a suspect completely.

That left West as the only other King that Nix knew of.

If he could hack into West's computer and discover the identities of the other Kings, he could investigate them and eventually make his way to those who'd graduated last year if need be. That would also solve the problem Lake had presented the other day. If Branwen's King had graduated and was no longer on the active list, West should still have a copy of all the past members.

This was it.

This was the break he'd been looking for.

And all he had to do was sell himself to three Demons.

Yejun was too busy working on his drawing to notice when Nix shivered at that thought.

CHAPTER 14:

"Nix!" Grady called out to him from across the library when he entered. His roommate was seated with a group of three, two male and one female. They'd chosen a spot in the corner of the room, furthest from the stacks and the scolding eyes of the librarian who was usually seated behind the front desk.

It'd only been a few days since the start of classes, and Nix hadn't really made many friends aside from Grady. In the past, that wouldn't have bothered him. He'd always been busy with his nose in his studies or playing the latest release of one of his favorite game series.

Branwen used to tease him over summer breaks when she'd visited his house that the entire world could end, and he wouldn't even know it until he pulled his head out of a book or away from a screen. She'd teased him, but she'd also been the first person to fully accept his dream to become a game developer and root for him.

The two of them had grown up apart, only seeing each other at major family events once or twice a year. It hadn't been until they'd gotten older and been allowed to have their own multi-slates that they'd started communicating more frequently. He hadn't been a complete loner in high school, but there also wasn't a single person from that period of his life he'd kept in touch with.

It was the same with Hyacinth Academy. He'd gotten along with his roommate there and the other students he attended regular classes with. They'd joked around, and there'd always been someone to sit with at lunch. When the professors had assigned group projects, he'd never feared being left the last one standing with no one wanting to work with him. A couple of those people had reached out after the death of his cousin, but none of them had known her, and none of them had been close enough with him to push the issue when he'd made it clear by giving them only offhand replies that he wanted distance.

Call him crazy, but friendship was never something Nix had felt the need for. He'd had Branwen for when he needed to talk to someone, and online friends he gamed with to help blow off steam. He understood it was unconventional, but it'd worked for him. When Branwen had called and gossiped about her friends, he'd laughed along with her and secretly thought he'd made the right choice not to get close to anyone.

The old version of him would have waved absently at Grady and gone on his way. Instead, he found himself approaching the table, a smile already set in place. He nodded in greeting and when one of the guys he didn't know offered the empty seat next to him, Nix took it.

"You're new this year, right?" the female student propped her elbows on the table and asked. She was pretty, with curly black hair and wide violet eyes. The crimson eyeshadow she'd chosen helped to highlight them, and when she smiled, Nix could tell it was with genuine happiness. "I've seen you around campus. I'm Khloe."

"Hi," he waved. "Nix."

The male sitting closest to Grady was giving him a funny look, almost as though he were trying to place him. He had a similar coloring to Khloe, but it was hard to tell if they were related or not, especially since his hair was a deep shade of red. Before Nix could formulate a good way to ask, the guy snapped his fingers and pointed at him excitedly.

"You were in Hunters Cross the other day, weren't you?" He nodded, answering his own question. "I saw you with Yejun Sang!"

Grady groaned and pulled his friend back into his chair. "Man, don't encourage him. In fact," he motioned to the student who'd offered Nix the seat, "Juri, please help me out here. We all know what the Demons are like. Explain to my roommate why they're bad news. Maybe if someone else tries to warn him off of them, it'll actually get through to him."

Juri was a dirty blond who seemed laid back, but he frowned at Grady's comment. "You're trying to make friends with the Demons?"

"Not trying," the redhead interrupted. "From what I saw the other day, they're already pretty chummy. They were walking down the hall and Yejun was whispering something to him. Seemed like they were close."

After being super normal the entire time they'd been in his studio, Yejun had finished up, walked Nix out, and threatened him. It hadn't been anything too extreme, just a passing comment about how if Nix planned on ruining their plan, or Light forbid, had any thoughts of siding with the hacker if he came calling, Yejun wouldn't hesitate to destroy him.

It'd gotten a little colorful toward the end, when he'd leaned in and said he'd make Nix wish he were never born if it came to that, but it'd been said with that same flirtatious smirk, and afterward, he'd winked and bid Nix farewell on the path. He'd gone right toward the Roost, and Nix had gone left toward his dorm.

If that's what the redhead had seen...

"I wouldn't exactly put it that way," Nix replied, uncomfortable with this topic.

"According to gossip," Khole said, "that's not true, like, at all. Aren't you dating them?"

The redhead gasped. "Like all three of them?! At the same time?!"

"Man, shut up," Grady hissed, glancing toward the head of the room. Fortunately, the librarian still wasn't at her station, so there was no one there to scold them. Once that was settled, he turned back to Nix. "Seriously though, I've been wanting to ask…Is it true?"

"Sort of." He couldn't deny it, but it felt strange admitting to something like that to a group of strangers, especially when the vibe was so torn.

Half of them seemed interested and excited about the news and the other half…

"Are they blackmailing you?" Juri asked.

"Oh," the redhead set his chin on his fist and stared, "are they? Scandalous."

"You're such an asshole." Grady pinched the bridge of his nose.

"What? I've been trying to make it into the Bishop tier for two years now and nothing," he whined. "But the newcomer somehow makes it in less than five days? How even?" He pushed out his lower lip, pouting in Nix's direction. "Tell me your secrets, new guy."

"Um," Nix wasn't sure how to proceed here, "I don't have any? I just…Ran into them the first day. Grady was with me."

Grady shook his head. "Seemed like you already knew them before that."

Well shit. Looked like he hadn't formed a strong enough friendship with his roommate either.

"Only Lake," he admitted. "He and I had talked a couple of times before."

"On the app, right?" the redhead said. He pulled up his multi-slate and opened the app, showing Nix his screen. "This is me. What about you?"

The username was RedHotLover and Nix barely caught himself from chuckling. He'd used a picture of the back of his head as his photo, and the tiny icon showed that he was a part of the Knight tier.

"Aren't these supposed to be anonymous?" Nix managed to point out, only to have the rest of them snort at him.

"Please," Khloe rolled her eyes. "Half of us have hooked up in real life thanks to that app, so for the most part, our identities have already been revealed."

"So," he didn't want to hope but felt it anyway, "you all use it?"

"Not me," Grady stated, but the others all nodded, even Juri.

When they'd first spoken about the Demons, Grady had seemed to have something personal against them. He'd said it had to do with his friend, and considering how he'd asked Juri to back him up...

"Have any of you interacted with one of the Kings before?" he directed the question to the table as a whole, but his eyes were on Juri, searching for any hint that he'd hit a nerve.

"Most people don't," Khloe was the one to reply, and she sounded bummed. "And if they are lucky enough, they're usually ordered to sign an NDA after so they can't talk about it."

"That's because the Demons don't play around," Grady insisted bitterly. "They're monsters. The shit they're into isn't normal."

"How do you know that if you've never been with one and don't personally know anyone who was?" the redhead said, giving off the impression that he was used to listening to Grady complain about them.

"Shut up, Dew. You don't know what you're talking about."

"No, man," the redhead, Dew, snapped back, "you don't. A couple of the guys on the swim team have slept with Yejun and West, and even though they can't give details, they all say it was a good time."

"Not Rase," Juri said.

It was only two words, but it instantly dampened the mood. Even Dew conceded, his shoulders caving in as he dropped his gaze to his folded hands.

Nix frowned. If they used the app, there was a chance they'd interacted with Branwen. He needed to find out more, but curiosity got the better of him, and instead of asking about that, he found himself saying, "Who's Rase?"

"Don't say his name so loudly," Khloe warned, inching her chair closer to the table. "Rase was a senior last year, super popular. Rumors were he'd made it to the King level, but that was never confirmed, and if asked, he'd deny it. He was all set to graduate top of his class, even had a job lined up at Granton Hills, the law firm?"

Nix nodded even though he didn't really know what she was talking about. Didn't really matter since he got the idea that it was a fancy firm around here. "And?"

"He pissed off one of the Demons," Juri picked up the story, looking over his shoulder as if to check and be sure they weren't being listened in on. It was fairly late in the afternoon and pouring out, so there weren't many others around.

"He pissed off *all* of the Demons," Khloe corrected, and gone was any semblance of playfulness or cheer. She actually shuddered. "Maybe we shouldn't continue. Nix is involved with them already and—"

"I won't say anything," he promised, unwilling to give up this chance to learn more. So far, he'd heard whispers about how the Demons were coveted yet feared, but aside from that time at the Roost, that hadn't been his experience.

Or, at least, not entirely.

The other day, Yejun had been rather kind, hadn't he? Pleasant and almost…friendly, and Lake, well. Lake was cold and hard to get a read on, and he'd forced Nix's hand in that office, but he also hadn't forced that massive cock inside of him when he'd shown a hint of fear and—

Nix inwardly cursed at himself.

He was doing that thing again. Being grateful for scraps instead of taking the abuse for what it was at face value.

Fact of the matter was, while being tied to them helped his plans to root out the person responsible for Branwen, this wasn't at all what he'd intended when he'd enrolled here. He'd never planned to get this entangled with Lake and his friends. Definitely never thought he'd find himself sitting on a dildo in an office building or brutally face fucked by a stranger.

He'd almost managed to convince himself they weren't actually that bad thanks to Yejun, but what if that was all an act? The difference between Nix and everyone else was that they needed him. Maybe they were only being somewhat nice because of that. It would certainly help explain it.

"It's not like he can't find out from someone else," Dew said.

"Was your friend one of the guys who were told to have sex on the field?" Nix guessed.

"That would have been kind." Khloe picked at the edge of her mutli-slate. "We don't know what Rase did, but whatever it was, it was bad. The Demons rule this school, hell, this city, and sometimes they can take things to the extreme but this…" She shivered again, and when it became apparent it would be difficult for her to continue, Juri picked up for her.

"I was there when it happened. We were eating in Café Soul when West stormed in and went straight for him. Rase had to have known what he'd done because he actually got up and tried running. Only Yejun was entering through the other exit and caught him first."

"Beautiful," Dew grimaced, "but deadly."

"West beat the shit out of Rase right in front of all of us," Juri said. "It was a nightmare. The guy fights professionally, did you know that?"

Nix shook his head in the negative.

"He's won competitions all over the country. Rase was a waif player, so not small and could hold his own against a normal person but not someone like West. Have you ever heard the sound a bone makes when it snaps? I have."

"He broke bones?" Nix felt his stomach churn uncomfortably.

"He broke eight," Juri corrected.

"Okay," he blew out a breath. "Note to self, stay on West's good side."

"West is bad," Khloe hummed in agreement, "but Yejun is the one to look out for."

His brow furrowed. That wasn't the first time he was hearing something along those lines, but it didn't really make sense to him. Yejun had followed Lake's orders at the Roost, but aside from that, he hadn't done anything untoward to Nix. He seemed more interested in holing up in his studio with his art than anything else.

It'd actually sort of reminded Nix of himself and how he'd rather be left to his own devices.

"If all you're doing is fucking them," Dew patted Nix on the back and gave him a reassuring smile, "then no big deal. Yejun is a super charmer, everyone knows that."

"Just like how everyone knows he's also the scariest," Khloe added.

"Why?" Nix really didn't get it. Sure, he'd only heard two real stories thus far, but out of them, Yejun had ordered two guys to fuck in the field leading to their suspension. West had sent a guy to the hospital. As far as he was concerned, one of those things was way more serious than the other. "Seems like West is the scariest."

"West left Rase a bloodied mess in the middle of the cafeteria floor," Juri said. "But it was Yejun who finished him off."

"Finished him off…how?"

"He stabbed him in the left eye with a fork and then pissed on him."

For a lengthy moment, he thought for sure he'd misheard and could only stare at Juri, waiting for him to repeat himself or correct himself. When that didn't happen, Nix opened his mouth to say something, anything, only to come up blank.

"I did get to see his dick though," Dew broke the silence with a sigh. "Probably the only chance I'll ever get to."

"Good Light." Khloe tossed her stylus at his head. "Can you not right now? This is a super shitty story we're telling. Stop being horny for five seconds."

"I can't help it," he whined.

Had Nix been feeling bad about himself earlier? Nope. There was something seriously wrong with someone at this table, but it wasn't him. "You…Want to get with Yejun even after having witnessed that?"

"Well, yeah." He shrugged like it wasn't a big deal. "He's a Demon. That means he's a King on the app and is a shoo-in for a spot in Club Essential. Are you kidding? Of course I want to get with that. Being the property of one of them means being set for life, man, don't you already know that?" He laughed at his own comment. "Of course you do. Why else would you be with them?" He clapped him on the back, unaffected when Nix leaned away.

"You see why I tried to warn you now?" Grady flung a hand out toward Dew. "Some idiots at this school can't see past their greed, and half the time, that gets them hurt."

"You seem nice, Nix," Juri told him. "Quiet, a good student. If they aren't blackmailing you, I suggest you try and distance yourself as soon as possible."

"How's he supposed to do that?" Khloe asked dryly. "The whole campus is already talking about how it's been three generations since the last time a group of Demons publicly dated the same person. He'll turn them into a laughingstock if he tries to dump them now. You really think they'll let him get away with that?"

She clearly didn't.

And neither did Nix, if he were being honest. The problem was he couldn't actually be honest with them. Couldn't explain what he was really doing with the Demons, or what they were really doing with him.

So he did the only thing he could do and nodded solemnly at them.

"I'll try my best," he said.

He just left out the part about how he meant he'd try his best to use them back every bit as much as they were using him.

CHAPTER 15:

Yejun stared out the window, over the drop of the mountain down at the murky tops of the nearest school buildings. Lights flickered through the foggy haze as water pelted against the thick pane of glass separating him from the elements.

He swirled the dark blue contents of his half-filled glass, the same one he'd been nursing since his arrival over an hour ago. The lounge area of the club was quieter than usual, though every now and again he felt the burning stares of others and caught wind of their whispered words.

It'd had gotten around that the Demons had chosen their sacrifice, and curiosity was brewing amongst the Essential who understood what that truly meant.

Their plan was convoluted, but it wasn't like Yejun could come up with a better one, especially not in the short amount of time they had. He'd been against using Nix in the beginning, mostly because allowing anyone to get close to them like that made his skin crawl, but in the end, it'd been two against one.

When he'd called Nix to Hunters Cross yesterday, he'd intended to make his displeasure known, only…Nix had arrived looking like a partially drowned kitten, his hackles risen and all, and Yejun hadn't been able to do it.

It wasn't Nix's fault that he'd been roped into this. Lake might seem like a frozen ice prince, but when he wanted something, he was more like an avalanche crashing his way through. He'd bulldoze anything in his way to get his way. Yejun had always admired that in him, even though it was also a trait that could get them into trouble.

"Yo." West appeared at his side, bumping his elbow against his before taking up a spot against the window next to him. He was holding a beer, his sharp gaze taking in the scenery below.

Even though he appeared relaxed with his shoulder propped against the glass, Yejun recognized the coiled tension in the set of his best friend's shoulders. Of the three of them, West was the most explosive, the most chaotic and out of touch with his emotions. He liked to pretend things away over dealing with them, but Light help anyone who tried to tell him as much.

They all had their own ways of coping, and who was Yejun to interfere or lecture?

He moved his glass forward, waiting for West to notice before they clinked them together. West wouldn't admit it, but he'd been on edge since Lake's return. Probably because he was torn between several different feelings on the matter.

The three of them were one, painted on the same shitty canvas, their splotches bleeding into one another. But that didn't mean there weren't issues. They'd both wanted Lake to come home, had missed him while he'd been away. West, however, had to deal with the inferiority complex he'd been gifted from his father, and that was always more difficult when in the presence of their Imperial bestie.

"Did you get any sleep last night?" Yejun had gotten up to get something to drink and had passed by West's bedroom. The sound of clicking keys had drifted through the door.

"Some," West said.

"Was it worth it at least?"

"I didn't find anything new, if that's what you're asked. Whoever this guy is, they're good."

"Better than you?"

The corner of West's mouth tipped up. "They have the advantage since I couldn't predict they were coming. Does that mean they're better?" He lifted a hand and rocked it back and forth. "I guess only time will tell."

"You still think we should bring Nix into this?"

West soured some. "Lake isn't onboard. He doesn't trust him."

West had suggested allowing Nix to take a look at the old hacks, but Lake had refused, preferring to keep their pretty little boy toy in the dark as much as possible.

"Ironic, considering the whole reason Nix is even involved is because he wanted him to be," Yejun sighed.

"He's involved," a dry voice carried to them, and when they turned, it was to find Lake slowly approaching, "because he broke into the app. The only person to blame for that is Nix himself."

"Oh," West drawled, "so it's his fault you want the three of us to pretend to date him, too, I suppose?"

"*Casually*," Yejun pointed a finger and waved at them both, "date him." Not that they could call what they intended to do with Nix *dating*. Giving something a proper label tended to cause people to relax. It gave them something tangent to hold on to, a name to call the thing. When people were comfortable, it was easier to slip a fast one by them.

Of course, being known as the dude dating the Demons probably would have the opposite effect for Nix, but that's what they wanted. They needed everyone's attention to be on the Firebird.

Including the Order's.

"I didn't see you complaining when your dick was in his mouth," Lake said to West, snatching the beer out of his hand. He took a deep drag but didn't offer it back, gaze sweeping out the window at the darkening sky.

"No, but you seemed pretty okay about it all," Yejun told him, grinning when Lake's upper lip twitched slightly.

"What's mine is—"

"Yeah, yeah, yeah." He shook his hand to stop him. "Still, if sharing a person was that simple, we should have tried it sooner."

"Oh?" West turned his back to the window, leaning against the glass. He crossed his arms and quirked a dark brow. He'd changed his hair again, the color a deep magenta. "Coming from the guy who can't remember the names of his various bedpartners, that's rich."

Yejun tapped his head. "Maybe that would hold more weight if you weren't constantly changing your dye job, bro. As it is..."

"This is only temporary," Lake stated. "Don't get attached."

Yejun snorted. "As if."

"Yeah, right," West chimed in at the same time. "He's cute, and he's got a fantastic tongue, but attached? Us? I just want to pick his brain apart a little and worm around it, that's all."

"Lovely." Yejun downed the rest of his drink.

"Maybe get back inside him," he added. "For real this time."

"That I can agree with." The two of them high-fived, and Lake rolled his eyes.

"Fucking children," Lake said it like he wasn't picturing the same thing.

"Jokes aside, it doesn't have to be temporary, you know," Yejun went in for the kill, figuring why the hell not. The lingering burn of the alcohol down his throat spurred him on. "Who says we can't just keep him?"

"Um," West gave him a look, "the Order?"

"Screw them."

"Gross, my dad sits at that table."

"Screw all of them except your dad."

"You fucking would, you perv."

"Why did I come back to this planet again?" Lake interrupted, but it made the three of them laugh as intended.

Partially because they knew he didn't mean it.

Mostly because they knew he hadn't had a choice.

Yejun and West were both Royals by blood, but Lake was an Imperial and part of the Imperial family despite not sharing their last name. He was always destined to settle on Tulniri, no matter how much he may have enjoyed his time on Vitality.

"Tell us the truth," West said then. "You replaced us there, didn't you?"

Yejun sighed, wishing he still had something to drink in his hand. The question had been circling for weeks now, ever since Lake's return, but it was still uncomfortable hearing it voiced.

West's feelings were like cotton candy. There one second, gone the next. All it took was one single drop to make them disappear. The problem was Lake was less predictable and far too honest. Even knowing it would bruise their egos if he had formed a tighter bond with his new friends on Vitality, he wouldn't lie to them about it.

It kind of sucked admitting, even to himself, that Yejun wouldn't like it if he had any more than West would. For as long as he could remember, it'd been the three of them against the universe. Change was a necessary and unavoidable part of life, but he'd always believed they were unshakable.

Had he been wrong?

"Would the two of you stop looking like jilted lovers?" Lake shook his head. "Like I could replace you idiots even if I wanted to."

"So you wanted to?" West grunted, but it was obvious this time he was one hundred percent joking.

"Can we just get down to business?"

"Is that what you came here for?" Yejun asked. "Business?"

"Yeah, like how much of Nix's we can get into." West shrugged when that earned him a dark look from Lake. "What? That's what this is really, right? Ground rules now that the game has been set. Well," he rolled his wrist in the air, "don't keep us waiting, your majesty."

"We share him," Lake didn't waste any more time denying it, "but no one else gets to touch him."

"That goes without saying." None of them were big on sharing, West least of all. "Someone else so much as glances at what's mine once and I'll break their face."

"Descriptive," Yejun said.

"How long they look and where at will determine which part of their face I destroy."

"You're an aggressive asshole, but at least you're a fair aggressive asshole."

"I do mean no one else," Lake reiterated, like they really were the idiots he'd claimed and weren't following. "Not another Enigma or Essential. Not even an Order member."

"Fuck no," Yejun agreed. "Nix is *our* sacrifice."

Lake nodded, relieved that they were all on the same page. It was obvious this had been hanging over his head for a while, possibly even before he'd made the suggestion to the two of them. Since he'd been back, he'd been playing on the app more and more. Yejun wasn't sure if West had noticed, but he certainly had.

It all made sense once he'd found out about Nix when they'd walked into him on campus that first day. Before, the app had been a means to an end for Lake. He'd only created it to guarantee their spots, and once that was confirmed, he'd all but handed off the responsibility of running it to him and West. As far as Yejun knew, Lake had only used the app once, maybe twice, to hook up, and even then, that'd mostly been to test it out after they'd entered college. He'd only been trying to decide if they needed to upgrade it.

They'd been freshmen at the time, but Lake had already been looking ahead. Already plotting what they could do come senior year to prove themselves further. They'd had no way of knowing that eventually he'd be shipped off planet, or that he'd be called back after the unexpected deaths of the Emperor and her Royal Consort.

Even though it'd brought him several steps closer to the throne, the whole ordeal had left Lake unsettled. He didn't like working with unknown factors, preferred seeing all of the pieces in advance so he could sort through them and line them up to his liking.

Poor Firebird. Had no clue what he'd gotten himself into.

Ultimately, the real reason Yejun was going along with

this was because he understood Lake needed an outlet. West was more than capable of finding this hacker on his own—even if it wasn't until the last minute. Until he did, though, there wasn't really anything for Lake or Yejun to do.

Neither of them could work with computers the same way West and Nix could. When they first told him about Nix manipulating his way up the tiers, Yejun didn't understand how —and he still didn't. Something about codes and doors and... Ugh. He was getting a headache just thinking about it.

"He'll be useful," Lake promised.

"He's got the right look," Yejun agreed. "If our hacker really is watching us the way we assume, he'll take the bait. Nix seems timid and out of place with us. The hacker will think we're blackmailing him into it or something and try to get to him that way."

"The only worry I have," West said, "is that he'll see through us. Nixie does look too naïve to play with us, and this guy we're after is smart. He might put two and two together and realize the blackmail is actually bait."

"That's why you're still going to try and hunt him down through other avenues," Lake reminded. "We aren't stopping the search. If Nix does help us lure him out? Great. If he doesn't? At least we've got our sacrifice already sorted."

Yejun wasn't so certain. "Are you sure you can do it?"

Lake frowned.

"Sacrifice him," he elaborated. "Are you sure you'll be able to when the time comes?"

"Of course he can do it," West jumped to his defense, but then set a hard stare on Lake, "Right?"

"Of course." Lake's expression never changed, but the air around them seemed to grow heavy and thicken.

Yejun cleared his throat, and straightened from the window to slap a hand down over Lake's shoulder. "It won't be a big deal if I call him right now then."

"You can call him whenever you fucking want to," Lake stated. "You don't need my permission."

"Never did." West blew him a kiss.

"Well then." Yejun made a big show of detaching his multi-slate from his wrist. He entered the Enigma app and hit the call button, bringing the device up to his ear instead of putting it on speaker like he typically did. When Lake noticeably tensed, he grinned, but before he could say anything, the line connected. "What are you up to, Firebird?"

Nix inhaled on the other end of the line and then said calmly, "I'm in my room studying. Why?"

"Studying?" He snickered. "Cute."

"Um, is there something you needed, Yejun?"

That was cute too, the way he said his name, kind of breathy. Almost as though he wasn't sure if he was allowed to or something. Had Lake brought the name-game into the bedroom perhaps? Or was it just regular nerves?

"Yeah, actually," he replied, figuring he'd get to the bottom of that later. "You at Hunters Cross in the next fifteen minutes."

It would take him longer than that to make it down the mountain, but there was something kind of hot about the idea of making Nix wait for him.

Something thrilling about knowing Lake was well aware that's what he was doing.

West wasn't the only one who sometimes liked to rattle the Imperial's cage.

The sound of a chair scraping lightly against the floor echoed through then, and a moment later, Nix spoke again. "It's pouring out. Can we maybe meet tomorrow?"

"Nope," he popped the p for good measure. "Gotta be tonight, Firebird."

It really did, because Yejun was starting to feel that thrumming beneath his skin, shaking his insides. That kind of wild energy needed to be dispersed as soon as possible. They all felt it in one form or another, the three of them. They just dealt with it differently.

Yejun dispersed his.

West let his consume him.

And Lake bottled it up.

"All right," Nix sighed. "I'll head out now."

Yejun stared Lake right in the eye and cooed, "Good boy."

West chortled as Yejun ended the call and placed his device back on his wrist.

With a wink at them both, Yejun spun on his heels and made his way toward the other side of the room where the elevators were located. When he finally reached them and turned inside, it was to find Lake still glaring.

He winked again as the elevator doors slid shut.

CHAPTER 16:

Nix waited for Yejun outside the locked door of his private studio in Hunters Cross. Even though it was well into the evening, the lights in the building were all left on, and he'd passed more than a handful of rooms that were clearly occupied. Apparently, it wasn't abnormal for artists to work this late.

He was used to late hours himself. Back home, he'd studied so long that more often than not he'd be heading to bed while the sun was waking. Nix had known what he wanted to do with his life since he was eight, and everything he'd done since had all been toward that goal.

Until now.

His mind wandered back to what Yejun had said the other day, about how this could potentially give him an in. Star Eye Holding was the largest gaming company on the planet, and had been Nix's dream job for years. He'd been well on his way to achieving it, top of his class at his old university, good reputation with his seniors and professors…He'd been so close.

An inkling of anger toward Branwen flickered to life in the center of his chest, and he did his best to try and bank it down, like he did every other time this occurred. It wasn't right to blame the dead, and yet…

No. No, the only person to blame was whoever pushed her past her limits. That was who Nix needed to hang all of this on. If he was lucky, he'd discover their identity sooner rather than later. If he were really lucky, it wouldn't be one of the Demons.

Not because he liked any of them, but because he really could kiss his dream goodbye if that ended up being the case.

There was a chance he could discreetly handle this himself if he found out the King's identity and it wasn't one of them. He'd get his revenge and complete his contract with Lake and the others. All he had to do was make it two months to Demons Passing, then he'd be in the clear. After that, he could get back on track and pretend like all of this had never happened. And if Yejun kept his word and also helped him get his foot in the door?

Nix wasn't above accepting that offer. He knew his skills were good enough, but this was Tulniri. Nepotism wasn't just a possibility, it was practically part of their culture. Everyone knew you could be replaced at the drop of a hat if an Essential got involved.

Grady hadn't been pleased when Nix had started getting dressed earlier. Even without saying as much, he'd known where Nix was heading off to. He'd bid him farewell with yet another warning that the Demons were bad news, but it wasn't like Nix had a choice here. His roommate seemed like a nice guy, but there was no way Nix could risk telling him the truth.

He couldn't admit he was using them every bit as much as they were using him.

"Firebird," Yejun arrived then, calling down the hall. He didn't have anything with him, his hands tucked into the front pockets of his black jeans, water droplets dripping off the shoulders of his leather jacket and his hair.

Nix frowned but didn't straighten from the wall where he'd been leaning, the folded umbrella at his feet having formed a small puddle he was practically standing in. "Did you walk through the rain?"

"Why?" Yejun asked as he reached him, and it was obvious by the mocking lift of his full lips he was teasing.

"You could catch a cold," Nix said anyway, shrugging as he finally straightened when the Demon reached for the keypad next to the locked door.

"Worried about me?"

"Worried about myself, more like."

Yejun laughed. "Are you this brazen with the others? Or am I special?"

"Lake mentioned something about my sunshiny disposition when he had me sign the contract."

The door popped open and Yejun pushed it the rest of the way, motioning for Nix to enter first. "Leave the umbrella out here."

Nix shrugged and walked in, moving off to the side so Yejun could pass him. "Why did you call me out so late?"

Yejun chucked off his leather jacket, careful not to get water on any of the easels, and went to the corner where there was a coatrack Nix hadn't noticed the last time. He hung his jacket and then held out an arm, turning to lift a brow at him when Nix didn't immediately respond. "Jacket, Firebird. Come on."

"Oh." He removed it and crossed the room, holding it out, watching as it was hung next to the Demons.

"You remember what I was working on the other day?" Yejun asked, rolling up the sleeves of his black dress shirt. In the sharp overhead lighting, it became apparent the shirt itself was see-through.

"Yeah."

"It's all crap. I had to toss it, but the project is due tomorrow, which is why you're going to help me get it done in time."

Nix frowned as the other man moved away to the center of the room. There was a circular wooden slab there, and Yejun lifted a stool and set it on top. "I'm sorry? Are you asking me to... model for you?"

"That's exactly what I'm doing." Yejun paused. "Well, ask is a strong word, don't you think?"

"I have to pretend to date you out in public," he reminded. "I don't recall there being any mention of acting like your guys' slave." He motioned to the empty room. "There isn't even anyone else here to see this."

"The windows are currently in dark mode, which means no one outside will be able to see in. Same for the one on the door," he pointed over Nix's shoulder at it. "But we can change that if an audience is really something you want."

"That's not at all what I meant and you know it."

"Do I?" Yejun set his hands on his hips. "We don't really know one another well, Firebird. Right now, we're still in the learning stages."

It was on the tip of his tongue that he didn't want to get to know any of them, but Nix caught himself. Hadn't he just been thinking about using this opportunity to his advantage? Pissing off the Demon wouldn't benefit him in any sense of the word, if anything, it'd be more akin to shooting himself in the foot.

"Want to know what I've picked up on so far?" Yejun asked. "You've got pride, more than I would have guessed considering how you ended up here, under our thumbs. Maybe Lake is onto something after all. Maybe there really is a bigger secret you're keeping."

The mood in the room shifted, and Nix could sense it like a live thing. If he wasn't careful, the scales could tip unfavorably toward him. He'd always been good at reading people, and so far, Yejun wasn't that hard.

He wasn't Lake, in any case.

Lake, who kept his feelings so close to the chest even Nix was unable to figure out what he was thinking.

Yejun was different. He wore his emotions proudly, not bothering to hide them. In fact, he gave the impression he wanted them to be seen. Like, maybe, he wanted to just *be seen* in general.

"Or," Nix tentatively tried his luck, "maybe that's exactly why you should believe me. My cousin was aware of just how small my sphere of comfort goes."

"And that's all it took for you to step out of your bubble?" He bristled. "*All* it took? She *died*."

That cavern within him yawned and Nix momentarily

was at risk of falling into it. The grief was still potent when he allowed himself to feel it, when he gave into the sorrow and the pain and the fury. It was the latter that had been driving him forward, allowing him to focus on the task at hand instead of crawling into bed and staying there for weeks on end like Branwen's older brother, Braint, supposedly was.

Yejun tipped his head, that suspicious gleam in his dark eyes unwavering. "How'd she die?"

He didn't want to tell him. Prior to this moment, Nix had foolishly believed that perhaps Yejun wasn't as bad as everyone had made him out to be. So far, he'd been the calmest—although, that was based off of their last encounter. Somehow, Nix must have forgotten that Yejun was the one who'd held him down at the Roost.

Had been the one to strip him at Lake's behest...

"Grady is right," he found himself saying, his distaste ringing clear. "You're all monsters." He took a step toward the door.

"You think you can escape just by walking out?" Yejun tsked. "You signed a contract, Firebird. Since it was made with Essentials, it's legally binding, no matter what you want to believe."

On most planets within the universe, a contract like that wouldn't hold much weight in court. Sure, Nix had signed his name to it, but he could easily claim—and rightly so—that it'd been under duress. Since most civilizations considered consent to be important, they wouldn't allow it to be given away lightly. They'd stand by him if he tried to fight it.

But Tulniri wasn't like the majority of other planets. Nix had had the misfortune of being born on a planet and in a galaxy, in particular, that had murky laws where things like consent were concerned. A lot of that had to do with the fact it was jointly run. The Imperial family had a say, but so did Club Essential.

And the Demons of Foxglove Grove? They were the future of the club. Which meant they might as well *be* the club.

"You guys could have chosen anyone," Nix stated. "Why me?"

"Because Lake wanted you," he told him matter-of-factly.

"And you and West just roll with whatever he wants?"

"I want Lake to be content," Yejun corrected, "and West... West wants what Lake wants. In more ways than one. We stick together."

Nix crossed his arms stubbornly. "If I contest this contract, yeah, I'll lose against you. But I won't be the only one screwed over. You need me to draw out this hacker, right? What happens when this person finds out I'm not actually as invested in this arrangement as you all want him to think?"

Yejun chuckled darkly. "Actually, that'd also work in our favor. Chances are very good that would only make him come to you sooner."

"What?" Nix didn't understand.

"The hacker is out to get us," Yejun shared. "So if he thinks you'd help him achieve that goal?"

"Is that what I'm being used for?" He shook his head. "That's what you both meant when you called me naïve?"

So the real plan was that the hacker would approach him and try to recruit him. If he believed that Nix hated the Demons, he would be more likely to do so, but they'd painted themselves into a corner by trying to appease all sides. The club was under the impression Nix was here willingly and helping them out in exchange for sexual gratification. In order to maintain that illusion...

"Essential wouldn't view it the same way," Nix dared point out.

"Which is why you're going to continue to be the good little birdie I know you can be," Yejun said without skipping a beat. "Put your stubbornness and pride aside and look at it this way: it's either a lose-lose or a win-win situation. At the end of the day, the three of us might be in charge, but I'll let you in on a secret Lake and West would never." He moved closer.

"What's that?" Nix forced himself to hold still as the other man approached, not wanting to come off weak even though his nerves were thrumming.

"You've got the power here." Yejun stopped so close he could feel his warm breath gust across his face and captured his chin between two fingers. "You're right. You could play the victim and make it publicly known that we're forcing you. The Order would be displeased with us and probably call us in for a scolding. They wouldn't trust you and you'd be number one on their shit list—you could kiss Star Eye goodbye, that's for sure. They won't do favors for anyone they don't trust.

"Or, you can lean into things. Convince the rest of the world that you want to be here, lavished by our glorious attention. The hacker will eventually come to you and try to sway you to his side, and the Order will believe that's all part of our plan—because it is. We catch the bad guy, you get that fancy job, and the story ends with a happily ever after."

It sounded great when he laid it all out like that, but...

"That's not how the real world works," Nix said.

"Maybe that's not how things ended for your cousin," Yejun corrected. "But your story could be different. It can be better."

He slapped his hand away and glared. "You don't know what you're talking about."

"How did she die, Nix?"

"That's none of your business."

"How did she die?" he repeated, but his tone changed. It was no longer demanding, now low and almost soothing. Like he was trying to coax the answer out of him.

Nix hated that it worked. There was a good chance that it did only because he'd been bottling it up, unable to talk to anyone about it. His family had been absent most of the time he'd been home, and he'd only really seen them at the funeral. His friends hadn't known Branwen, so there'd been no point in discussing things with them, especially since they weren't all that close.

He hadn't been lying about the part where he'd spent

most of his time as a bookworm, locked in his studies. Since transferring, he'd only spoken to his old roommate twice, and they'd lived together since freshman year.

There was no way Nix could trust any of the Demons with the full truth, not until he had one hundred percent certainty none of them had been involved, but if this was a give and take like Yejun was trying to make him believe, perhaps using him to get this off his chest wasn't so bad?

"She took her own life," the words felt foreign on his tongue, practically whispered in the small space between them.

To his credit, Yejun winced.

"She left me a note," he continued, all of it suddenly pouring out of him. "Just me. Her older brother had to sneak it to me even, because he didn't want their parents getting hurt by that fact."

"Did she tell you why she did it?"

"Someone hurt her."

Yejun's hand cupped Nix's chin, but before he could shove him off a second time, the Demon was pulling him in. He wrapped his arms around him tightly and held him close, patting his back as if he were a small child in need of comfort.

Frustratingly, that also had the desired effect, and before long, Nix was responding, reciprocating the hug. He inhaled and breathed in Yejun's scent, a mixture of pomegranate and turpentine with a hint of musk. It wasn't entirely unpleasant.

"I'm sorry, Firebird," Yejun said.

"You mean that, don't you."

"Of course I mean it. And I understand now how something like that could push you into making these types of extreme changes. Running from your emotions is never the answer though. If you came to Foxglove to escape your demons —"

Nix snorted before he could help it, finding that morbidly funny.

"Right," Yejun grunted, pulling away. "Poor choice of words."

"Anyway," Nix cleared his throat, "we're done arguing now, yeah?"

He chuckled. "Yeah, we're done. I hereby call a truce."

Nix smiled and nodded, acknowledging that he actually felt a little bit grateful for that. Being on decent terms with one out of three was something, and even though the moment had been fleeting, being able to confide in another person had been... elevating. He didn't feel *better*, but he didn't feel worse.

"You needed me to model?" Nix took a step toward the circular dais, figuring cooperation was the least he could do now. Only to be stopped by a hand on his wrist.

"I do," Yejun confirmed, but that glint of something mischievous was back in his eyes. "But not like that."

Nix's brow furrowed. "Like what?"

"You didn't pay much attention to my work the last time you were here, did you?" Yejun grinned and leaned in, holding his gaze all the while. "Get undressed, Firebird. I need you naked." His grin widened when Nix sucked in a breath and he added in a teasing lilt, "Your state of arousal is up to you. Your choice."

Choice.

Bullshit.

CHAPTER 17:

Nix held his breath as Yejun rearranged his legs, propping his right foot up on the wrung of the stool, extending his left slightly. He'd had Nix rest his right hand on the edge of the seat and turn his head slightly so he was partially looking over his shoulder.

Stripped of his clothing, Nix watched out of the corner of his eye as Yejun focused on getting the angles just right, seemingly unaffected by the fact Nix's junk was right there at eye level. Aside from a single whistle when Nix had removed his pants, Yejun had been the epitome of professionalism.

Why did that...bother Nix?

He shouldn't feel slighted, he should be happy. It wasn't like he wanted anything sexual to happen between them, here or anywhere else.

But that didn't change the fact that Yejun was pretty. Like, freakishly, unfairly, next-level gorgeous. Out of all the Demons, he was the one talked about the most on campus. No one had approached him about his situation with them yet, but Nix was sure when it finally happened, the first one they'd ask him about would be Yejun.

Although, according to rumors, more than half the student body already had stories of their own to tell of him. To say he slept around would be an understatement. That was probably why Nix had assumed Yejun would use his good looks to try and seduce him, used to getting whatever he wanted with that face of his.

Satisfied with the pose, Yejun stood and wandered over to another stool he'd set nearby, lifting his sketchpad from the floor to settle it in his lap. He stared at Nix silently for a moment before finally taking up a stick of charcoal from the ledge of an easel.

For a while, there was only the sound of the charcoal scratching lightly against the page and the pitter-patter of the rain against the windows. Nix was turned in such a way that his privates weren't in view, which meant he didn't have to worry about them showing up in the sketches or the final work, and it wasn't like this was the first time he'd been nude in front of the other guy.

All in all, he should have been able to relax.

Instead, his heart seemed to ricochet every time Yejun glanced up from his pad and set that entranced gaze on him. There wasn't anything sexual about it, and yet having all of that intense attention made Nix's skin hum and heat uncomfortably.

He shifted on the stool.

"Stay still," Yejun scolded, though his voice lacked any bite. He flipped the page to a fresh one and started again.

He'd seriously asked him here to model.

Wow.

That...

Wow.

Nix should have realized. If the number of easels in this place were any indicator, Yejun considered his art earnestly.

"Why did you start drawing?" the question slipped out before he could help it and he immediately apologized. "Sorry. No moving. My bad."

"My parents are both artists," Yejun answered anyway, not the least bit affected by Nix's break in silence. "I'm surprised you haven't heard of them. Insu and Sayda Sang?"

Nix thought about it and then his eyes widened. "The famous composer and—"

"The Royal portrait artist," Yejun finished for him. "That's them."

Insu Sang was world-renowned for his skills with the xix, a chordophone instrument. He was marketed as a genius and had been playing since he'd been a child. It helped that he came from a royal bloodline, but there was no doubting his talent.

"I bought tickets for my dad to one of his concerts for his birthday a few years ago," Nix admitted, and Yejun smiled.

"Yeah? That's cool. Did he enjoy it?"

"He did." He'd talked about how great of a son he'd had for months afterward, bragging to anyone who'd listen. "I had to save up almost an entire year for those tickets."

"I'll let you know the next time he plans on performing near your hometown," Yejun offered. "I can have tickets delivered to your house."

"Oh, thanks, but I don't think I could afford to buy them again."

He paused, scrunching up his nose. "I'm giving them to you for free, Firebird. Do you really think I'd make you pay? You're supposed to be my man, remember?"

Nix didn't know what to say to that, so he went quiet once more.

Sayda Sang had been the Royal portrait artist for two generations. She'd started at a young age, brought into the palace at twelve after the death of her predecessor. Every portrait drawn of the Imperial family and their branches since had been done by her hands. Even Lake's which was supposedly hanging in the Right Wing, would have been her work.

Yejun didn't just come from Royalty in the sense of blood or their ties to Club Essential. He came from artistic royalty. No wonder he took this so seriously and was so passionate. If Nix had been following in the footsteps of creative geniuses, he'd do the same.

"What about yours?" Yejun asked then. "What do your parents do?"

Nix watched him apply a few more strokes to the sketch pad. "They're typical office workers. Nothing special."

"What offices?"

"Braxton and Wilde," Nix said.

"They work together?"

"They met there."

"Cute. Office romance." He flipped to another fresh page. "Braxton and Wilde? Never heard of it. What do they do?"

"It's a law firm."

That got his attention and he momentarily looked up, blinking at Nix. "Lawyers?"

"Yup."

"And they're okay with their one and only son wanting to be a game developer?"

Nix shrugged. "Not at first."

"Ah, wore them down." Yejun smiled and started drawing again. "Good for you."

It'd been tough to convince them, had taken a while, but eventually they'd realized he wasn't going to change his mind. It'd been harder for them to argue when Nix had earned himself a full scholarship to Hyacinth University, something he'd successfully maintained throughout all four years.

That was another reason they'd been so against him transferring. He'd given up his full ride at the final hour, and they couldn't fully comprehend why. Branwen was the only reason they hadn't fought him on it.

"You've got a fantastic body, Firebird," Yejun said, and the note was different, less conversational and more…suggestive. But when Nix searched his face, his expression was still focused on his drawing.

"Thanks?"

"Do you work out?"

"Not really." He used to make himself hit the gym for at least an hour every other day, mostly because most of his time otherwise was spent studying. Travel to and from classes had helped keep him lean though, since he hadn't had a car at his old school.

"West will be disappointed to hear that," Yejun told him.

"Watching your muscles bunch and seeing you covered in sweat will turn him on."

Nix swallowed and licked his lips, going still when Yejun's gaze shot to his mouth and lingered.

"Lake's birthday is in a couple of weeks," Yejun stated, the change of subject momentarily confusing Nix. "I just came up with an idea of what to get him." He stood with a flourish and then motioned at Nix to stand.

He hesitated but eventually did as instructed, covering himself at the last second.

Yejun grunted at him. "Don't bother, Firebird. I've seen something once and I've got it memorized forever." He tapped the side of his head and then swirled that same finger in the air. "Now, turn around."

Nix slowly did, giving the other man his back.

"You've got a great ass. Round but firm." Yejun paused and Nix felt his gaze practically searing into him. "Put your hands on the stool."

He glanced over his shoulder at the Demon. "What?"

"You heard me. Bend over and put your hands on the stool. Do you need me to come over and help you?"

Nix shook his head, not sure how he'd handle having Yejun that close again. He squeezed his eyes shut and focused on his breathing when he leaned over and planted his palms against the wooden surface of the stool.

"Arch your back slightly," Yejun instructed next, either unaware of how Nix was now blushing or uncaring. "And adjust your stance so your legs are half an inch further apart. Just like that, there you go."

"Is this necessary?" Nix asked the second he heard the sound of the other stool scraping as Yejun undoubtedly moved it closer and then settled back into it.

"Absolutely," Yejun replied. He started to sketch, only speaking again once he noticed that Nix was shaking a little. "Are you cold?"

"No." Was that a joke? He felt like he was about to

spontaneously combust.

"Embarrassed?"

He didn't bother dignifying that with a response.

"There's no point in being self-conscious. I'll have those thighs spread around my waist eventually. Oh," Yejun chuckled, "did you like that? Your hole just fluttered."

"It did not." Had it? Shit. "Just keep drawing so we can finish this and I can go back to my room."

"Eager to escape now that I'm starting to turn you on?"

"You are not." Nix couldn't be that easy...Could he? No. No, absolutely not.

"No?" Yejun set the sketchpad down and the sound of clothing ruffling had Nix's spine stiffening. "So the thought of me unbuttoning my shirt doesn't do anything for you?"

"No." Nix listened intently to the sound of him doing just that, followed by the unmistakable hiss of a zipper being undone. He shifted on his feet, grimacing when he felt his balls draw up a second before his dick twitched.

Yejun tossed his pants across the room, making sure they landed in an area where Nix could see and laughed. "Look down, Firebird. Someone didn't get the memo."

He ground his teeth, not having to look to know what he was talking about. "Do not refer to my dick like a separate entity."

"Is that your way of admitting you're horny for me?"

"No!" Nix straightened and spun around, but anything else he'd been about to say died on his tongue as soon as he did.

Yejun had moved closer and was now standing less than a foot away. True to his word, he was naked, all that tanned and inked up skin on full display. A detailed snake coiled its way up his right arm, its head resting over his shoulder, tongue flicked out and aimed toward his burgundy nipple. On the other arm, a dragon made its way down the other direction. There were loose flower petals and vines with sharp thorns through both designs and over Yejun's chest, a couple fully formed flowers blooming on the side of his neck.

Enthralled, Nix's gaze inadvertently trailed lower, following the twist of one vine down his side. He'd mentioned that West was the one who liked to work out, but from the looks of things, Yejun had to as well. His abs were defined and he had that perfect v that acted like an arrow aimed straight at the prize.

Yejun's cock was just as weirdly beautiful as the rest of him—which wasn't something Nix thought he'd ever think in regards to genitalia, but here they were. It was long, longer than West's had been by at least an inch, though not as wide. His head was flushed and rosy, his shaft straight and not too veiny. Even his balls hung in perfect proportion to the rest of him.

He looked like someone had sculpted him from golden marble.

"Wow." It took Nix far too long to realize that single word had been uttered by him, and he froze all over again the second he did.

"Gee, Firebird," Yejun laughed and then stepped onto the dais, putting himself chest to chest with Nix in one swift move. "Thanks."

"I—" Nix was cut off by Yejun's tongue before he could finish. It darted past his parted lips and stroked against his as if it had the right to invade him, the rest of Yejun's mouth following quickly after.

Nix didn't struggle to break free, instead he went still, his hands coming up to settle against the rise of Yejun's hips as the Demon continued to coax him into submission with his skilled kisses, the hard press of his lip piercings forcing Nix to acknowledge this was real and not some twisted dream he was having.

The Demon tasted a bit sweet, almost as if he'd been eating candy recently, and his touch was gentle when his fingers combed through Nix's hair and tilted his head for a better angle.

Yejun kissed him like making out was simply another art form he'd perfected, carefully, but with the right amount of pressure to keep things interesting. To keep the heat in Nix's gut rising and the thoughts in his mind spinning.

"Can I touch you?" Yejun pulled away just far enough to breathe the question against Nix's mouth.

"You're already touching me."

He chuckled and then reached around Nix to grab onto the stool. With one swift move, he tossed it off the daze, laughing a second time when that had Nix jumping.

"Shh," he cooed at him, slowly tugging Nix down so they were both kneeling on the dais. Once there, he set a palm at the center of Nix's chest and eased him the rest of the way until he was lying on his back. Yejun rearranged his legs so they were spread out on either side of him before he leaned back in and kissed him again.

This time was softer, slower, as though he were attempting to mollify Nix. His left hand skated between them, traveling down until he found Nix's hard dick.

The second his fingers wrapped around his solid length, Nix gasped, his back arching.

"You're so hot, Firebird," Yejun said, gripping him with just enough pressure to tease as he started to stroke his hand up and down his length. His other hand tangled in Nix's bangs, sweeping them off his forehead. "All flushed and bothered. You're pink all over, especially," he glanced down pointedly at his dick, "here."

Nix groaned and draped an arm over his face, but that only made the other man chuckle.

"Why are you so embarrassed? I know for a fact that Lake has watched you do worse than this. I bet he fucked you the other day too, didn't he? When he had you alone in the office. It would have been the perfect opportunity."

"No, he—" Nix gasped again when Yejun wrung his hand, momentarily losing his train of thought. "He...With...A toy."

Yejun paused. "He fucked you with a dildo?"

When put like that it was even more humiliating and all he could do was nod his head once.

"Poor baby."

That was not the reaction he'd been expecting, and Nix risked moving his arm just so he could frown at Yejun.

"Plastic isn't the same as the real thing," Yejun said. "No wonder you're so needy." His hand let go of his dick to move lower, his middle finger prodding at his entrance. "Does this feel neglected, Firebird? Need a cock to fill you up the right way?"

"Don't," his frown deepened, "talk to me like I'm a child."

"Is that what you think I'm doing?" Yejun slowly eased that finger inside, smiling when Nix's lips parted and his hands grabbed onto his arms. "Would you rather me be rough with you? Is that what it takes to get you off?" He stared at Nix's dick again, quirking a brow when a thick drop of precome seeped out. "I don't think that's the case."

"No, this is..." Nix shifted on his back. "...fine."

"Fine is definitely one way of putting it." He dragged his gaze down Nix's body and then slowly inserted a second finger, delving them deep and scissoring them on the way out. As he continued to pump into him, he lowered his head to Nix's chest, planting open-mouth kisses across his collarbone and down before capturing his left nipple. He sucked hard enough to cause Nix to cry out, then licked at it and did it again.

He lavished that one bud with so much attention that it started to become hyper-sensitive, and he only stopped once he had Nix squirming beneath him. Then, he transferred his mouth to his other nipple and repeated the process. At the same time, he slipped in a third finger, his thumb pressing against Nix's taint as he drove them in and out of his body.

When he'd had sex in the past, it'd been quick. The men he'd slept with had prepped him so it wouldn't hurt, but they'd been fast about it, only opening him up enough that he wouldn't tear once they took what they wanted. Even with Lake, things had been explosive and raw.

This was so different, and Nix was lost to sensation for a while, reduced to a writhing bundle of nerves and chaotic energy even as he was touched and tasted tenderly. Even those fingers inside of him worked slowly, stretching him until they slid in with ease and with no resistance.

"There you go," Yejun said, slipping his hand free. He tutted down at him when Nix whined at the loss, shifting between his spread thighs. His long cock was leaking as well, and he rubbed the tip around Nix's entrance, slicking it up further. "I lubed my hand earlier. Did you even notice?"

Nix had not.

What the hell.

His cock positioned at his hole and then pushed past that ring of muscle, gliding in with a slow roll of his hips. They both moaned as he inserted himself, filling Nix up until he was fully seated, his balls brushing up against the swell of Nix's ass. He rocked forward, resting his arms on either side of Nix's head as they both adjusted to the fit.

"You're so tight, baby," Yejun growled, capturing Nix's mouth a third time. His tongue stroked in tandem with his cock as he pulled out and thrust back in. "Good Light, fucking you with a toy is a travesty. He has no idea what he's missing."

Nix wanted to mention he and Lake had still gotten off, but then Yejun changed the angle, scraping his cock against his prostate with every inward stroke, and he forgot about everything else.

Yejun blanketed his body over his, careful not to crush him. "Plant your feet on the floor, there you go. Open your thighs wider for me, good boy, just like that." He kissed beneath Nix's chin and across the length of his jaw. "How the hell did Lake wait for you? If it were me, I would have come found you immediately after our first play session on Enigma."

The bright lights in the room made everything visible, but the feeling of embarrassment was gone, replaced with a strong need that had Nix lifting his hips to meet with each and every thrust. There was something almost sensual about the whole thing, about the way Yejun was careful not to hurt him, about how he was staring down as though fascinated by what he saw.

Even though it was purely physical, Nix hadn't felt truly seen in a long time, and having all of that raw attention on him while he was taken in the middle of an open space like this…It was similar to fucking Lake in the office, and yet so incredibly different.

"Yejun." He was close, so close. His muscles clenched and his dick, trapped between them was leaking so much there was a pool of come already forming on his stomach.

"Come, Firebird," the order came the same as everything else had, smooth and easy, spoken with a kiss at the end and a ravishing smile that turned Yejun's dark eyes into tiny stars. "Combust for me. I want to watch you burn and come alive beneath me."

The next time that cock pushed in Nix lost it. He cried out and clawed at Yejun's back, squeezing his thighs around him as he continued to fuck in as deep as he could go. He came, his orgasm sending waves of pure electricity coursing through his entire body as he jerked under Yejun's toned form.

"Ready to feel why real cock is better than a toy?" Yejun asked, and before Nix could follow, he thrust in and ground himself against him. A second later he came, hot shoots of come squirting into Nix's body.

He felt the warmth spread inside of him, felt it fill him up as Yejun continued to pump into him. It seemed to last an impossibly long time before the Demon started to soften.

Nix went boneless all at once, eyes slipping shut even as he felt Yejun pull himself free. He listened, only partially paying attention as the other guy got up and started moving about, only looking when he was suddenly lifted up.

"What are you doing?" he asked as he was brought back to his feet and held there by Yejun until the Demon was certain he could stand on his own.

Yejun picked up the stool he'd tossed earlier and returned it to the dais before twisting Nix around and bending him into a mirror of the position he'd had him in earlier before the crazy, intimate sex.

"You can't be serious?" Nix growled, but he didn't move, keeping the position. He winced when he felt something warm and sticky seep out of his hole and drip down his inner thigh.

"I'm always serious about art," Yejun said teasingly before kissing his jaw and slapping him once across the ass. Then he left him there and returned to his seat, picking up his sketchpad. "This is so much better than the last one. The view is…"

There was a moment of quiet, followed by what sounded like a click that had Nix tensing. "Did you just—"

"Stay still, Firebird," Yejun ordered and started drawing. "If I can get this sketch done within five minutes, we'll have enough time for a second round."

"Second round?!"

"Going to pretend not to want me again?" Yejun asked. "That worked out so well for you the first time."

Nix clamped his jaw shut and pretended not to hear when the Demon laughed at him.

CHAPTER 18:

West tossed the drea in the air and caught it, the circular fruit's shiny blood red skin reflecting the harsh overhead lighting of the classroom as he waited for the rest of the students to poor out.

"Are you planning on eating that or just going to play with it all day?" Beck Bardin, Imperial seventh in line for the throne, and also a professor at Foxglove, asked dryly. He flipped through the screen on his tablet, standing behind his desk with his other hand in his pocket.

"You've really got this whole teacher look down," West said.

"That's because I am one," he reminded, finally looking up to send him a questioning look. "Do you need something?"

"Just hanging out." He snapped his fingers almost as soon as he'd finished the sentence. "Actually, yeah. Has Lake spoken to you yet?"

Beck straightened, brow furrowing. "About?"

"Your father."

The Imperial family was always a hot mess as far as West was concerned, but they'd really taken it to the extreme in recent generations. Beck's father, Hendrix, was Lake's cousin on his father's side, though through marriage. Because it'd been a fairly political merger of two bloodlines, Hendrix had been given the title of Imperial and placed in the line of succession. His son, Lake's cousin once removed, Beck was also in line, though one step below his dad.

Lake wasn't particularly close with his family, even less so after the deaths of his parents had left him an orphan and Hendrix had refused to take him in. Since they had no blood relation, he'd claimed he wasn't suitable.

Even though they were only two years apart in age, Lake had never been interested in trying to form a relationship with Beck, either. They'd attend the same Essential events and exchange pleasantries if Beck initiated it, but that was about the extent of it. Which was why it wasn't all that surprising that Lake hadn't talked to him yet, despite promising West and Yejun he would.

Beck pinched the bridge of his nose and leaned back against the projection board. "What has he done now?"

This was one of the reasons West liked Beck. He wasn't a slave to his father's bullshit the same way West allowed himself to be. More often than not, he wished he could be more like Beck, borrow some of that indifference. Unfortunately, no matter how much he talked himself up beforehand, the second West was in the same room as his father all of those preparations were dashed to smithereens.

It wasn't so much that he wanted to please his old man. West just wanted to be acknowledged. That was something people like Lake and Yejun would never understand, the first because he'd never cared about such things, and the later because his parents both showered him with adoration.

"Maybe nothing," West admitted, tossing the fruit again, relishing the satisfying thump it made when it hit the center of his palm. "We were hoping you could tell us."

"I haven't heard anything," he said, thinking it over. "What's made you suspicious?"

"You know that hacker the Order is after?"

"The one they've tasked you to find?"

"Yeah," he nodded. "We've managed to establish they're most likely trying to stop Lake from ascending."

Beck frowned again. "He's next in line."

"Yup."

"There's really nothing they can do to prevent him from taking the throne," he pointed out. "The only reason he hasn't already is because the mourning period on this planet lasts so long."

Six months. That was how long they had to wait before Lake could officially be announced as the next emperor. Of course, they'd only been given two to unearth their enemy and present him to the club.

"If we fail this task, it'll give someone reason to argue against Lake claiming the crown." They both knew who West was referring to. The Order didn't have many seats, but out of them, almost half followed behind Hendrix like lost little lambs. "The only thing that could stand against following the line of succession are the Essentials."

It was a precarious situation. The government was so entangled between its two rulers—the Emperor who sat as the face of command, and the club who operated in the shadows. No one would dare try to argue against things if the entire Essential Order as a whole called for a change in the process and demanded someone other than Lake be named. The only way that would be possible?

If Hendrix could prove to the rest of the Order that Lake was unfit to rule, either because of his age, incompetence, or both.

"Lake's wanted the crown for as long as I've known him," Beck said. "He won't give it up so easily."

"Neither will I," West confirmed. "I've hitched my star to his and we're both in it to win it."

"And Yejun?"

"Yejun goes where we go." West cocked his head, unable to hold back the smirk. "When are you gonna grow a pair and confess to him? You wait any longer and you might miss your chance."

"I don't know what you're talking about," Beck lied, unable to meet his gaze while he did. He moved back over to his tablet and started flicking through reports again, clearly not staring at any of them long enough to actually process what was written on them. "But even if I did...What do you mean exactly?"

West grunted. As far as he knew, the others had yet to pick up on Beck's crush, but he'd noticed. It'd been a while, too. Whenever they were all at those fancy events, Beck could be found sending Yejun longing glances from the corner of the room. He pretended like that wasn't the case whenever he actually interacted with Yejun, which was probably why Yejun hadn't realized himself since he was typically pretty good at picking up on things like that.

It was tempting to help them out and move things along by saying something himself, but it wasn't West's place, and he was no cupid. Besides, Yejun had never once shown any sort of interest in Beck aside from being friendly and polite.

He certainly had never looked at Beck the way he'd looked at Nix the other day.

"What? Don't tell me you haven't heard the rumors," West teased, knowing that Beck absolutely had. Hell, some of the students in the class that had just ended had been not so quietly discussing it amongst themselves when West had walked in.

Beck's finger paused over the screen before he got a hold of himself. "Even if the three of you have decided to choose a fourth, that doesn't mean anything. Yejun is hardly the monogamous type."

"I don't know," he drawled. "Maybe he just hasn't found the right one yet." Movement out in the halls caught his attention and he glanced out, grinning when he spotted Nix just as he passed by. "Speak of the devil."

Beck followed his gaze, but Nix was already out of sight.

West dropped the fruit onto Beck's desk. "Let me know if you end up hearing anything." He waved but didn't stick around to see if there was anything else Beck wanted to say to him, too focused on catching up to Nix in the halls.

It didn't take long. West draped an arm around Nix's shoulders, laughing when the slightly smaller man tried to pull away and set a surprised look on him before it registered who he was.

"West," he said his name tentatively, almost as though he was gearing up for something crazy.

The two of them hadn't interacted much since the blowjob. Maybe that was why. Admittedly, that hadn't been the best first impression he could have made, but Lake had been the one calling the shots. West had simply been rolling with the punches.

"Where you off to, Nixie?" West pulled him to the side, stopping them by a row of coffee-colored lockers. "Can I make a suggestion?" He caught Nix's chin and forced his face to turn back to his when a couple of giggling girls passing by had him looking away. "Focus."

"I have class," Nix said, brushing his hand off.

West allowed it since he didn't make any moves to leave, standing there quietly as though waiting for him to finish whatever it was he'd stopped him for. "You adjust quick, huh."

Most people would be freaking out if within their first week of school they were publicly claimed by a group like the Demons. Not only that, but Nix had been placed in several uncomfortable situations thanks to them. Maybe someone else had already smoothed things over?

"How was last night? With Yejun?" West asked.

"I don't kiss and tell," Nix replied.

"Ah, so you've kissed." He propped a shoulder against the lockers. "Have I fallen behind? That won't do."

"I really do have class right now, West."

"What about that comment you made to Lake?" he pressed anyway, a bit irked by the reminder that Nix had said his bestie tasted better. "Sounds like you need a refresher."

"Comment?" Nix frowned and clearly thought it over. He sucked in a sharp breath the second he seemed to recall, glancing around at the audience they'd collected.

Students were not so subtly pretending not to be watching, but they were too silent or leaning in too closely for that to be even slightly believable. Since it was so obviously making Nix uncomfortable, West considered shooing them off. If he were Yejun, he would. As it were…

"You've got to get used to that too," he suggested. "It's only going to get more intense from here. Why don't we start practicing by," he hooked a finger into the band of Nix's pants, laughing when he stepped away, "playing."

"Stop messing with me," Nix said, keeping his voice down.

"Make you a deal." He pushed in closer. "You promise to give my dick another try after, and I'll let you run off to class like the good little boy you're pretending to be."

He scrunched his nose but caught himself, dropping his gaze before he'd fully set that displeased expression on West.

Which, oddly, West wasn't a fan of.

"Hey." He gripped the short hairs at the back of Nix's skull and yanked them just enough to tip his head up. "You're scared of me. Why?"

"Oh, I don't know," Nix drawled. "Maybe it has something to do with how you almost killed me our first meeting?"

He blinked. "Did you really think I was going to choke you to death? Come on, Nixie. Have a little faith."

"I don't know you," he reminded.

West was about to argue but…That was fair. His fingers uncurled and he patted the tender spot he'd just assaulted before dropping his arm. "There's no time like the present to get to. After," he added when Nix stubbornly opened his mouth and it was clear what he was about to say, "your class."

Nix eyed him suspiciously but didn't argue when West spun him around and wrapped an arm over his shoulders again.

"Which room?" he asked, pulling Nix in close when they passed by a guy and a girl staring at him with more interest than West was comfortable with. He sent them a dark look the moment they passed, and the two quickly shot down the hall as though they'd forgotten they needed to be somewhere.

"You aren't seriously walking me to my class," Nix said.

"We could always return to my earlier suggestion and

duck into a broom closet instead," West offered. He reached down and pointedly adjusted his semi-hard cock, drawing Nix's attention to it. Remembering how it'd felt to have that plush mouth wrapped around him had him instantly aroused, and it was taking all his willpower—willpower he wouldn't have bothered with if Nix had been anyone else—not to carry through on his threat and simply force Nix to give him what he wanted.

This was a long game though, and after the way Yejun spoke about Nix at the clubhouse...West couldn't be the only one of the three that Nix didn't like. He'd apparently been nice to Yejun, and he and Lake had come into this with some weird connection already established. That just left West in the lurch.

He hated coming in last place.

"It's this one," Nix pointed to the class they were coming up on the right.

"Not my preferred choice, but I'll accept it." West pulled them both into the class and let Nix go so the other guy could lead them to his seat. Then he followed behind, taking the empty one on his left. He shrugged when Nix frowned at him.

"What are you doing?" Nix asked.

"Here's that broken record thing again," West rolled a finger in the air. "Relax. I'll let you concentrate."

"Don't you have something else to do?"

"Nope."

"...West."

He shushed him and motioned to the front of the room just as the professor entered.

Nix continued to stare at him for a moment, but then he sighed and gave in.

Which was good.

Pretty soon, West was going to have him ready to give in to all of his demands at any given notice.

CHAPTER 19:

"If you're bored," Nix mumbled out of the corner of his mouth so as not to be caught by the professor, "you can go."

It was a class in a lecture hall, with several rows curved to face the small stage at the head of the room where the professor stood. The man was about ten years older than them and spoke with a steady voice. It was clear he knew his stuff but...

"Of course I'm bored," West replied, leaning in. He rested his arm on the back of Nix's chair and then dove his fingers through the strands of hair at the back of his skull. "Aren't you? You know all of this already."

This was one of the classes required for them to get their degree in their particular major, but yes, he was right. Nix did already know about all of the source material. That didn't mean it was okay to cause a disturbance in the middle of it, however. He still needed a good grade, and respecting Professor Michaelson should have been a given.

"Cut it out." Nix tried to brush West off, a pained sound slipping past his lips when those fingers tightened and tugged. He was yanked a full inch back in his chair, instinctively reaching to grab onto West's wrist.

Professor Michaelson glanced their way, paused, and then continued as though nothing were happening. Nearby, a few students also turned to look, one or two staring longer than the rest before they turned back and pretended not to have seen.

"You seem to have gotten too comfortable, Nixie," West

growled against the curve of his ear, at least keeping his voice down. "What, because Yejun was a little bit nice to you, did you mistake that the four of us are somehow tight?" His tongue darted out, flicking against his earlobe once. "I'm not Lake. I'm not infatuated by you. I've been friendly because you promised to go along with things. If you're choosing to misbehave instead…"

"Stop," he risked saying, clenching his jaw when that had his hair pulled a second time. "We're in the middle of class."

"Exactly," West said. "Half the point of this little game of ours is to be seen with you. Bet every single person in here rushes out the second the bell rings, eager to gossip about how I disciplined you in front of all of them."

Nix *had* forgotten his situation. He'd also made the poor assumption that because the three of them were best friends, they must be alike. Yejun had stripped him and held him down that first night, and yet he'd been almost sweet since. Stupidly, Nix had hoped it would be the same with West.

Things were already hard enough as it was with Lake and his frosty disposition. Hell, Nix hadn't even heard from the guy in the past couple of days, not even through the Enigma app. It was almost as though he'd made him sign that contract and then had pushed him off on his friends as soon as he was done with him.

Nix didn't like how that made him feel.

"Believe it or not, you aren't the only one who's afraid of me," West continued, hand dropping to Nix's left thigh when Nix snorted in response. "Oh? Not so shocking, that it?"

Considering the guy was built like a fighter and supposedly liked to blow off steam in a boxing ring? No, not really. This time, however, Nix smartly kept his mouth shut, thinking perhaps things would go smoother if he remained silent and just allowed West to do and say as he pleased.

Wrong.

West's hand on his thigh lifted and went for the button of his pants.

"No!" Nix whisper-yelled, latching onto him and trying to push him away. The closest student in their row had only left a single empty seat between them, and they were in the middle of the room, which meant all of the rows behind would simply need to lean forward to catch an eyeful of— "West. Please, stop."

The Demon paused, observing him. "Are you...crying, Nixie?"

Tears burned at the corner of his eyes, but they'd yet to spill. Stubbornly, he fought them back, biting down on his tongue. He was too afraid to do more than that, not wanting to risk moving or letting go of West's hand, which was still in his lap.

He tensed when West's tongue flicked out again, this time over the rise of his cheek. "Going to cry for me, baby? I won't mind that at all. In fact, I'll most likely get off on it."

Nix gave a single, curt shake of his head.

"I've been thinking about it, you know," West carried on. "The way you sobbed for me our first time. How hot you were with spit dripping down your chin and your eyes all puffy."

"Later," Nix blurted, pretty much willing to agree to anything at this point just to get this to end. They'd given more than enough fuel to the rest of the students for gossip.

West cocked his head, waiting for him to elaborate.

"You wanted me to blow you again," he reminded. "I'll do it. After—"

"We already agreed you'd suck me off once class ends," West stopped him, nosing the underside of his jaw before he followed the same path with the tip of his tongue.

It was somewhat ticklish and Nix pulled away before he could stop himself, hissing when he was yanked back into place by that same harsh grip on his hair. At least the hand in his lap was still, no longer trying to get into his pants.

And now he was grateful for things like not being sexually assaulted in public.

What the hell was wrong with him?

What the hell was wrong with this school? He'd known

about the power imbalance, of course, but this...The Demons were just allowed to do whatever they pleased, even if it meant forcing one of their fellow classmates?

"You're clever, Nixie," West said, as though having read his mind. "You should have picked up on the fact that if I chose to bend you over this table right now and fuck you through your protests, no one would come to your rescue. In fact, if I allowed it, I bet half of them would pull out their multi-slates and start filming even."

Nix's chest constricted. Tulniri might be a planet open to sex, but that didn't mean something like that wouldn't haunt him throughout the rest of his adult life. Getting any sort of respectable job would be seven times harder. His dream of working for a major game development company? He could kiss that goodbye as easily as Yejun had kissed him the other night.

As easily as West was laving at him with his tongue.

The real problem here was that it seemed like West was the type who really would be into that sort of thing. This wasn't just a threat—the growing bulge in the Demon's pants was proof of that. He was turned on by the thought of publicly overpowering him.

If a blow job wasn't enough, he was going to have to debase himself further.

"I'll cry for you," Nix offered quietly. He had no real concept of what that even meant or how he'd go about it, but since West had seemed eager for his tears...Maybe that could work.

Amazingly enough, it seemed to catch the Demon's attention the way he'd hoped. West's hand loosened some, allowing Nix's tender scalp a small reprieve as he considered the new proposal.

"My time and place?" West asked, as though this really were some deal.

"Not in public."

For a moment, Nix feared West would push that issue, sinking into his chair when he was suddenly released.

West swiveled to face forward once more. "Well played, Nixie. There's hope for you yet."

He didn't know what that meant.

But he sure as shit wasn't willing to push his luck and ask for an explanation.

Nix didn't want them to, but his thoughts turned to Branwen. There weren't any indicators that she'd had any type of interaction with the Demons during her years in attendance here, but considering the way the rest of the student body treated them like gods, that wasn't as comforting as it'd once been.

What if this King she had been involved with was close to them? What if she'd done something to upset that person and they'd gotten the Demons involved anyway? With his mere presence alone, West controlled the room—even the professor pretended not to have noticed the scene they'd just put on.

This wouldn't do. Nix needed to speed the process up. He'd been too afraid of misstepping, hadn't even risked bringing his cousin's name up to Grady, but that had to change. If he was able to find at least one of Branwen's old friends, maybe they'd be able to point him in the right direction.

The rest of class went without a hitch. West surprised him by keeping his word. He left Nix alone and played on his multi-slate quietly for the next half hour, not even glancing in his direction once.

It should have made it easier for him to concentrate, but Nix found himself hyperaware of the man at his side, unable to focus. Every time West shifted he tensed, but the Demon never even brushed up against him. His first week at Foxglove and Nix was discovering things about himself that he maybe could have lived without knowing. Least of which, that apparently he had fucked up preferences when it came to the bedroom.

He still drew a line at public humiliation, and no part of him wanted to be fucked in front of a live audience but...His reaction whenever one of the guys used that threat against him wasn't...normal. His heart rate kicked up into overdrive, and he panicked, sure, but there were other sensations as well.

Nix didn't want them to follow through, but something about their controlling nature seemed to call to him and he wasn't sure how he felt about that. Bad, mostly. Guilty, definitely. He hadn't come all this way to be used by three dicks—both literally and figuratively.

West was hotheaded and aggressive, not Branwen's type even a little, so Nix highly doubted he was the King he was looking for. Still, he needed to confirm as much. He'd talk to Grady and see if his roommate recognized her name, if he got a lead from it, great. Either way, his first matter of business had to be clearing the Demons off his suspect list, that way he could turn his attention elsewhere.

He recalled his talk with Yejun the other day, tuning out the professor entirely now to the point he no longer bothered to fake taking notes. Out of the three of them, West was technically the one Nix *should* be trying to get closer to. He needed an invite into the man's bedroom and a way to sneak onto his computer to search through the King accounts. That definitely wouldn't happen if he pushed him away.

But Nix couldn't exactly stop resisting either, not only because it would be highly suspicious for him to suddenly have a change of heart, but also because he really just wasn't sure he had it in him. Was he turned on whenever one of them cornered him? Yes. Did that mean he wanted to be coerced into giving sexual favors and having intercourse whenever they wanted it? No.

Well…not really.

Mostly.

What was happening to him? Since when had he been the type of pathetic loser that caved for decent cock? His sex life prior to arriving had been lackluster at best, but also not something he'd actively ever thought about. He'd never found himself studying in the middle of the night, wishing he was screwing instead.

Then again, his fantasies had also always been relatively

tame. The types of boring daydreams he was certain the Demons would all laugh at if he voiced them out loud. Things like flowers and first dates leading to making out in the corner of a dark movie theater or at most, passionate lovemaking in a locked bedroom with the lights dimmed.

Nix was grateful that he was adaptable. Adjusting to his surroundings had always been easy for him, but he couldn't help but wonder if he might not be taking that too far in this case. How much of himself was he willing to change or lose here?

The anger that had driven him to upend his entire life was still simmering beneath the surface despite everything that had been done to him so far, but he needed to speed things along. The initial plan had been to get in and get out. He'd given himself one semester to wrap things up, find answers for himself and Branwen's brother, and then he was meant to reenroll at Hyacinth.

The only person he'd said as much to was Briant, since there'd been no good way to explain that to his parents. That was still the goal. Nix had no intentions of graduating from Foxglove Grove, which meant he would only be here for four months.

Surely he could keep himself together in that brief amount of time?

If he had to suck a few more dicks and spread his thighs, who cared?

And if he secretly kind of liked it sometimes? What did that matter either?

Nix was merely immersing himself in the role. That was all.

The bell rang and he started collecting his things on autopilot, mind still circling. He was so caught up in his own world, he didn't notice West until an arm came into view and stole his backpack just as he was closing it.

"Stalling, Nixie?" West asked. He'd already stood and was now sitting on the edge of the long table that connected the row, eyeing him down with mild suspicion like he thought there was a chance Nix might try and bolt now that it'd come time to pay up.

"No," he said. "I keep my word."

"Something we have in common."

He didn't bother mentioning it was probably the only thing they did. Just as he was about to rise, his mutli-slate went off and Maestro flashed across the surface.

West snorted and snatched Nix's arm, lifting it into the air and taping the accept call button before he could stop him. Since he left the earbud attachment set in the side of the device, it automatically switched to speaker, Lake's monotone voice cutting the air between them a moment later.

"I'm almost done with practice," he stated. No hello or anything of the sort. "Come to the stadium."

"Nixie's a little busy at the moment," West answered before Nix could think of anything to say.

Lake was quiet for a breath before asking, "With what?"

"A taste test." West grinned when Nix tried to end the call, grabbing his hand roughly and shaking his head. "I've been eating kuy berries for days in preparation for this, so you better be prepared to hear how much better *I* taste when you get home later."

Nix's mouth dropped open. He couldn't be serious...could he?

Kuy berries were a sweet fruit found on the opposite side of the planet in the hotter regions. It was considered to be an aphrodisiac, not because they legitimately increased a person's sex drive, but because they had the odd after-effect of altering the taste of...well. There'd been more than a few studies on it, of course, but like with most things, taste was subjective. Some people swore by the kuy effects and others claimed there'd been no difference.

Nix had never even considered trying it out for himself, whether as the one consuming the berries or the one feasting on come after someone else had.

"You should seriously get that complex of yours checked," Lake stated, only for West to snort.

"Says the guy who's clearly jealous right now."

Was he? Nix hadn't picked up on any changes in his tone, how could West tell?

"Fuck off, West."

"I'm about to, *Maestro*," he dragged out the username, laughing when Lake actually cursed on the other end of the line. "Have fun jerking off on your own." He clicked the end button and dropped Nix's arm. "Ready to go?"

Nix stared at him. "I really wish you two would stop using me as a pawn between you. What's even up with you guys? I thought you were best friends."

"We are," West confirmed. "What? Never heard of friendly competition before?"

"If it were friendly, you wouldn't have spent days eating fruit." Although...Nix's eyes narrowed. "You didn't really, right?"

West leaned in. "How about you get up so we can leave and you can find out for yourself?" He swung Nix's backpack over his shoulder, dropping his gaze to the ground when something slipped out and hit the floor with a heavy thump. "What is that?"

Nix moved over to see, frowning when he spotted something rolled up in paper. "I don't know."

"It came from your bag."

"It's not mine."

West read his face and seemed to conclude he was telling the truth, then he reached down to pick it up.

They both yelped like little bitches the second they saw what it was.

CHAPTER 20:

Lake very rarely, if ever, lost his cool, but he came very close to slamming his fist into the wall when West hung up on him. It'd been days since the last time he'd properly seen Nix, and he'd finally been able to carve out some time in his schedule only for West to cock block him.

Not that he'd been planning on fucking Nix, necessarily. A part of him still didn't trust the other guy, no matter how badly he was also fascinated by him.

And Lake was fascinated. He was drawn to the Songbird in an inexplicable way he couldn't describe and had never experienced before. Back on Vitality, he'd witnessed Kelevra fall seemingly head over heels for another person and found the whole process absolutely ridiculous.

By making Nix their sacrifice, he'd secured a good enough reason to keep him around, but not just because Lake was attracted to him.

There was something he was hiding. He was certain of it. Normal people didn't hack into an app like Enigma for fun, and while the death of his cousin definitely posed a better excuse, it still wasn't enough in Lake's mind. From what he already understood of Nix, it would have taken a lot more than a letter to get him to abandon his lifelong dreams and plans.

Nix was meticulous. Crafty.

He thought he was hiding those features away by rolling with the punches and going along with this whole scheme, but

Lake could see right through him. He knew why he was doing this. He wanted to keep the Songbird close, to sort through these weird emotions and also uncover his secrets.

But what was Nix's real reason?

Why was Nix pretending like he didn't mind the idea of being screwed by three people at once?

Because he did. He was an ace at adjusting, but that was an *adjustment.* Relationships between more than two people weren't abnormal on their planet. There'd been Demons in the past who'd all chosen the same lover, and this wasn't the first time Lake and the boys had shared a person either, though not in such a serious context.

They'd never publicly claimed anyone, in any case.

Yejun had his suspicions, that was why he'd goaded him the other day. He'd been trying to get a rise out of Lake, to get him to admit his interest in Nix. It wouldn't change anything even if he did, however, so he'd kept his mouth shut and had shrugged the whole thing off.

It was a bit harder to do with West. Before his parents' deaths, the two of them had been inseparable. They'd never fought about anything. Then Lake had moved in with him and Demitrious's already tenuous relationship with his son had splintered further thanks to Lake's presence. He put up with West's backhanded remarks and his overly competitive nature because he understood where his friend was coming from. He'd been there all through it. Knew his dad was a real piece of work.

When he'd been on Vitality, Lake had missed West the most, and yet...

He closed his eyes and inhaled slowly, trying to soothe his annoyance before he gave in and reacted negatively. He was the one who'd wanted Nix to get involved with them all, and not just because it made sense toward their plans or would help them flush out the hacker.

Lake had wanted to gather their opinions on the Songbird. Wanted to see if there was a chance he affected them the same way. They'd never openly discussed sharing a person in the future, but others had done so for them. The three of them had heard the whispered rumors, both at the club and out of it.

They were so close, people wondered if they weren't fucking each other.

If perhaps they'd choose a fourth.

If someone could ever come between them and tear through their bond.

Lake had always shrugged the comments off, but now… he was curious. He trusted West and Yejun, they were family. But his time on Vitality had given him a different perspective of what that sort of thing could actually mean.

Kelevra had his Retinue and Lake had been a part of it. There, having a tight-knit group in support of the Imperial Prince was the norm. Here? The Demons of the past had all gotten along, for the most part, but none of them had grown up together as closely as Lake, West, and Yejun had.

If Lake could break the crown into thirds, he would do so in a heartbeat. Half the reason he even wanted the damn throne was for them in the first place. As Emperor, he'd be able to punish Demitrious for his crimes against West, and he'd be able to break Yejun free from his parents' shackles. Right now, they gave the impression of being untouchable to the rest of the planet, but in reality, they were merely pawns to the Order, same as everyone else.

That would change if he became emperor.

When he became emperor.

Just a little longer. All they had to do was make it to Demon Passing, which happened to fall around the same time that the mourning period would end. Once it did and he beat this final challenge, there'd be no reason for anyone to speak against his ascension.

Lake would take the throne, and the three of them would be free to be the monsters they were always meant to be.

His multi-slate went off and when he saw the caller ID he almost ignored it, too high-strung at the moment to deal with speaking to West's father. Knowing it would only cause problems for him later, however, he ended up caving and pulled out the earbud attachment, slipping it in before he hit accept, making sure to make the caller wait for as long as possible between.

"Lake," Demitrious's sharp voice came through, causing Lake to wince, "has practice just ended?"

He was standing in the middle of the stables, the last to leave. Next to him, his waif snickered and circled its pen before lying down. The creature was three times his size with four legs and a powerful back. It was strong enough to carry a rider even Lake's size, with smooth scales the color of burnished bronze.

It'd been the last gift his mother had given him before the accident, and the only reason he'd agreed to continue playing the game had been the stipulation that he could only bring the waif with him to campus if he was on the team. Even the Order had refused to speak with the dean to waive the rule for him, mostly because Demitrious had always enjoyed watching Lake play.

Bastard.

As kids, West had been the better rider and better at the sport, but had his father noticed?

No.

"Yes," Lake replied, checking to be sure the pen was locked before he started down the long, wide path toward the end of the building where the changing rooms were located. "Is there something I can help you with?"

"I just called to see if there's a progress report," he told him. "If there's anything I can help *you* with, you know all you have to do is ask."

It was against the rules for any of the club members to help out the Demons with their final task, but Lake didn't bother mentioning that. Demitrious didn't care for rules, not even ones set by Essential that he'd given a blood oath to uphold.

"We've got it under control," he replied. "West is close to tracing the hacker."

Demitrious hummed noncommittally. "How is your backup plan coming along? I know you two are close, but don't rely solely on my son's abilities to get you through this."

Lake didn't want to discuss Nix with him, but if it meant taking the attention away from West, he would. West was top of his class and had already been scouted by several of the galaxy's top tech companies, and yet if you asked Demitrious, he'd shrug and say his son was just all right with computers.

If Lake hadn't owed the past ten years of his life to the man, he would have told him off several times already. Hell, if the guy weren't seated on the Order, he and Yejun would have plotted a dozen and half different ways they could take him out without getting caught.

Alas.

"We're still waiting to see if the hacker will take the bait," Lake said. "But word is spreading throughout campus, so it's only a matter of time."

Hopefully. Though, to be honest, he wasn't entirely sure this plan would actually pan out. He just wouldn't say as much out loud to anyone, especially not the Order. They were making a risky move bringing in someone like Nix, someone unknown to them. Someone with a secret...There was always the chance for betrayal.

He'd long since learned the only people he could rely on were West and Yejun—maybe the Retinue when he was on Vitality. But this wasn't Vitality, and Lake needed to gather as many reinforcements as he could.

Perhaps it was a good thing he'd returned home sooner than expected. If he'd stayed any longer, what other ideas would have been put into his head? West and Yejun were more than enough for him, and yet...

If they could make it through this, and if what Nix was hiding wasn't all that bad, then maybe Lake could allow himself to consider something more concrete in the future. If the others didn't want Nix in a more permanent fashion, that would be fine. They only needed to share the same sacrifice up until Demon's Passing occurred. Then it was fair game and Lake could claim the Songbird for his own.

If.

There were too many unknown factors involved here. Too many questions. He didn't like that. Liked to be in control and five steps ahead. The confusion had started right from the beginning, though.

Lake had signed into the Enigma app to check things out. Yejun was still too pissed about his situation with the member who'd been working with the hacker, and that left Lake and West to search for a sacrifice they liked. He'd stumbled into the forums and had actually selected someone at random, only mildly paying attention while he filed re-enrollment paperwork for the university.

Then Nix's masked face had popped up on his screen, and it'd been so obvious how uncomfortable he'd been. He'd nibbled on his bottom lip and then turned, presenting himself to Lake's view and something about the whole thing had gotten to him.

He'd seen a million and one naked bodies before. Had slept with more men than he cared to keep track of. Sex was an itch that needed scratching, but once the deed was done, his bedpartner was sent on their merry way. Lake had been shocked to find himself glued to the screen, his hand wandering down to cup himself through his pants as he watched Nix awkwardly stroke himself.

Since only students of Foxglove could sign up for the app, Lake had known he'd be able to track him down as soon as the semester started. With each meeting, he'd told himself he'd get it out of his system and wouldn't bother once they were in person. That seeing Nix through the screen would be enough to satiate this hunger.

He'd of course been wrong.

He needed to uncover Nix's secret before he grew even more attached. If it came to that...There was nothing Lake couldn't have if he wanted it, and that included people. Right now, they were being collectively considerate toward Nix and this sudden change, mostly because the three of them had learned the best way to catch someone was with honey and not vinegar. Hiding their monstrous sides was easy enough, but eventually, it would all come to a head one way or another.

"And this guy, Nix," Demitrious asked, "you trust him to keep his word?"

Lake ground his teeth as he entered the changing rooms and stripped out of his tight riding jacket. "He's smart enough to know he'd have all of Essential against him if otherwise."

"Yes, that's true." There was a pause, and then, "You like him?"

"We're partial to him." There was no way in hell he was going to give Demitrious that sort of power over him. His feelings toward Nix were his own business, no one else's, and while he'd always been held high on a pedestal by West's father, he knew better than to expect that to always be the case.

Look how easily he'd tossed his own son aside.

Demitrious was only paternal toward Lake because he had a spot in succession. If they somehow failed to procure his place and he lost the crown? There was very little doubt in his mind that he would be kicked to the curb just as quickly as West had been. Demitrious only kept people around who were useful to him.

Lake would judge, but up until Nix, he'd been the same way. Even after, hadn't he needed to come up with this plan to convince himself that he wasn't keeping the Songbird around just because?

"Once he's sacrificed—"

"That will be something we'll deal with then," Lake cut him off. He opened and slammed his metal locker with enough force he knew the sound could make its way through his earpiece.

"Oh, are you getting ready to leave?" Demitrious asked, like he knew he would. "I'll let you go. Just remember, if you ever need anything I'm here for you."

Lake hung up without giving a reply. He yanked his shirt off, tossed it into the locker, and was just in the process of reaching for his hanging uniform when his device chimed again.

Cursing, he slammed on the button and growled out, "What?"

"Come to the Roost." West didn't sound anything like he had only ten or so minutes ago, and that had Lake stiffening. "Now. We'll meet you there. I've called Yejun home as well."

"Nix?" He grabbed his uniform shirt off the hanger, sending the metal pinging around, but he was already turning for the door, not even bothering to close his locker in his haste.

"He's fine, but…" West blew out a breath. "Some freak put a dead thing in his backpack."

"What?" Lake slammed a palm on the door leading out and stormed across the parking lot toward his car. "Forget it, I'll see for myself. I'm on my way."

Some freak was about to become a dead thing if Lake had any say in the matter.

And as the Imperial soon-to-be prince?

He had a say in everything on this planet.

CHAPTER 21:

Nix clasped his hands and stared down at the muddied tips of his boots as they waited in the Roost. West had dragged him there—though, to be honest, it hadn't taken much effort on the Demon's part. He'd been too in shock to really argue, and the thought of returning to his dorm and acting like nothing had happened...

His stomach tightened and he swallowed the bile that threatened to climb up the back of his throat. He was in the leather lounge chair, the one West had been in when Nix had been forced to blow him. Yejun had already come and gone, taking the mysterious—and disgusting—package with him.

The front door clattered and a moment later Lake entered, gaze instantly seeking out Nix. He was halfway to him before he seemed to compose himself, coming to a complete stop. "Where is it?"

West, who was seated on the couch nearest Nix opened his mouth to reply, but Yejun gracefully dropped down the winding wooden steps that led to the second level, interrupting them.

"Here." He walked over and then chucked the wrapped item onto the center of the coffee table.

Both Nix and West shot back in their seats, the latter cursing.

"Relax," Yejun reassured. "It's fake."

"Huh?" West pointed at the item. "It looks fucking real to me."

"Well, it isn't." He turned to Lake, crossing his arms. "It's a believable fake. They even added fur. Whoever did this, they've got some art skills."

"What is it?" Lake peered down at the item.

"A dead luk," Nix said, staring at the item as well. Part of the back legs of the small rodent-like creature poked out from the paper that was wrapped around its tiny body. "And a note warning me to stay the hell away from you guys."

"It's a *fake* dead luk," Yejun corrected, seemingly losing his patience.

"Oh, and I supposed the note is fake, too, then?"

Yejun stilled, but West beat him to the punchline.

"Thinking about bailing now that you've been threatened by an outsider?" He leaned in and planted a heavy palm possessively to the back of Nix's neck, jostling him slightly. "Sorry, Nixie, not an option."

"Is this what you wanted?" He ignored West and instead glared at Lake. "Is this the kind of attention you wanted me to have?"

"We don't know this came from the hacker," Lake said.

As badly as he wanted to push the issue, Nix had to admit he was right. He deflated and dropped back in the chair, freeing himself from West's hold in the process. When he batted the Demon's arm away, West even let him, probably sensing how freaked out he was.

"I've never been threatened before in my life." Nix hadn't really known anyone or done anything worth receiving threats over either, but he kept that to himself.

"Come on," West drawled. "That's not true. We've been threatening you since your arrival on campus."

He blinked at him. "Is that supposed to make me feel better?"

Yejun snorted.

"Focus," Lake ordered. "What are the odds this came from the hacker?"

"Considering the note was scrawled in red paint and

warned him against associating with us," Yejun said, "slim. The hacker we're after would want to try and use him, not scare him off."

"Unless he came to his senses and gave up," West pointed out, shrugging when his friends both sent him droll looks. "Yeah, I don't think that's the case either, but it's worth mentioning."

"Who else could it be then?" Lake asked.

"Could be one of your crazy fans," Nix guessed, "telling me to get out of the way. Or one of the people who hate you."

"No one hates us," West stated, frowning when Nix quirked a brow at him. "What?"

"Tons of students hate you," he corrected. "They're scared of you and think you're all actual demons."

"And you've spoken to some of these people before?" Lake's eyes narrowed. "Who are they?"

Nix opened his mouth, caught himself, and slammed it shut again.

"Names, Songbird."

"No." He ran a hand through his hair, realizing too late that he'd walked straight into a spiderweb. Grady and his friends were the first to come to mind, but the last thing Nix wanted was to throw them into a snake den without any proof. "I'm sure it wasn't them."

"How sure?" Yejun said. "You can't trust anyone. People screw other people over. It's in their nature."

"Dark, man," West shook his head at him. "When are you going to get over that and move on already?"

"Hey." Lake obviously didn't agree with that sentiment.

"Don't hey me," West snapped. "You weren't even here. Who do you think had to pick up the pieces after?" He motioned to Yejun while scowling at Lake. "You want to know how much carnage I had to clean up because of his piss poor mood?"

"You stabbed someone in the eye," Nix's voice, quiet yet firm, caught all of their attention, and they turned to him. He blew out a breath and met Yejun's gaze. "Right?"

It was hard to put those two images together. The one of a man capable of blinding someone out of rage and the one who'd been so gentle with him in the studio. The Yejun Nix had been introduced to had the ability to be cruel, sure, but aside from that first night, he hadn't shown it.

Even knowing that, Nix had allowed him to lay him down, spread his legs, and enter his body. He hadn't just accepted it either. He'd *welcomed* it.

He covered his mouth as another wave of bile threatened to come up.

"How could you do something like that?" he demanded when none of them denied it.

"He deserved it," Yejun said.

"He—" Nix stood. "And you all wonder why there are students willing to do shit like this." He pointed to the fake dead animal in the center of their coffee table with a grimace.

"We don't know why they did it," Lake began, only for Nix to chuckle humorlessly.

"If that shit doesn't scream 'I hate you' I don't know what does," he told them. "Whoever sent that to me wants me to back off. I agreed to help you find a hacker, not whatever the hell this is."

"West is right, Firebird," Yejun's voice softened, as though he were trying to lessen the sting of the following blow. "You don't get to leave."

"We own you," Lake stated, a lot more aggressively than his friend had tried to be. "You signed a contract."

If it weren't for Branwen, Nix would have told them all to go screw themselves right then and there. But if he did that, he'd lose any chance at a lead he had, and no matter how freaked out he currently was, he couldn't give that up. Besides, the animal was a fake, and the letter, while scary, was crass and a bit cliché.

Whoever had sent it was just trying to warn him off, not harm him. Now that he'd had time to consider everything, that became more and more apparent.

"Give us names, Songbird."

He shook his head. "I'll talk to them myself."

"As if."

"It wasn't them," he insisted, holding up a hand to stop Yejun from speaking when he went to argue. "I know, I know. There's no way for me to be sure. But there's also no way I'm going to potentially feed innocent people to you guys either."

"We don't stab everyone in the eye," Yejun drawled.

"Just beat them up in the middle of a cafeteria," Nix let on he knew more than he'd brought up.

"Who's been whispering in your ear, Nixie?" West asked. "I don't like it."

"Which is why he's going to tell us their names," Lake insisted.

"Fuck off, no, I'm not." The room went dead silent and Nix plopped back down into the chair, hoping that he could appease them by showing he'd at least stay put. Which pissed him off even more because since when had he started to automatically cater to them?

From the beginning?

Probably.

Shit.

He groaned and covered his face. "This is so messed up."

"We'll find who sent you the dead luk," West tried reassuring him, but it didn't really stick the way the other man clearly hoped it would.

"And then what?" Nix asked, meeting his gaze. "You guys beat them up? Cripple them?"

"It's unlikely, but we can't rule out that it's the hacker," Yejun said, completely ignoring that question.

"Oh, so it's cool if you maim someone so long as they're this hacker you've been after, that it?" Nix straightened, lips pursing. "Wait. Is that what I'm helping you guys do? Am I going to become some accomplice in a horrible crime? Because that's not—"

"No one is going to make you personally harm anyone," Lake cut him off.

"Just because I'm not the bullet doesn't make me innocent if I'm the one aiming the blaster." He'd been so caught up in his thoughts of vengeance for Branwen, he hadn't taken a moment to stop and *think*. Anger for his cousin had driven him, but now that they were here and he'd learned about the types of things the Demons did to those who'd crossed him... "I don't belong here."

Not just in the Roost either.

Nix didn't belong at Foxglove Grove.

He stood again, head swimming. How absolutely foolish he'd been to think he was the type of person who could come all this way and enact revenge like some storybook character. Mentally, he could hold his own, but physically...He'd never so much as harmed a fly before. How the hell had he believed he could harm another person?

Sure, he'd wanted answers, but deep down he'd known that wasn't all he was coming here for. That wasn't everything he was going to demand of whoever had dragged Branwen down to that pit of despair. Did he know exactly what kind of punishment he would mete out? No. But the plan for punishment had always been there.

How could he stand here and scold Yejun and West when he'd had half a mind to torture someone himself?

"It's late," Lake said, waiting until Nix had lifted his head before adding, "You'll stay the night."

"Here?" He couldn't do that. The last thing he wanted right now was to be coerced into sex with one or more of them. "No. I can walk back. My dorm isn't far."

"Someone threatened you today," Yejun reminded, coming over to rest a hand on his shoulder.

"So then," Nix latched onto the first compromise he could think of, "walk me there. That'll be fine, right?"

"You're staying," Lake stated before Yejun could answer. In a few steps, he was at Nix's other side, latching onto his wrist. He ignored it when Nix made a pained sound as he was tugged and half dragged across the room toward the stairs.

"Dude," Yejun called after them.

"Be careful with him," West urged.

Lake merely lifted a hand and flipped them the bird, stomping up the steps two at a time as he pulled Nix behind him.

He almost stumbled on the stairs but righted himself just in time, fear and irritation only taking a backseat once they'd made it to the second level. It had the same cozy, mysterious vibe as the main floor, but the hallway branched off in two directions, encircling a center room with the door closed.

Lake led him to the left and down the hall before taking a right and selecting the first door. As soon as he had it open, he shoved Nix through and secured it, the flick of a lock drowned out by the sound of rain hitting the domed skylight.

It took up most of the ceiling, casting moonlight down on the king-sized bed and the crisp white sheets that covered it for a second before Lake flicked the lights on. Six orbs hovering around the room blared to life all at once, and Nix got a good look at the rest of the space Lake called his own.

"The Roost is built around the mountain," Lake said, still standing by the closed door, watching Nix explore with his gaze. "The structure is unique because of that. Some of the rooms are circular, like this one. Others are more angular or standard rectangles."

"You like to read?" Nix dared to run his fingers over a low bookshelf, noting it was one of many cluttering the walls. All of the furniture was made of the same dark and polished wood, but the accents, things like his bedding, the throw rug, and the blanket tossed over the leather chair by the window, were all white.

It was so...normal. Everything about it screamed cozy and relaxed, the very opposite of where his mind went whenever he thought about the man at his back.

That ease was shattered fairly quickly though.

"Get undressed."

Nix startled and spun to face him. "What?"

"You heard me, Songbird." Lake took a single step away

from the door. "Take off your clothes."

CHAPTER 22:

Lake watched a wide range of emotions play across Nix's face before he settled on reservation. His mouth was good at lying, but he tended to give himself away with his expression, even someone as self-absorbed as West had to have picked up on it.

"Why do you want me to do that?" Nix asked, then threw up a hand to stop him from answering. "Look, it's been a really long day, and honestly? That whole dead thing, fake or not, totally freaked me out, so if we could just—"

"The bathroom is that way." He motioned with his chin to his right at the door that had been left ajar this morning.

Nix stared at it and frowned.

"I'm telling you to wash up, Songbird," he said.

"Like..." he swallowed, "alone?"

"Is that an invitation?" Lake knew it wasn't. The other guy wasn't lying right now. He really was spooked and out of sorts, the real question was why? When Lake had first arrived, West had seemed more uncomfortable than Nix—most likely due to his fear of luk, not that he would have shared that information. It wasn't until after they'd started discussing what could potentially be done to the hacker that Nix started acting strangely.

Which put Lake on edge.

He'd been certain he'd chosen correctly, that, while he had a secret, that secret wouldn't have anything to do with the hacker. But...If Nix was this concerned for him, did that mean they weren't strangers?

Was he playing them?

Lake shifted slightly on his feet, not liking that idea at all. If that were the case, and Yejun found out...

It was too soon after the last one, and he'd yet to heal fully. Yejun very rarely let people get close to him. He had his flings and other friends from the art department, but they were "friends" not people he actually confided in or trusted. Lake hadn't been here to witness it, but according to West, their boy had fully let his guard down with this one girl last year.

The one who'd turned out to be working with the hacker.

When he'd discovered she'd only been using him to climb the ranks on the app and glean information about the Demons to send back to her partner he'd lost his mind.

"I'd rather it not be," Nix confessed, noticeably holding his breath as though he were afraid his rejection would set Lake off.

"Did West fuck you before you found the luk?"

Nix's brow furrowed deeper and he shook his head.

Lake sighed. "Pretty sure I promised not to have sex with you until they both had already. Relax, Songbird. It's just a shower, and you can help yourself. Unless you're so freaked out you need me to hold your hand and wash your hair for you?"

"No." Nix started for the door, halting halfway there. "My clothes..."

"Pretty sure I ordered you to take them off." He retreated the single step forward he'd taken and leaned back against the closed door, crossing his arms. The distance should make Nix more comfortable, should make it apparent he had no intentions of touching him right now. "I just want a show, Songbird. That's all."

"A show," he repeated dumbly before clearing his throat. Determinedly, he reached for the buttons of his shirt, slipping them through the holes one by one with ease.

"The first time I asked you to strip on camera, your hands shook so bad." Lake felt the corner of his mouth tip upwards, but he didn't stop it. That was a pleasing memory. He'd invited Nix into a private chatroom and offered up a Favor. He'd been a bit worried at the time that Nightingale, whoever he was, would refuse. "You surprised me by how quickly you took me up on my offer that afternoon."

Nix undid the last button and pulled the shirt off, biceps flexing as he exposed himself to Lake's hungry gaze.

"Feel free to toss it on the bed," Lake suggested, and when Nix snorted, he tipped his head in silent question.

"Free is a funny word coming from you, that's all."

"You're very honest tonight."

"Don't you mean brazen?" He folded the shirt and carefully set it on the end of the bed before reaching for his jeans. He slid the zipper down and pulled them off without hesitation, moving on to his boxers next.

"I don't mind how you are," Lake said. "Most people flirt with us or get shy."

"Scared," Nix corrected, and this time it was Lake's turn to snort.

"Believe it or not, Songbird, you're in a favorable position. People at this school would kill to spend even an hour in your shoes. You've got the attention of all three of us."

"Even if I don't want it?"

"You do." Lake had seen that truth clear as day. "Maybe not in the beginning. But now…" Something had changed Nix's mind, swayed him toward them. "Could it be the sex? You fucked Yejun a couple of days ago, didn't you? Was it that good?"

He'd always been a little bit curious, considering his friend's revolving bedroom door. That was as far as it went though. Lake had never desired to try Yejun out himself, and fortunately, Yejun hadn't either.

"I've seen him screw before," Lake continued, mostly to distract himself as Nix stepped out of his black boxer briefs and straightened. "It appeared as though he was good at it."

"He is," Nix replied. Then he just stood there, legs slightly parted, shoulders pulled back.

He was giving Lake the chance to look his fill.

Cute.

"You weren't this confident before either," Lake pointed out.

"Yeah, well, a lot's happened in a short amount of time. I adjusted." Nix shrugged like it was no big deal. Like he hadn't just been trying to renege on their agreement less than fifteen minutes ago downstairs.

Something sharp sliced through the center of his chest and Lake clenched his jaw against it. "Tell me."

"Tell you what?" the frown returned tenfold.

"What you're hiding," Lake reiterated. "Tell me now, Songbird, while there's still time to forgive you."

He glanced away. "I don't know what you're talking about."

"You're a better liar than that." Was he trying to hint to Lake that he was on to something out of guilt? Or had that been a mere slip in his armor? Perhaps he really was too unnerved after the day's events.

Meaning it was the best time for Lake to push, to poke at him until he caved and spilled the big secret he'd been hiding from them.

Lake inwardly cursed. "Go take your shower."

Nix bolted across the room and disappeared into the bathroom, practically slamming the door behind him. This was another mistake he usually wouldn't have made. He was careless. But why? Whatever the reason, it couldn't be in Lake's favor.

As soon as the sound of running water came through the wooden door, Lake lifted his multi-slate and sent a message in the group chat he shared with West and Yejun.

Maestro: One of us has to stay with him all day tomorrow. He can never be left alone. Understood?

West replied first, his response coming in a second before the sound of classical music picked up down the hall.

Hellhound: Why? You worried about him?

Lake moved away from the door to avoid the music and started to undress as their messages kept coming in.

Incubus: I don't think this person intends to hurt him. They just wanted to shake him up a bit, that's all. Convince him to ditch us and save himself or whatever. Don't read too far into it. You've got enough on your plate.

Hellhound: June is right. We'll take care of it and find whoever slipped that in Nixie's bag. You don't need to worry. I'm hacking into Foxy U right now. If anyone mentioned it to anyone through posts or DMs, I'll know.

Foxy U was the university's private social media. Everyone on campus used it, including professors and alumni.

Lake pulled on a pair of gray sweatpants and a plain white t-shirt before pouring a glass of water from the pitcher left by the windowsill. The large bay window looked out to the side of the mountain, so the view was mostly stone and hanging branches from two large oaks growing out of the side. On nights like this, where it poured, water ran like a river down it, reflecting in the lights of his bedroom. It was soothing, and usually he'd stand there and watch it for a while, allow it to help ease the tension in his shoulders and relieve him of whatever had stressed him out that day.

But he could hear Nix moving around in the bathroom and knew he wouldn't spend too long in there for fear of Lake changing his mind and trying to come in while he was nude.

Lake moved back around the bed and set the glass on the end table built into the wall before responding to his friends.

Maestro: That's not what I'm worried about. Didn't you see the way he was acting? He's thinking about running.

Hellhound: He wouldn't get very far.

That sounded possessive. Had West formed an attachment to Nix already? When? As far as Lake was aware, the Songbird had spent most of his time with Yejun as of late.

Incubus: I'll talk to him.

Maestro: I don't want you to talk to him. We tell him we're onto him and that'll just make him want to run more. Just make sure he isn't left on his own. Got it?

He undid the strap of his device and tossed it onto his desk before he could get a hold of his frustration. Bowing his head, he clenched and unclenched his fists and focused on inhaling and exhaling to the beat of four, like his father had taught him when he was a child.

Emotions were dangerous. They were tricky and controlling. Only a fool would allow something like that to rule over him.

Lake was no fool.

Hellhound: Jealous much?

Incubus: Understood. None of us want him to run.

The bathroom door opened and Lake remained hunched over the desk, listening to Nix's footsteps come to a stop.

"Quit hovering and get in here," he snapped, cringing as he lost his cool a second time. Lake straightened and turned just as Nix entered.

His hair was damp, and he'd slung a towel around his narrow hips, his right hand clutching the white material with a death grip. It would have been annoying to see, but after everything they'd already put him through his first week here, Lake couldn't really blame him for being suspicious.

"Those are for you," he motioned to the clothing he'd set out when he'd been getting dressed himself and dropped down into the wooden chair in front of his desk. The desk was set against the same wall as the bed, part of the same attached piece of dark wood that made up the end table.

Seeing him seated helped ease some of the tension in Nix's shoulders, but it didn't last. The second the Songbird picked up the bundle of clothing, he hesitated all over again.

Lake propped an elbow against the surface of his desk and then rested his chin in his palm. "It's not like you've got anything I haven't already seen. Literally ten minutes ago even."

He had enough self-control not to force the guy to sleep with him tonight, but that didn't make him a saint. Lake wouldn't pass up the opportunity to see all that toned form on full display. He'd make Nix dress for him.

Would make him dress up in *his* clothing.

Nix unraveled the snow-white sweatpants first, holding them up in front of him. They weren't the same height exactly, but a couple of inches wouldn't make too much of a difference. He set them aside and grabbed the shirt, also in the same pale shade, yanking that on over his head.

"Underwear?" Nix stared at the pants as though unable to meet Lake's gaze.

"Is it due to pride that you have to ask, or embarrassment?" Lake couldn't tell, and that bothered him. He wanted to know everything there was to know about the Songbird. Right down to the way he took his toast in the morning.

"I'm used to taking care of myself," Nix finally admitted after a lengthy pause where it appeared as though he was trying to get out of it.

Well then he was going to absolutely hate this next part.

Lake rose from his chair and stalked forward, noting when Nix sucked in a sharp breath, though he remained where he stood and didn't try to back away. Once he reached him, he hooked a finger into the top of the towel and tugged, the thick material falling away. He smirked when Nix's hands fisted.

"Put your pants on, Songbird." He gave him a second, turning to grab the smaller towel he'd left on the top of his dresser.

Nix had one leg in the pants and was balancing to get in the other when he came back, his cheeks stained that bright pink shade that Lake had found endearing right from the start. He was brave, even when he was terrified, and had impeccable self-control.

It was the latter that fascinated Lake the most. As someone who'd always prided himself on that very thing, it was interesting to see someone else display similar features. The difference was, Lake understood why he did it. Why he contained his true self and forced himself to do things he didn't actually want to do.

But why did Nix?

Why was Nix here with him right now instead of tucked safely in his dorm room with his annoying roommate? Or better yet, why wasn't he still at Hyacinth University on the other side of the planet?

Once Nix was fully clothed, Lake draped the smaller towel over his head and began to dry his hair.

"Why are you like this?" Nix asked, his voice cutting through the quiet between them, giving Lake momentary pause.

"Like what?" He went back to his task, taking care with the silky strands. Wet like this, they looked a lot like spun gold, and he found himself distracted by the glint and gleam. The Songbird was so pretty, a mixture of delicate yet firm. If Lake hadn't claimed him right away, there was little doubt in his mind that students would have flocked to him trying to get a taste for themselves—male, female, didn't matter. They'd all want a piece of Nix if they had the chance.

"I wish you wouldn't be this gentle," Nix admitted. "It confuses me."

"So you'd rather I toss you around and mess you up?" He wasn't West.

"You know that's not at all what I mean."

"Do I?"

"Forget it." Nix pushed him away and ran his fingers through his hair. "There. All dry."

Lake sighed. "There's really no pleasing you, Songbird."

"This isn't about pleasing me and we both know it."

He cocked his head and waited for him to explain.

"You're luring me into a false sense of security," Nix stated. "I'm well aware of what you're doing here, Lake. I just can't figure out your motive."

"I'll tell you my secret if you tell me yours."

"This again." Nix took a deliberate step back.

"I won't let it go until I uncover what you're hiding."

"Why? I'm doing everything you want me to do. Why

can't you just be satisfied with that? I'm not even convinced this whole hacker thing is even real at this point or if you three just made it up to trick me. Is this fun for you? Using me?"

He snorted. "I haven't even begun to use you." Lake captured a strand of his hair between two fingers. "And the hacker is very real. I wouldn't joke about Essential business."

They weren't going to get anywhere tonight. Even though he'd had the most interaction with Nix out of them all, it was clear he'd fallen behind somewhere. For a moment, he'd worried that Nix was about to suggest staying with Yejun instead, and he wasn't sure how he would react to that.

Not well, that was sure.

"Have some water and then get into bed," he instructed, returning to his desk.

"You're not sleeping?" Nix followed and eyed the glass of water, but Lake waited until he'd picked it up and taken a sip before answering.

"I have a paper due in a couple of days," he said. "I'll work on that while you rest."

"You're going to do homework?" Nix pursed his lips. "All night?"

"Why? Need me to hold you until you fall asleep?"

He slammed the glass back down on the end table and then yanked the covers off the bed and slipped beneath them. Nix settled on his side, facing Lake, and it was obvious he wanted to ask something but was debating how well that might be received.

"What?" Lake helped him out, flicking his tablet on and lifting his stylus so he could begin going over his notes.

"Before, when you'd send me Favors," Nix said, "they'd always come at random hours."

"So?"

"Do you actually sleep? Do you even have a paper due?"

Lake set the tablet back down and met his curious gaze. Sometimes, it was wiser to give an inch to take a mile. "I have sleep anxiety. Have ever since I was a child. Back then, West used to sneak into my room after his father had gone to bed. It wasn't so bad then, knowing that he was with me."

"He made you feel safe." Nix nodded his head on the pillow, and there was no judgment in his tone. If he thought that it was pathetic for a grown man to still have childlike fears, he didn't show it. "What are you afraid is going to happen? Anything specific?"

He considered it. "I suffered from fairly terrible insomnia after my parent's deaths. At some point, the stress over whether or not I'd be able to fall asleep at night got to me."

Lake would spend the entire day worrying over it. Fearing another restless night where he stared up at his ceiling blankly, praying for sleep to take him. Those first couple of months after were the worst when he was awake. His parents' faces appeared constantly, or he'd recall the last words they'd spoken to him.

The smell of his mother's perfume…

His father's laugh.

"We were close," he found himself revealing, giving Nix far more than he'd initially asked for, yet unable to make himself stop. "It's rare for families of our station, but we were. Growing up with them as my parents was like a dream."

And then that dream had shattered, ripped from his fourteen-year-old hands.

"How did they die?"

"An intruder," Lake said, digging his fingernails into his palm to keep himself from giving into the sweeping anger. Instead, he kept his expression controlled and his back straight as he held Nix's unwavering gaze. "My parents ran a successful investment company; that sort of thing comes with risk. A client blamed them and chose the worst course of action available."

Nix slowly sat up, swiveling so he was sitting cross-legged and fully facing him. "He broke into your house at night intending to kill them?"

Lake nodded.

"I'm so sorry."

"You sound like you really mean that."

"You're pretty great at reading people," Nix pointed out. "So you know that I do."

Yes, he did, but for some reason that made him uncomfortable. Not talking about his parents, but this. Nix's reaction. The way he was looking at him, not with pity, but something else. Something a lot like compassion.

"What about your cousin?" Lake needed to change the subject and get it off of him. "What was her name?"

"Branwen," he hesitated, yet eventually answered.

"How did she die?"

Nix started picking at the comforter, but just before Lake could say never mind, he whispered, "She took her own life."

That...was unexpected. He'd assumed sudden accident or illness. But that...Nix was so strong-willed. Lake had figured he'd learned that type of strength from his family. Perhaps not?

"Did she have a good reason?"

Nix's gaze instantly darkened, his shoulders drawing back in clear insult. "Is there ever a good reason to kill yourself?"

"There are understandable ones," he shrugged. "I'm not saying it's forgivable."

"She doesn't need my forgiveness," Nix snapped. "She was in pain. So much pain that she decided dying would be better than living."

Lake searched his face. "And you're not mad about that? That she gave up?"

"That's a horrible way of putting it."

"Maybe," he agreed. "But I'm also not wrong."

"That's..." Nix dropped his head into his hand and rubbed at his forehead. "Someone bullied her. Someone pushed her to that point."

"Ah," one of the pieces clicked into place, "so you are angry, just not at her. You've chosen to place all of that blame and anguish on someone else. Were the two of you really that close? So much so that you can't even stand the idea of her doing something wrong? Of making the wrong choice?"

"Stop."

"Who was the bully?"

Nix wavered and then admitted, "I don't know."

Was that the secret? Lake needed to thread carefully from here on.

"Is that why you really upended your entire life, Nix?" he asked. "Is that really why you're attending Foxglove Grove?" When he wasn't met with denial, he pressed further. "Was she a student here?"

Lake stood after a moment of silence, but that seemed to be all it took to shake Nix out of it.

He lifted his head stubbornly and replied in a tight voice, "Yes."

CHAPTER 23:

Lake ran through all of the information he already had.

According to Nix, his cousin only just recently passed, and it happened before he'd signed onto the app and created a false account. That meant Lake hadn't been on planet, so it couldn't have been him Nix was after.

Still, that left West and Yejun…

If it turned out Nix was here for revenge against them, Lake couldn't allow him to stay. No matter how badly he wanted him, the Demons came first. Always. As far as he was aware, neither of his friends went out of their way to harm females, but that didn't mean it never happened.

"I know what you're thinking," Nix cut into his thoughts, "but you're only partially right."

"Enlighten me, Songbird." He wanted to warn him to make it convincing, but that wouldn't be fair to the others. Just because Lake wanted to be lied to at the moment so he had an excuse to hold onto Nix, that didn't make it the right call.

"I did come here to find out who hurt my cousin," he said. "But I had no idea about any of you before I arrived. I know she was speaking to one of the Kings, but…That could be anyone."

"Anyone?"

"Not you," he corrected. "The timeline doesn't add up. I don't think it was Yejun either since he was busy with—"

"He told you about that?" Lake was surprised. Yejun typically didn't share personal things. The fact that he'd let Nix in like that must mean he liked him more than he'd let on before. "He doesn't have many real friends. When he found out she was helping the hacker get to us and using him..."

Lake had tried getting on the first spaceship back home once he'd found out, but he'd been ordered by the Emperor not to return. He'd been furious and would have gone against her if Yejun hadn't gotten wind of his intentions and called to tell him not to.

When it came to the throne, it wasn't just him on his own who'd been fighting for it all of this time. West and Yejun had been there with him every step of the way. Inciting the Emperor's ire meant throwing all their efforts down the drain. That, and the knowledge that West was there and would take care of Yejun were the only reasons Lake had held off.

"How did you guys find out that she was sent by the hacker?" Nix asked.

"Another time, Songbird," he stated. "We're still talking about you."

"I don't know about West."

"It wasn't West."

"How can you be sure?"

"He doesn't do girls." Lake shrugged. "Neither of us do. Yejun is pansexual—if he's attracted to them, he'll fuck them. West and I are both gay, and the only people he has any interest in getting to know are those who've joined the school's fight club or frequent the gym."

Nix rubbed at his forehead again. "She wasn't into either of those things."

"Then it wasn't West." He pulled open the desk drawer on the left and took out a bottle of painkillers, shaking a single pill into his palm. He leaned forward and held it out to Nix, picking up the water to present that as well.

"I'm fine."

"Take the medicine, Songbird." He'd force it down his throat if he had to, but he'd rather not.

Grumbling something under his breath that Lake couldn't

catch, he snatched the pill and popped it into his mouth, then took the water and gulped down half of the glass's contents. "Good?"

"Golden."

Nix blew out a breath. "Are you mad?"

"That you suspected us?" He shook his head. "No. I would have as well."

"You're mad."

Lake frowned. "I'm not."

"Whatever you say." Nix clearly didn't believe him, but he moved on. "That's it. That's the real reason I broke into your app."

"You're looking for a King." He steepled his fingers. "That's why you were curious about the others."

"If there are seven of them, and we make up four, that leaves three. Any one of them could be who I'm looking for."

The way he so casually lumped them together like that did something odd to Lake's chest, but he carefully kept his composure so as not to let on.

"You said this took place last year?" he asked. "That means it could also be any of the Kings who graduated. Once they do, they're removed from the top tier to make way for active students."

"So how many Kings were there last year?"

"I don't know." He hadn't exactly been around to help manage things.

"But West and Yejun do."

"Why haven't you asked them then, Songbird?"

"The same reason I didn't want to tell any of this to you," he stated. "I don't trust you, any of you. Look where I am right now." He motioned to the room. "I came here for my cousin, not so I could become a fuck toy."

"You're more than that," Lake said.

"What if the hacker never approaches me?" It almost appeared as though Nix was hopeful that would be the case. "What then? Will you let me go?"

"We have until Demons Passing," he reminded. "There's still plenty of time for him to take the bait. It's only been a week. As long as we focus on being seen with you, it should draw him in. He'll want to warn you off of us."

"Like whoever left me that package." Nix shuddered. "We're really sure it can't be the same person?"

"You know we aren't. But it wouldn't make much sense."

"He could have given up."

"It's possible."

"And you're all right with that?" Nix eyed him down. "If there's no hacker left to find, you can't complete the task that's been given to you."

"It'll complicate things," more than he wanted to admit or share, "but I'll make due if that happens."

He licked his lips. "And me?"

"What about you?"

"What exactly was written in that contract you had me sign, Lake? How long do I have to do this? Be here? You said it was until Demons Passing. What happens if you can't find who you're looking for by then? Do I still get to walk away?"

He would never be allowed to do that, but it was obvious now wasn't the time to say as much, so Lake kept that to himself as well. Whether Nix liked it or not, he was a part of their world now, and once someone was let in, they weren't given a simple pass if they wanted to leave.

"You don't have access to your cousin's chats," Lake said instead of answering, and even though Nix had to catch onto what he was doing, he let him. "If you did, that would solve everything. You'd find the person you're looking for."

Would he leave afterward?

He could try.

"What?" Nix pulled back slightly. "What are you mad about now?"

"I'm debating whether I should help you or hinder your search," he replied cooly.

"Why would you do that?"

"Prevent you from finding this King?" Lake hummed. "Oh, I don't know, perhaps it's because chasing after you would be a tedious waste of my time. Are you going to deny that you'd make a break for it the second you've settled what you really came here for?"

Nix cursed under his breath, but Lake heard it.

"Exactly. Since it's pointless for me to pretend, as you've already proven you can see right through me, do you want me to even bother?"

"Bother with?"

"I can give you another false sense of security, Songbird," he offered. "If that's what you need."

He considered it and, in a small voice, said, "I just need to solve this thing for my cousin."

"Then I'll help you," he held up a hand, "with the understanding that you're trapped, no matter what we find. The contract, using you to find the hacker, these were mere excuses to keep you around. This will be no different."

"Why?"

"Truthfully? I don't know." Lake hated that he didn't, but it was what it was. If he were Yejun, he'd understand, but he'd never been as good at sorting through and naming his tumultuous emotions. "Does it matter? Having an answer won't change anything. For now, you're mine, Nix Monroe; that's the only answer I need."

He sighed and got up, clicking his tongue when Nix braced himself at his approach. Lake was sure to be gentle when he pushed on his shoulder, easing the other guy back onto the bed. Once he had him lying on his side, he pulled the comforter up.

"Are you seriously tucking me in right now?" Nix grunted. "Would anyone else on this campus believe it if I told them?"

"Probably not." He didn't exactly have a reputation for being the caring sort. "I'll speak to West tomorrow about getting you access to your cousin's account. We'll just need her username."

Nix settled more comfortably against the pillow. "Okay."

"That's it?"

"Why would I fight you on this?" he asked.

"I could be lying to you," Lake suggested, mostly to gauge his response.

Nix snorted and closed his eyes. "You could be, but eventually, I'd find out. Nothing can stay hidden forever, Lake, and you aren't the only one who's good at getting what they want."

All of the teacher reports Nix had received since grade school said roughly the same thing.

Determined, driven, and hyper fixated on his future.

"I'll help you get what you want, Songbird," Lake promised. "So long as you help me get what I want in return."

Even though he didn't mention what that could be, Nix's eyes reopened and he gave him a small smile.

"Deal."

* * *

Nix must have been exhausted because, despite his present company, he was out like a light in less than half an hour.

Lake waited just to be sure, giving it an extra ten minutes before he stood and carefully undid the strap of the Songbird's multi-slate. It wasn't that he didn't believe Nix's story about his cousin, he did, but he couldn't rely solely on his instincts, not when there was a very solid way to collect physical evidence.

He used Nix's finger to unlock the device and then perched on the edge of his chair, glancing back and forth between it and the sleeping Nix. There was no Branwen in his contacts list, and a spark of uncertainty came alive in his chest. Not wanting to feed it further, he opted to check out his messages, scrolling through them until he came to one that fit the bill.

Planets Best Cousin: Don't come. You were right. This place is hell...

Lake clicked on the chat feed, opened it, and scrolled up, stopping at a random place in the log. The two of them spoke frequently, but a lot of it was just general pleasantries and check-ins. It seemed like more often than not it was Nix reaching out first asking how his cousin was doing, and him receiving a pretty generic response.

But there were moments when things became insightful and every time he encountered them, he paused and paid close attention.

Nix: Will you be home for the holidays this year? I miss you.

Planets Best Cousin: Sorry, no. I promised a friend I'd spend it with him. Don't tell my parents! They'd be so annoyed with me for choosing a boy over family.

Nix: Are you seeing someone? Congrats! Why didn't you tell me sooner?

Planets Best Cousin: It's…complicated. We're not officially together, but we see each other every day and we talk just as frequently. I've never felt this way before, Nix. I think you'd really like him.

Nix: He's a student?

Planets Best Cousin: Sometimes we sneak off to the history section of the library for lunch, just the two of us. No one goes back there because the textbooks are so dated, so it's like our own little world!

Nix: That's great, but if things are going so well, why aren't you officially dating?

Planets Best Cousin: We will, when the timing is right.

Nix: What does that even mean?

Planets Best Cousin: You wouldn't understand, you aren't a Foxglove student. Things operate differently here.

Nix: You mean because you're so close to Club Essential's base of operations?

Planets Best Cousin: Something like that.

Nix: He's not like, a member, is he? Do you have classes together?

Planets Best Cousin: We met on an app! It sounds strange, but everyone here is doing it.

The rest of that particular conversation was just more of Nix trying to pry answers out of her and her mostly deflecting or divulging snippets. It was pretty apparent that she was hiding something, and considering how smart Nix was, there was no way he'd missed that.

Lake moved on to another lengthy chat.

Planets Best Cousin: Do you ever wonder what you'd do if you found your soulmate, but it was the wrong place and the wrong time? I didn't believe in that type of thing before, but now...Nix. It sucks. Should I give up?

Nix: What's wrong? What happened?

Planets Best Cousin: I just feel like I constantly have to prove myself. Why can't he just accept me as I am? Am I not good enough?

Nix: You're literally the best person I know. If this guy can't see that, he isn't worthy of you. Dump him and move on.

Planets Best Cousin: You wouldn't understand. Thanks for saying that anyway, though.

There was a span of about two weeks between that and the final conversation, where the feed was filled with one-sided messages sent by Nix that had all gone ignored.

Nix: Are you feeling any better? How are things going with the guy?

Nix: We missed you this weekend. I know you said you were busy, but the festivities just aren't as fun without you. Call me later, yeah?

Nix: Hey, your mom mentioned yesterday she hadn't heard from you in a bit. You aren't getting back to me either. Can you just text me so I know you're okay?

Nix: Seriously, Tulniri to the world's best cousin?

Nix: Where the hell are you?

Nix: That's it. I'm hoping on the first plane to you.

That last one seemed to have done the trick, because afterward his cousin had finally responded.

Planets Best Cousin: Don't come. You were right. This place is hell. And even if you do, I won't be here when you arrive.

I'm sorry, Nix. I'm really, really sorry.

He'd sent a slew of text messages after that begging her to explain, but she never replied again. Lake assumed she must have taken her life shortly after this. There was no mention of the Enigma app by name or anything about a King, but he recalled Nix talking about a letter he'd received early on. Was that where he'd gotten the rest of those details?

If that were true, then all of this checked out. He really was here in search of the man who'd hurt his cousin's feelings badly enough to make her want to end it all.

Lake watched as Nix burrowed deeper into the pillow and sighed. This whole thing had clearly hurt him deeply, enough that he'd upended his life to come here for justice. If Lake were a better person, he'd probably feel bad for the cousin and all that she'd gone through. As it were...

Since her death had been the driving force that had brought him and his Songbird together, Lake's time would be better served visiting her grave and thanking her cold, decaying corpse.

"You'd probably say that makes me a villain," he murmured to the sleeping man in his bed.

In his bed.

In his clothes.

In his home.

His.

His.

His.

Lake liked the sound of that more than he should. Liked the thought of keeping Nix there, forever. If the rest of his future were already set, Lake would probably do just that. He was confident he could find a way to convince Nix this was where he belonged. But for now, there was too much going on. Other things that needed his attention.

"Soon," he promised, though it was unclear who he was making the dark pledge to.

Nix.

Or himself.

CHAPTER 24:

Nix moaned and shoved at whatever was on top of him, a cool breeze tickling at his skin.

Which was bare.

His eyes popped open a second before it registered there was a tongue snaking its way up his torso, and with a gasp, he shoved again, freezing when he finally focused on the large form lying partially on top of him.

"Morning, Nixie." West was settled between his legs, lying on his stomach with his arms on either side of him. While maintaining eye contact, his tongue stroked out, lapping at the spot just above Nix's navel.

"What are you doing?" he sounded out of breath, and when he tried to move, West held him down. "Wait. Why am I naked?"

He wracked his brain for his last memory, and he was pretty sure he'd fallen asleep fully clothed last night with Lake typing away at his tablet. A quick search of the room now, however, showed that they were alone. There weren't even sounds coming from the bathroom.

"They were in the way so I removed them for you," West said casually, licking him again. "As for what I'm doing, I'm making my way down your body, duh. I started at your neck, which you seemed to enjoy, but it's taken you a surprisingly long time to wake up. At least," he leaned off of him a bit and motioned down with his chin, "parts of you, anyway."

Nix groaned when he saw he was hard and dripping and covered his face, dropping back down onto the pillow. "Can you please get off of me now?"

"No can do," he said. "I'm not finished with breakfast."

"You can't be serious."

"Oh, I am. My time and my place, remember?"

Nix scowled at him, annoyed at them both for that stupid agreement they'd made in class yesterday. "This is Lake's room."

"Which is why the only one of us who's going to blow their load is you. Lucky." He slid down until his head hovered by Nix's dick, but instead of touching it, he turned and lapped at the rise of his hip bone. "Lake would be pissed if I got my come on his bed. But your bodily fluids? I'm sure he'll be all right with that."

"I don't think—" Nix gasped and arched his back when West pressed his lips to his inner thigh.

"I've been working you for over ten minutes," he confessed, laughing when Nix's eyes went wide. "You're not as sensitive when you're asleep. You were practically drooling when I came in, too. It was hot as hell. Did you sleep well, Nixie?"

"I..." The words died in his throat as West nudged his dick with his jaw and licked at the base where it met the rest of his body. He nipped on the delicate skin there, chuckling again when Nix winced before moving to plant a single kiss on his tip.

West resituated, folding Nix's legs up so that his knees were practically at his shoulders, ignoring his protests all the while. Suddenly, his face was at Nix's entrance, tongue corkscrewing straight past that tight ring of muscle.

The invasion was so sudden that Nix flinched and tried to wiggle away, crying out when that earned him a sharp nip at his balls.

"I like causing pain in the bedroom, Nixie," West warned. "It really gets me going. Since all I'm doing today is feasting, I'm going to try and take things easy. So don't push me, yeah? Then we can both get through this with a few minor bruises and, ideally, no blood loss."

"What?" Nix tried to sit up but was forced back down with

a growl and a firm grip behind his knees.

"What'd I just say?"

"West." He grabbed the comforter, clutching at the material as his eyes tracked a storm cloud through the skylight above. "Please."

How was this his life? He'd been reduced to this thing that constantly begged. Tears pricked at the corner of his eyes as he thought about how he'd been left alone in here, an easy target for West to come and gobble up.

Last night, he'd thought he and Lake had made a breakthrough. Not necessarily gotten closer but…something.

Had he been wrong?

"Did you talk to Lake?" he asked, mewling when that tongue circled his hole and then flicked back inside of him, pushing all the way in. It wiggled and felt around, the sensations as odd as they were electric. He peered back down in time to watch his dick dribble precome onto his stomach.

"Haven't seen him this morning," West pulled back and replied, sucking on the tender skin of his sack. When he didn't get an immediate response from Nix, he sucked harder, grinning when that had him crying out again. "Why?"

Lake had left without speaking to West about Branwen's account, but that didn't mean he wasn't going to, right?

The sound of West hacking came a second before a wet glob hit Nix's puckered hole.

"Did you just spit on me?" he demanded.

"Yup." West used his thumb to press that wad of saliva into him, stretching him further in the process. Then, leaving that digit buried as deep as he could, he lowered Nix's legs around him and finally wrapped his lips around his cock.

With one drop, he took Nix deep, allowing him to hit the back of his throat. He started bobbing in a quick rhythm, sucking the entire time to the point it was almost as painful as it was pleasurable.

Nix writhed on the mattress, that thumb hooked in his hole pulling him back down when his hips tried to rise of their own accord. He sobbed when West's other hand slapped at his balls and then grabbed at them, squeezing as he continued to swallow him down.

It was the most violent sexual encounter he'd ever been subjected to, somehow even more intense than the blowjob he'd been ordered to give, and it wasn't long before Nix felt his entire body coil, ready to explode.

Only for West to pull off of him all at once.

His hand slipped free the same moment his mouth did, and West planted his palms at either side of Nix's hips and lifted himself so that no part of them touched. Intensely, he watched as Nix struggled to breathe, grinning when a desperate whine rumbled up his chest.

"What are you doing?" Nix asked again, only this time he meant it in an entirely different way.

"Ever been edged before, Nixie?" West chortled. "From the horrified look you're now giving me, I guess the answer is no."

"No," he confirmed anyway, "and I don't want to experience it now."

"That's too bad," West smacked his lips. "That's the game for today I'm afraid. You promised you'd cry for me, right? Here's your chance."

Nix started to shake his head, but West wasn't having any of that.

"That seemed to shock you enough to cool you down," he noted. "Round two."

"West—" He squeezed his eyes shut when two fingers speared into him. Then West's mouth was back on his dick, his tongue circling his flushed crown, teasing his slit until his hips were wriggling in a poor attempt to find any sort of friction.

Those fingers pressed against his prostate and he moaned, the sound turning into a hiss when West finally took him back into his mouth. Saliva poured out of the corners, coating Nix's cock in a slick mixture of both of their fluids which seemed to please the Demon immensely. If the time in the living room was any indication, West liked it messy.

Typically, Nix wasn't into that sort of thing, but then, before meeting them, he hadn't been into any of this.

Now, his dick was leaking, and his balls were drawn up, his hole tightening around those fingers as if in a bid to keep them buried deep. He moaned wantonly, momentarily forgetting where he was, lost to the sensations of West's hot mouth and wide fingers.

Just a few more pumps and he'd—

West pulled out a second time and lifted his face with a loud pop.

When Nix reached for him, he tutted at him and shot away, kneeling on his knees just out of reach.

Nix cried out in frustration and dropped back again, cursing.

"Pinch your nipples," West demanded, barring his teeth like some animal when Nix didn't instantly follow his command. "Should I do it for you?"

The slight maniacal gleam in his eyes made it clear that if Nix chose that option, he'd regret it. West would probably twist them so hard they'd tear off, or if nothing else, feel like it.

Nix brought his hands up to his chest and carefully rolled the pads of his forefingers over his perk buds. They were sensitive already and he startled, only for the Demon to laugh at him.

"I told you," he said, "I worked you good while you were out."

Had he sucked him off here as well?

Nix risked a glance down, inhaling sharply when he noticed the purplish splotches on and around both areola. Hickies? Where else—He slapped a palm to the side of his neck, recalling West's earlier comment about having started there.

"Yejun would be proud," West drawled in self-satisfaction. "The artwork I left on you is a masterpiece—Nipples, Nixie. Don't make me repeat myself or I'll keep you here all day. Actually," he tipped his head, "maybe you'd like that. Imagine Lake walking in on us later tonight, you reduced to a puddle of come, sweat, and tears. Wanna see how long it'll take for us to drench his bedding straight down to the mattress?"

He vehemently shook his head, because no, no he really, really didn't.

Nix covered his chest and tugged at his nipples, his legs opening wider at the contact as that sent jolts throughout his entire body. His dick twitched and gushed some more, and before long, he was thrusting lightly up into the air, grinding his ass down against the silky comforter.

"Beg for my mouth, Nixie."

"Please," he didn't even think to hesitate, the desperation clawing at his insides. "Please, West, touch me."

"If you can take four of my fingers, I'll let you come, deal?"

Nix hadn't been prepped enough for that, but even knowing it would sting, he found himself nodding his head. "Yes. Yes, please."

West shifted on his knees and then brought his right hand to Nix's entrance, his other circled around the base of his dick, tightening around him in a makeshift cock ring as he drove those fingers into Nix's body with one hard shove.

He screamed, but there wasn't actually as much pain as he feared, more like a quick burn and then nothing but bliss as that hand stretched him nice and good.

The Demon lapped at him, licking all around his dick from root to tip and back down again, teasing him by applying pressure here and there with his flattened tongue while his hand fucked his hole open.

Tears poured freely from Nix's eyes now as the frustration boiled over, his dick achy and full. It felt like he'd burst at any moment, yet West's tight hold kept him from being able to.

"West, please. It's too much. Please."

Like with everything else he'd done, West switched gears without warning. Suddenly he was swallowing Nix's dick, hollowing his cheeks and sucking him in time with the thrusts of his fingers. He brought him straight to the edge with only a few pumps, and just as Nix began to fear he was going to cut him off again, West dropped all the way down and hummed.

The vibrations at the back of his throat traveled over Nix and the orgasm hit him like a meteorite making impact.

He made a slew of noises as he came, his vision darkening and winking in and out as his entire body jerked and spasmed. He was still twitching when West released him and climbed up him, still partially blinded when his chin was captured and his face was positioned. When those firm lips pressed against his own and an insistent tongue urged him to open.

He did, gasping when West forced the come he'd just collected into his mouth. His struggles returned, but the Demon flattened himself over him, easily pinning him to the mattress as he continued to force-feed him his own spunk.

West's hand came down over his mouth when he pulled away. "Swallow it all, babe. Don't disappoint me now."

It was disgusting, but it wasn't like he had another choice. Nix swallowed, gagging the second West released him. He turned onto his side, head hanging over the edge of the bed as he hacked, but fortunately—or unfortunately, depending on how you looked at it—nothing came up.

"Don't be so dramatic," West chided, climbing off the bed. He bent down and licked at the stream of tears coating Nix's left cheek. "Tasty."

Nix shoved him away but fell back onto the mattress, completely spent and out of energy.

"Stay here until you get the feeling in your legs back," West suggested, grabbing a backpack off the ground by the desk. He checked his multi-slate and swore. "Damn. I'm late. Coach is going to be pissed."

Nix was pissed.

West yanked open the door and took a single step into the hall before pausing and turning back. He grinned at him. "Thanks for breakfast, Nixie."

CHAPTER 25:

After showering off all of West's dried spit, Nix got dressed in the uniform that'd been left out for him on the bathroom sink. The clothes fit perfectly and he vaguely wondered if Lake had washed his set or if he'd ordered one with the correct measurements to be delivered to the Roost at the crack of dawn.

It was quiet when he stepped out into the hall, pausing with his head poking out just in case. A part of him was still annoyed that Lake had left him on his own, but the other worriedly wondered if that had something to do with the promises he'd made last night.

What if he'd already changed his mind?

What if, even now, he was gathering with the others and telling them all about Nix's true purpose for being here?

It's not like Nix had done any real harm, if anything, they were getting use out of him they otherwise wouldn't if he'd never enrolled here. Did it really matter if he was looking for his cousin's toxic ex if it wasn't one of them?

He'd only kept the secret in case it turned out to be, but if he trusted Lake—which he didn't, not fully, he wasn't stupid —but *if he did*, that meant none of the Demons were involved. There was no reason for this to cause any sort of problems between the four of them. Still…Nix stepped out into the hall and glanced down both directions.

West wasn't here, which meant his room was empty… Lake might eventually talk to him, but it might be smarter for

Nix to stick with his original plan. He was used to doing things on his own. All his life, that was how it'd been. The only other person he could count on had been Branwen. He wasn't like Lake with his forever best friends and their childhood memories.

No matter how sweet he'd been last night, or how physically attracted to him Nix was, he had to remember the stakes here.

Branwen was what mattered.

Period.

Last night he'd freaked out and almost lost sight of that. It wouldn't happen again.

Mind made up, he selected a direction at random and slowly made his way down the hall, on a mission to locate West's bedroom. He assumed all three of them slept somewhere on this level of the Roost, he just needed to find the right door.

The first he came across led to a closet. The next, a communal bathroom. The first door on the right attached to the center room he'd seen when they'd first come up the main stairs. It was a library of sorts and he didn't linger since it was clearly not what he was looking for.

After almost fifteen minutes, he finally found another bedroom, stepping inside cautiously to make sure he was alone before fully entering.

The room was clearly in use, with clothes strewn about and the bed unmade. There was a computer on the desk to the left, but it quickly became apparent this space didn't belong to West.

He should just go, yet Nix found himself pausing in front of an easel by the window, staring at the curve of dark black lines on the bright white canvas. It was a drawing of a woman, long hair strewn out around her as she sat on the ground with her face hidden behind her hands. He didn't know much about art, but looking at it made him kind of sad.

"Looking for something, Firebird?" Yejun's voice coming from off to the side startled Nix and he spun around to find the Demon standing in the open bathroom doorway. He was dressed in only a low-hanging deep red towel, strands of his hair sticking to the sides of his neck as he cocked his head and stared Nix down.

Nix struggled to come up with a viable excuse but, in the end, only managed to mutter, "Sorry."

Yejun snorted and made his way over. "What are you doing?"

"I was looking at your drawing," he admitted, turning back to it.

"That?" He shrugged. "It's not finished. I just can't seem to bring myself to throw it away."

"Why would you do that? It's good."

He scoffed. "Don't insult me."

"No, really," Nix insisted. "I don't really understand art, but isn't it supposed to make you feel something? That's how you know it's good, right? When I look at it…I feel kind of depressed."

Yejun hesitated and then asked, "Do you?"

He nodded. "Why is she crying?"

"She made a mistake," he replied. "And it cost her everything."

That sounded personal…

"Is this her?" he asked. "The friend you mentioned before?"

"A version of her," Yejun confirmed. "So don't feel too bad for her."

"I don't." Nix took in the drawing. "It makes me sad, but not for her. It's like…I can tell you were upset while drawing it? I don't know. Maybe that sounds stupid." Put him in front of a computer and he could pick it apart and piece it back together again. He wanted to be a part of a gaming company after graduation, but he wouldn't be applying for the graphics department, that was for certain. "She really left you frustrated, didn't she?"

It was on the tip of his tongue to confess like he had last night to Lake. If he explained things to Yejun now, there wouldn't be reason for him to be mad at Nix, right? It wasn't like he was betraying him the same way this female friend had.

"She was the first person who was interested in my art purely because she enjoyed it," Yejun spoke before Nix could. "Or, at least, that's what she made me believe. Obviously I know now it was all a lie, but back then it was nice finally meeting someone who simply liked looking at my work. Who didn't want to get close to me because of my last name, or the fact that I'm Essential, or that I'm a Demon of Foxglove. She never made any type of move on me either, so I knew she wasn't after sex. I should have known it was a trap."

"Why?" Nix frowned. "Because there's no way someone could just be interested in getting to know you? Don't think like that."

"Why not?'"

"Because it's not true."

Yejun grunted. "Coming from the guy who is only here because he was forced to be? Admit it, Firebird, you wouldn't have fucked me if you thought you could get away with turning me down."

That was only partially true, but Nix didn't feel comfortable enough in his own skin to admit as much. To either of them.

"I think you can waste your whole life judging yourself for the things that were done to you," Nix said. "Or, you can choose to step back and look at the bigger picture."

"Which is?"

"Half the time, the shit you think is personal isn't. I was in the wrong place at the wrong time and ended up under Lake's thumb. Could have happened to anyone. You didn't know this girl beforehand, right? You'd never done anything to her in the past?"

"No," Yejun answered without hesitation.

"Then it wasn't your fault that you were played." Nix glanced back at the drawing. "Stop blaming yourself. Everyone on the planet wants to believe they can be liked for who they are."

"Who do you think I am, Nix?"

"I don't know," he admitted. "I'm still trying to figure that out."

He chuckled, but the mood seemed different. Lighter. "Fair enough. Well, right now, I'm hungry. I'm going to grab a change of clothes and go make breakfast. Interested?"

He'd skipped out on dinner last night because of the whole incident with the fake dead Iuk. "Yeah, food sounds great."

"Cool." Yejun undid the tie at his waist, laughing when Nix immediately averted his gaze when the towel dropped to the floor.

"I'm," he scrambled for literally any excuse to escape the naked Demon, eyes landing on the open bathroom door, "going to use the restroom."

"Knock yourself out," Yejun said. "I'll meet you downstairs after."

"Okay." Nix basically hid in the bathroom while Yejun dressed, not daring to come back out again until after he'd heard the Demon leave. Considering the way he'd been woken by a fervent tongue this morning, he wasn't in the mood to risk being pinned down by another one of them.

As soon as he was certain Yejun was gone, he slipped back out into the main room. It was set up completely differently from Lake's, most notably that it was square instead of circular. The window showcased a view of the stone pathways leading into campus, and Nix momentarily searched for his dorm building, only able to pick out the curved tip of the roof, the rest of the building concealed by others.

Yejun's bed was set against the right wall, his dresser across from it, with the desk next to that. Even though the walls were the same dark wood as Lake's room, the rest of the interior lacked the color scheme theme he'd gone with. Ironic, considering Yejun was the artist in the group.

He was also the slob, it appeared.

There were piles of clothing and stacks of art books.

Canvases set against the walls, some already finished or started, others blank. Yejun's computer was practically buried by paintbrushes and tubes of paint, the desk cluttered and hard to get to.

Nix found himself back by the drawing he'd been looking at earlier, mostly just stalling if he were being honest. Eating breakfast with the Demons like everything was normal felt... weird. Since he was already here, he opted to snoop a bit, opening one of the wardrobe doors almost absently.

The second he did, dozens of shoes toppled out, and he cursed, springing backward. At first, he thought it was just Yejun being a chaotic mess, but then he registered that a good portion of the shoes were high heels and clearly the size of more feminine feet.

"What the hell?" He stooped and picked up a neon yellow stiletto, searching through the mess for its partner. Which was missing. "Why does he only have one of each shoe?"

Not wanting to get caught, Nix began picking them up, opening both of the wardrobe doors so he could pile them back in. He'd only replaced a few before he noticed that there were also canvases in there, tucked behind hanging clothes, and he swept them to the side to get a better look.

There were only three, the first of a raven with gold eyes surrounded by pink flowers. The bird was perched on an extended wrist, the hand also painted, though the arm disappeared off the side.

The second and third paintings were side by side, but Nix didn't really see the second, his attention instantly captured by the last one, half of which was visible.

He pulled it the rest of the way into view and it was like the whole world came to a screeching halt.

A blond girl was sleeping on a desk, her head cradled by her arms. Her eyes were closed, but her full lips were curved slightly upward, almost as though she knew she was being watched and only pretending. It was a closeup, so there was only the partial part of the desk she was lying over, the hint of her black uniform shirt, and the depiction of a jade drop on her ear in the picture.

The jade drop earrings Nix had bought her.

"No." His arms fell, brain momentarily unable to process things.

Hadn't they said the name of Yejun's friend was named Iris? He'd even told Lake Branwen's and gotten no reaction, but there was no mistaking the girl in the painting was Nix's cousin.

Which meant Yejun, at least, had known her.

Nix took a step back and then glanced over at the black drawing one more time. Now that he knew what to look for, it could be said they were the same girl in both works. Even though the black and white one had her face covered and no color to help identify her hair, the style of the cut, the shape of her form...

He was moving before he even registered that was happening, his feet practically racing from the room. Blindly, he traveled down the halls, mindlessly seeking the exit. The second he found the stairs, he took them, eyes landing on the front door the moment it came into view. Someone called his name from the kitchen area, but he barely heard and he absolutely wasn't going to stop to find out who it was.

Yejun had been friends with his cousin.

She'd betrayed him.

What the actual fuck was going on?

The door wasn't locked and he tugged it open with all of his strength and shot out onto the porch. He darted across the bridge and then kept going, only realizing he wasn't wearing socks or shoes when he'd made it around the bend and stepped on a stone hard enough it hurt and snapped him out of it.

Nix stumbled and cursed, lifting his heel to find he'd cut himself.

"Are you okay?" Juri was standing beneath the black awning of one of the small art stores on campus, a large portfolio case held in one hand.

"Are you an art student?" Nix blurted.

"Yeah...Why? Where are your shoes?"

"Can we talk for a minute?"

Juri hesitated but then glanced in the direction Nix had just come. A look of understanding morphed his expression and he ended up nodding. "Follow me."

Without bothering to ask where to, Nix did.

CHAPTER 26:

"Here." Juri handed Nix the can of coffee he'd just purchased from the vending machine. He'd brought them to a small snack area situated outside between one of the literary and science buildings. There were a couple of picnic tables, along with a row of machines that offered various snacks and beverages. He'd already pulled his shower shoes out of his bag and given them to Nix as well.

"Thanks." He rolled the can between his palms, collecting his thoughts as Grady's friend quietly took the spot next to him on the bench. "Do you major in art?"

"Yeah," Juri said. "Both Dew and I."

Right, the redhead at the library, Dew had mentioned seeing Nix and Yejun together.

"This is going to sound strange but," he blew out a breath and went for it, "do you happen to know of a student named Branwen?"

He considered it, but shook his head. "I don't think so."

"What about Iris?"

"Yeah, her I know. She was expelled last year though." Juri frowned. "What's this about? Did you hear something else about the Demons?"

"You and Grady are the only two people on campus who've warned me against them," he said. Everyone else either whispered about how jealous they were behind his back, or tried to suck up to him in class. "Aside from Grady, I haven't even been able to make any friends."

They'd come around his desk, clearly wanting something from him, sure, but the second he stopped engaging when asked about the Demons, all of the "friendly" students tended to return to their seats and go back to ignoring him. All this time, Nix had just assumed that was because he was the new guy and it being senior year, everyone had already established their clicks.

It'd made finding the right opportunity to ask about Branwen difficult, but since accessing the Enigma app files was the quickest way to discovering who she'd been chatting with anyway, he hadn't been too bent out of shape about it.

"Then, how do you know Iris?" Juri asked.

"I don't." Nix lifted his multi-slate and pulled up his saved photos, finding one of him and Branwen from a couple of years back at a family event. "This is her, right?"

Juri nodded. "Yeah. Iris Cherith."

"She must have changed her name on campus." But why? She'd kept her last name, so it clearly hadn't been to conceal her identity entirely. He was pretty sure she'd never mentioned anything about the name Iris to him or the rest of the family either. "She's my cousin. Her real name is Branwen."

"Oh." Juri seemed like he wasn't sure what to say for a moment. "Sucks she was kicked out. I didn't know her personally, but she seemed nice."

"Do you happen to know any of her friends?" Nix thought she'd majored in history, so he hadn't even considered checking with art students.

"Honestly?" Juri seemed uncomfortable. "The only person I know she was close with was Yejun. She took the beginners class in art as her elective and that's how the two of them met, but that was the only one she signed up for, so I never had any classes with her myself."

"What about West?" Lake was off-planet at the time, so Nix didn't bother asking about him. "Did she hang out with him too?"

"Not that I know of, but I could be wrong. Like I said,

I didn't really know her, just that she was someone who hung around Yejun a lot. Then toward the end of last year, rumors went around that she'd done something to piss him off and was expelled."

According to Yejun and the others, that something was working with the hacker after them. That didn't sound anything like the person Nix knew, but apparently, he didn't know her nearly as well as he'd thought. She'd been going by a different name and he'd never heard anything about that.

"When we spoke on the phone, it always sounded like she was hanging out with friends," Nix divulged. "She said she was having a good time here."

"She probably was," Juri tried to reassure. "For what it's worth, when I said she was close to him, I really mean it. They looked like they were legitimate friends. That's why it was surprising to hear she'd done something that warranted being blacklisted from school. It happened pretty quickly, too. There were only three or four days left of the semester, but as soon as word got around about her expulsion, she was already gone."

He'd foolishly convinced himself for over a week that the Demons had nothing to do with his cousin. Last night, his talk with Lake had only bolstered that idea, and yet now it felt like everything was falling apart and he was left standing on quicksand.

"Did you come here because of her?" Juri's voice dropped low, even though they were the only two currently in the area, and the students walking the path were too far away to listen in on them. "Is that why you've gotten close to them?"

"No!" Nix dropped his head in his hand and groaned, speaking at a more level tone himself when he reiterated, "No, it just sort of happened this way. That's why I'm so confused right now."

"I tried to warn you they're bad news," Juri sighed. "You aren't the first person they've fooled, and you won't be the last. It's sort of the price we all have to pay in order to attend this university. Deal with the revolving door of Demons. Keep our heads down. Pray they don't take notice. Or do, if you're into a quick fling."

"Branwen wouldn't have been," Nix stated. "She wasn't like that."

Juri hummed. "I don't think she and Yejun were in that kind of relationship either. It was actually a little weird to see them together. Usually, he sticks to himself while he works, but she was constantly around him and he never seemed bothered by her presence."

"She told me she was close to someone here, I just never imagined..."

"This group is particularly bad. The story I told you in the library? That's just one account of the things they've done since taking the mantel."

The Demons of Foxglove Grove was a title, but that didn't make every single person who bore the name the same.

"This is the first year in many that there are three of them, and they're all already such prestigious members of the club," Juri added. "They've been bred to control the planet through fear and aggression. Really, it's no wonder they rule campus that way."

"People still seem to like that," Nix replied, only *like* was a strong word and even he thought it wasn't entirely accurate in this situation. "Well. They want to fuck them, anyway."

"They want to use them to get ahead," Juri agreed. "To be frank, when we first met, I thought that's what you were doing as well, but now...You came here because of your cousin, right? Is she refusing to tell you why she was expelled or something?"

As far as his family was concerned, Branwen never had been. She'd returned the day she was supposed to at the start of the summer break and said nothing about being kicked out. Though, it wasn't too long after her arrival that she'd ended it, so there hadn't been much of a chance for anyone to notice something was up or for her to confess.

"No," Nix hadn't spoken about this with anyone, but he was so drained at this point, he didn't stop himself from saying,

"She killed herself."

"What?!"

His reaction proved to Nix that no one had heard anything about her death. Even thinking her name was Iris wouldn't change that fact for Juri, but he truly had no notion she was gone.

People weren't openly discussing her expulsion, but a part of Nix had assumed that was because they didn't want to think about how she'd died. He should have known better than to assume anyone here held respect for the deceased.

"I'm so sorry," Juri told him. "I had no idea. That's…awful."

"She didn't give a reason why," Nix said. "But she was clear someone here hurt her badly enough it drove her to it."

"Someone?" Juri rubbed at his face. "Shit."

"Now you're saying that the only person she hung out with was Yejun, and there's this whole thing about her using a fake name…" Nix swore and popped open the can, chugging half the contents in one gulp. "I don't know what's going on and it's driving me nuts."

"She could have had other friends," Juri corrected. "I just never saw her with anyone. Would you like me to ask around for you? I know a couple of people in the history department. Maybe they'll know something more."

Nix nodded. "Yes, thank you."

"You aren't going to like hearing this," Juri said then, "but I have to say it. Yejun is the one who got her expelled. I don't know why, but if the gossip is true, he was the one who went straight to the dean and demanded she be removed."

And the dean would have to listen to someone like Yejun.

"They aren't good people, Nix. Right now, they might seem like it to you because they want you to think that. You've caught their attention, and they're manipulators raised in the art of business and politics. They know the right way to approach someone, the right things to say to them to get them to let their guard down."

"This sounds like it's coming from experience," Nix

pointed out.

"If I tell you a secret, will you promise to keep it to yourself?" Juri nervously glanced toward the pathway.

Nix nodded. "I just told you about my cousin."

"I'm technically a Legacy," he said. "My older brother was a Demon when he came here five years ago. He hated the whole experience and ended up leaving the club instead of moving up in rank after graduation. My parents and I haven't heard from him since he graduated early last year, aside from a text he sent me on my birthday."

"What made it so bad for him?" Nix asked. "Aren't the Demons in charge?"

"Legacies are considered Demons and allowed to live at the Roost," Juri confirmed, "but there's still a hierarchy. In the beginning, it was just my brother, Joel, and Breck Bardin—he's Lake's cousin. The second year was when Lake and the others enrolled as freshmen, though, and that's when things went downhill. He wouldn't ever give me details, but those guys are straight-up monsters. I'm a junior and at first he tried to convince my parents to send me somewhere else. I eventually got him to drop it by agreeing to wave my Legacy rights."

"You can do that?"

"It's practically unheard of, but yeah. I'm probably the only one in all of history who ever has, but I did. And I don't regret it. Seeing the way he was forced to act on campus whenever those guys were around...Watching the toll it was taking on him...Joel was always a kind person, but you can't just bring kindness to the table against bullies like Yejun and West."

Had they done that to Branwen? Worn her down until she was a shell of the person she'd been?

"If they deemed someone unworthy, they'd turn the entire school against that person," Juri said. "If my brother tried refusing to participate, they'd scold him publicly. One time, West even made my brother cry. They have this way of uncovering weakness and exploiting it."

If Yejun's list of events was to be believed, it was Branwen who'd approached him though. She'd been the one who lied about her intentions, spying on him and delivering messages to whoever the hell this hacker accomplice was.

Why would she do that? She was many things, but vigilante wasn't one of them.

What did he really know about her? The deeper he got, the more he realized the answer was… nothing.

"Your brother," he said. "He's no longer around, but do you happen to know where he is?" Was there a chance that the hacker was Joel? Branwen was in the same grade as Yejun and the others, which meant she would have witnessed all of this. Could she have formed a friendship with Joel and cooked up this scheme with him?

It all sounded ridiculous. Like some bad detective tv show.

"He's not on planet," Juri replied. "He got a job on Drax and left almost immediately after graduation. He hasn't been back since. Why? If you're thinking he was friends with your cousin, I doubt the two knew each other."

"What was his major?" Nix shrugged when that earned him another frown. "Humor me."

"Sports therapy. He spent most of his time with the swim team and in the medical sciences buildings."

That explained why Juri had been so upset when talking about Rase. The student Yejun stabbed in the eye must have been friends with his brother.

"What about computers? Programing? He any good?"

"No," Juri shook his head, confusion growing. "I mean, he had an Enigma account, like practically everyone else on campus. But he didn't really do anything with computers. That's never been an interest of his."

So, most likely not the hacker.

If Juri was telling the truth.

And there was no way for Nix to know that with absolute certainty.

"Last question, and I swear I won't be mad if you come clean," Nix held his gaze. "Did you put something in my backpack yesterday?"

"What? No. Like what?"

"Like a dead luk," he left out how it was a fake.

"Good Light! Someone put a dead animal in your bag?!" Juri seemed honestly upset. "Who would do something like that?"

"That's what I want to know."

"And you thought it could be me?"

"It came with a note telling me to stay away from the Demons," he explained.

Juri exhaled. "Okay, I can sort of see how you might suspect me. But I swear I didn't send it. That's gross."

"Can you think of anyone else who might want me to stay away from them that badly?" Nix asked. "Either because they hate them or want them or something?" Had to cover his bases.

"There are a lot of students on campus currently hating on you for seemingly taking all of the Demons' attention," Juri replied. "But I can't think of anyone off the top of my head who'd go to these types of extremes. Most of us are well aware of what Yejun and the others would do to us if we were caught messing with their boyfriend."

Nix winced at the title. Boyfriend. Yeah, right.

"Have you considered..." It was clear that he didn't want to continue, only doing so when Nix motioned for him to, "What if it was actually them?"

"Huh?"

"I told you, using fear tactics to control people isn't out of the norm for them. What if that's what this is? What if one of them put that thing in your bag so they could convince you to stay with them?"

West had been with him when it'd happened but...Nix really didn't like this theory.

"You just came from the Roost, right?" Juri said. "You're wearing a waif sweatshirt and Lake's number is on the back."

Nix hadn't even noticed. Last night he'd been so quick to get dressed, not wanting to be naked in front of Lake for longer than necessary. Not because he was afraid of what the Demon might do to him if given the chance.

Because Nix had been afraid he'd enjoy it too much.

"Did they ask you to stay with them, or was that your suggestion?" Juri questioned.

Nix ran a hand through his hair. It made sense, but at the same time, that wasn't something they'd bother with. Right? To what end? They already had him coming when they called, and they hadn't tried asking him to stay the night normally. Why would they jump to such an extreme?

Just to scare him?

To tighten their control further?

It hadn't worked. All finding that luk had done was give Nix more of a drive. He'd been reminded why he'd truly come here and what his purpose was.

Nix rose to his feet. "I have to go."

"Where?" Juri stood as well but didn't try to stop him.

"Any chance you know where Lake is right now?" He needed to talk to him. Needed to look him in the eye when he asked if Lake had been aware this whole time that Iris and Branwen were the same person.

Needed to know if that moment of understanding between them last night had all been a lie he'd stupidly eaten up like a sucker.

"Um," Juri checked the time, "probably at the stadium. Usually, this is when the waif team practices."

"Thanks"

The stadium was across campus, and he'd seen Lake take his hovercar occasionally while Nix went to and from classes. Since he hadn't brought a car with him, and there was no time to waste, Nix mindlessly raced toward the large domed building in the distance, slipping between students as he went with only one goal in mind.

He had to get to Lake and demand answers. The longer he sat with this, the worse his thoughts became.

What if Lake had known all along and this had merely

been some game?

What if they all knew?

Juri seemed like a decent person, not the type to lie, and considering everyone else's reactions whenever the demons were around, it was obvious they were more than capable of doing horrible things. Hell, they'd already done some of those horrible things to Nix. But wouldn't a fake dead animal in his bag be a bit extreme?

It wasn't like they even needed to put in that much effort. All they had to do was order him to come and he did. He'd yet to go against their wishes, no matter how badly he wished he could.

He was playing the part they wanted him to play perfectly.

But was the part also a lie? Was this all a hoax? Maybe there wasn't even a hacker to find. What if Lake had known from the beginning that Nix had hacked the system and the three of them had come up with this scheme as a form of retaliation? Yejun was so upset over Branwen's betrayal Nix could more than see him willingly going along with a plan to screw over her cousin—both literally and figuratively.

Were they just out to humiliate him?

No. Wait. That wouldn't make sense either. If the hacker wasn't real, then Branwen wouldn't have betrayed Yejun for him. So the hacker had to be legitimate, unless there was another reason Yejun was upset with Branwen and the hacker was another fake story…

He hated this. Hated the uncertainty, and what's more, hated how something tightened in his chest at the thought of all of it being a farce.

Nix didn't know these people. A week in their company, in their beds, and what? Suddenly he had attachments to them? Bullshit. This strange sensation was simply because he wasn't sure if he was closer to finding out what happened to Branwen or further. That was all. This was about his cousin.

This could only ever be about that, whether it turned out they were playing him or not.

Still, Nix needed to know. Right now.

His thighs burned and he was slicked in a sheen of sweat by the time he made it to the stadium, bursting through the stable doors since he came to that part of the structure first. There were a few snickers from the waifs currently in their pens, large creatures with scales and reptilian faces, but Nix tried not to look at them, passing down the wide dirt hall, eyes glued to the opposite side.

The stable was set up with closed entrance doors, but opened up to the field. Nix could see the grassy ground and the curve of white wall, bleachers set up in rows behind it. He'd never been big on sports and was even less comfortable around creatures as large as waifs, but he set all of that aside as he made his way through.

He had no idea what his plans were once he made it to the field, but he figured he'd find Lake amongst the other players and call him over. Hopefully it wouldn't make too big of a scene and Lake wouldn't be too pissed off to talk with him openly.

Nix was so caught up in his head that he almost didn't catch the sound of footsteps jogging up behind him. He turned, brow furrowing, and already started stepping off to the side, figuring he must be in the way of one of the players late to the field or something. Only, he managed to catch a flash of a black robe, and before he could fully process what he was seeing, the person wearing it shoved him.

He let out a startled yelp and fell backward, hitting one of the stall doors and tumbling straight inside. His ass hit the straw-covered ground hard enough that he cried out a second time, the shooting pain vibrating up his spine, costing him precious seconds.

The cloaked figure took advantage of this, grabbing the door and slamming it shut. There was the distinct sound of a lock sliding into place and then the person's footsteps as they ran off.

For a moment, Nix sat there with his mouth hanging open, sure that he'd imagined the whole thing. It'd happened so fast and was so absolutely ridiculous he didn't think there was a way it could be real, and yet…His palms got pricked by the ends of straw as he lifted himself back onto his feet and made for the door. The handle didn't budge, and the thick wood shook when he tried to pound his shoulder against it but didn't give.

Sucking in a breath, he spun on his heels, taking in the large stall, grateful at least that it was empty. If there'd been a waif in here, he probably would have been trampled after startling the creature.

"Hello?!" Nix pounded on the door. "Is anyone out there?! Hey! Can anyone hear me?!"

He reached for his multi-slate, cursing when he saw the screen had cracked when he'd fallen. No matter how many times he tapped at it, the device refused to turn on.

CHAPTER 27:

Lake took a drink of water and eyed his teammate, Smith, as the other guy approached the dugout where he was standing. According to the others, Smith had been a shoo-in for the captain position before the announcement that Lake would be returning. He was still trying to gauge how pissed he was about that, but Smith was surprisingly good at keeping his thoughts close to his chest.

If Smith had tiered higher than Knight on the Enigma app, Lake would have considered offering him Favors to move up the ranks. He'd make a good addition to the club with a poker face like that.

"Good match," Smith said, coming up to Lake's side and stopping to reach for his own water bottle.

They'd just finished their morning practice, and coach had them split into two teams playing against each other. They'd been on opposing sides and Lake's had—unsurprisingly—beaten Smith's by several points.

He hummed in agreement but didn't share anything else. They'd been teammates since freshman year, but had always been more like friendly rivals than actual friends, and since that wasn't something Lake was currently in the market for anyway…

His multi-slate with its distinctive chime went off in his gym bag and he took it out, smiling slightly to himself when he saw the familiar name flash across the screen. Since this wasn't

Vitality, he didn't bother removing the earpiece, clicking the accept button and letting the call go straight to speaker.

"Want to hear something funny?" Kelevra's voice came through, a hint of humor in his tone.

"Sure," Lake replied.

"Ledger only just realized you were gone."

He chuckled. "Of course he did. I'm surprised he realized it at all."

The school period on Tulniri happened at a different time of the year than it did on Vitality. He'd been present for their first semester of their senior year, and now they were starting their second, whereas classes at Foxglove were only just beginning.

"How's being back?" Kelevra asked, and Lake paused, sipping at his water momentarily.

"How uncharacteristically curious of you."

"Rin says I need to work on being a better friend, whatever the hell that means."

Lake doubted Rin had even meant it at all, was mostly likely just egging Kel on for fun, but the Imperial was so hooked on his Royal Consort he wouldn't notice right away. "Things are relatively the same as when I left."

"Really? Pretty sure I heard word that you're about to be crowned."

Lake glanced at Smith, but the other guy was doing a great job pretending not to listen in on them. It was an act, because it would be impossible for him not to hear with Lake standing so close, but the show of respect was noted.

Perhaps Lake could use him after all...Maybe he'd speak to the boys about finding a way to get him on the potential membership list.

"Why? Jealous?" he teased, knowing that Kelevra couldn't give two shits about becoming an emperor. The guy's oldest sister held that position on Vitality, and that was the way Kel had always preferred it.

Sure enough, Kel grunted. "I also heard you and your crew are called Demons there. That's a step down from Devil, don't you think?"

"I don't know," he drawled. "For my coronation, why don't you bring Madden with you and we'll pit him against West? Or, better yet, see if you can borrow Kazimir?"

"And suffer the entire space flight over?" Kelevra clicked his tongue. "Pass."

He and Kazimir Ambrose, the underboss of the Brumal mafia, were like oil and water.

"Well, my point is, West can beat any of yours," Lake concluded.

"I'll consider it," Kelevra said. "Where are you? Don't you have classes at that fancy school of yours?"

"I just got done with practice."

"Oh, right. Waif? I've never played."

He'd mentioned that before, when he and Lake had first been introduced. Waifs were a creature native to Tulniri, so it made sense that a Vital wouldn't have learned the sport. Most of the creatures bonded with their riders at a young age as well, so it was a difficult game to get involved with later on in life.

Lake's waif, Raz, had been with him since he was six, a gift from his late mother, the last big one she'd given him before her death. His gaze cut across the field to the other side, where Raz was currently being washed down by one of the assistants. That was typically a job Lake preferred to do himself, but since he'd been eager for practice to end so he could return to the Roost and check on Nix, he'd outsourced the task this once.

"Giant lizard horses and fragile golden balls sound like an absurd combination to me still," Kelevra told him. "If I do come for your crowning, you have to promise to take me to a game."

"Deal." Lake would never admit this to anyone, not even the Imperial, but he missed Kelevra and the others. He didn't regret returning home and was relieved to be back with West and Yejun, but that didn't make the melancholy, almost wistful feeling he got now and again when thinking about his life on Vitality any less intense.

The sound of a door slamming shut in the background

came through the line a second before Kel said, "Someone's pissed off my Royal Consort again it seems. I'll talk to you later, Lake."

"No problem," he chuckled and hung up, already picturing all the ways Kelevra no doubt planned on putting Rin in a better mood. Sex was useful in that sense. Useful in many others as well.

Perhaps he should rethink waiting to take Nix. There was no telling how long West would put it off. His best friend was a dick like that. He'd go out of his way to come without penetrating just so Lake couldn't either.

"What's so funny?" Beck called suddenly, drawing Lake's attention up to the bleachers that swirled around the octagonal field. He was standing on the nearest level, elbows propped on the metal bar.

Though there was no blood relation between them, the two had often been told they were similar in visuals. Beck was around the same height with the same sharp jawline, though his green eyes were a shade deeper and his hair wasn't nearly as platinum as it was golden—sort of like Nix's but way less appealing.

"I haven't seen you smile like that in a long time, cousin," Beck continued when Lake didn't greet him. He glanced over his shoulder toward the field. "How was practice?"

"I dominated as per usual," Lake replied, a bit on edge. Like with Smith, he wasn't sure how to approach Beck. The two of them had never had any problems in the past, and West and he were actually really close, but… "Are you here because you've heard something about your father's antics?"

"Unfortunately," he sighed, "no. My father doesn't treat me as a confidant."

Lake was well aware. That was one of the reasons why he'd never felt any true animosity toward Beck. He knew what it was like to have family he couldn't stand.

It was no great loss to him that the emperor had passed.

"There's a meeting tonight," Beck said. "I was just

informed and figured you'd yet to check your messages."

Lake tilted his head. "You came all the way to the stadium for that?"

"No," he chuckled, "I had to see your coach already about another student."

"It's only two weeks into school. Don't tell me someone is already at risk of flunking your class?"

"I wish I could." He straightened, brow dipping into a deep furrow. Beck was like that. He cared about his students. When he'd announced during a rare family get-together with the Emperor and Royal Consort a few years ago that he planned on becoming a professor, his father blew a gasket. He'd wanted Beck to follow in his footsteps, but his son had adamantly refused.

Though he'd never taken one of his classes, Lake had only heard good things from others who had. His cousin was apparently great at his job, passionate and caring toward his pupils. He most likely would have made a good leader if only he'd been higher up the ladder and had actual blood relations with the Emperor.

"When's your first official match?" Beck asked. "I'd like to come and show my support."

"Your support, while appreciated, would be better placed elsewhere."

Beck started walking toward the stairs alongside Lake when he moved toward the opening of the stadium that was attached to the stables. They both went silent until he'd reached them and came down, falling into step at Lake's side.

"You know that's already done," Beck said. "Of course I support you, cousin."

"Even though your father is openly against it?"

"My father," disdain practically oozed from his lips, "wants the crown for himself, but he doesn't deserve it."

"And I do?"

"Much more so than he does," Beck smiled at him. "The meeting tonight is with the High Council. They'll discuss moving forward now that the mourning period is coming to an end. My father will no doubt try to argue you're incompetent, so it's best if you bring your friends along with you for the added verbal support."

The High Council, like the Order, appreciated a strong stance, and the fact that the Demons were best friends would go a long way in showing them Lake was prepared to take on such an important position. With the backing of two other members who would one day fill leading roles on the planet, he was the better choice.

And when considering he was the only remaining blood relative in the Imperial family?

Lake was the only choice.

"We'll be there," he replied as the two of them passed through the stables. He tugged off his riding gloves and slipped them into the back pockets of his tight black pants, already lost in thought.

If the meeting was scheduled this last minute, it must mean someone had something up their sleeves. As long as it wasn't his uncle, he'd be fine, but if it was…There was lots to plan for. Lake needed to go into this on the defensive, which meant rounding up the boys now so they could discuss all of the possibilities.

Sounds of penned waifs, their hooves clapping against the hard ground, their grunts and hisses, filled the stables, but as they passed by one of the stalls, Lake thought he caught a whimper.

He paused.

"What's the matter?" Beck asked, stopping at his side.

"Did you hear that?"

Before his cousin could reply, the sniffle came again, followed by a cautious voice to his right.

"Lake?" came through the wooden door of a closed stall, but was audible enough Lake immediately recognized it. "Is that you?"

He burst into motion, mind reeling as he undid the latch and practically yanked the door off its hinges to get it open. His breath caught in his throat the second he processed Nix, huddled in the middle of the dirty floor, his arms wrapped tightly around his knees.

Lake grabbed him under the arms and hoisted him up, eyes already scanning him from head to toe, searching for injury. When there didn't appear to be anything wrong, he took his hands, scowling when he saw his Songbird's palms were rubbed raw. "What the hell happened?!"

"Someone locked me in," he said, voice still low and weak. When he cleared it, it became obvious that it was probably because he'd been in here screaming for help for a while.

A tightness coiled within Lake, the anger raw and demanding, and his grip tightened before he could think better of it, causing Nix to wince and cry out. He loosened his hold and pulled Nix from the confined space, not letting him go even once they were back in the main area.

"Who?" he asked.

"I didn't get a good look at them," Nix replied. "They were wearing something, like a cloak or a big jacket. I don't know. It happened too fast."

"If they were walking around in disguise," Beck stated, reminding Lake that he was still there, "it sounds like they planned this."

Nix stared at him, and even though he didn't seem particularly uncomfortable in his cousin's presence, Lake still found himself slipping his hand into Nix's, careful not to apply too much pressure to his injuries this time.

Beck's gaze trailed down to it, and something unreadable passed over his expression, gone before Lake could decipher it and replaced by a small smile. He nodded his head at Nix. "Hello, I'm Professor Beck, Lake's cousin."

"Where are West and Yejun?" Lake demanded. "Why are you here alone?"

"I..." Nix's voice trailed off and he glanced between him and his cousin, but it was hard to tell if he simply didn't want to say in Beck's presence, or if he was stalling.

His Songbird was good at adapting, which meant he was also more than capable of hiding things. Case in point, the fact that Lake had only just managed to pry the truth of why he was really here out of him last night.

Whatever. It didn't matter right now. Lake's friends were going to hear from him later. He'd told them not to leave Nix alone; he understood he was more invested in this than they were, that neither of them felt the same connection he did with Nix, but he'd given them an order, and they should have fucking taken it seriously.

"Is there anyone you can think of who might want to do this to you?" Beck asked Nix. He turned to Lake before he could answer and added, "You three have thrust him into the limelight. Perhaps it's one of your fans?"

Lake scowled.

"Don't give me that look. Half the student body is obsessed with you and the other is terrified," Beck said. "This seems like a fairly childish prank, even if they did plan to do something to Nix ahead of time. A student is the likely guess."

"Are you saying this is my fault, cousin?" Lake's eyes narrowed. It wasn't like Beck wasn't well aware of the reason Nix had been brought in—or, at least the reason Lake had given the Order and the rest of the club.

"I'm saying you should have anticipated some type of blowback from your peers," he corrected. "Naming a fourth isn't unheard of, but to announce a brand new student as one and—"

"A what?" Nix frowned.

Forget finding who'd done this. Lake could strangle his cousin.

"We'll discuss this later," he said, but that only irritated his Songbird.

Nix shook his hand off of him and took a deliberate step back, stubborn, even as he was still clearly shaken up about being locked in the stall. "No, you'll tell me now. What does he mean by that?"

Beck set his hands on his hips and had the audacity to

give Lake a stern look. "You didn't explain things properly to him when you chose him?"

"He understands enough," Lake argued, but neither of them seemed to agree.

"What's a fourth?" Nix shook his head before Lake could speak. "Don't try and feed me any more bullshit. I'm at the end of my rope here. Tell me the truth. Now."

"Legacies are given the title Demons when they enter Foxglove Grove," Beck started to explain. "It's a rite of passage that only those with families high in Club Essential are allowed to partake in. You're aware of this at least, yes?"

Nix nodded his head in the affirmative. "Which actually has me wondering, what's the point of anonymity if everyone knows whose families are involved the second their kids enroll?"

"There's a point to that as well," Beck said, "but that's not the purpose of this talk. I just want to be sure you know exactly what it is you agreed to. My cousin can be rather...blunt."

"That's one way of putting it," Nix mumbled, pretending not to notice when Lake glared.

"In their final year, Demons are given another luxury," Beck continued. "They're allowed to bring in one other person. The catch is, all of the current Demons need to be in agreement, and only one can be selected. For this reason, it's rare for this to actually occur. They're named by number since the gender and identity of the chosen person can differ. Because there are already three Demons this year, your signifier is the fourth when you're spoken of amongst club members."

"I told you to pretend to be our boyfriend," Lake stated. "It's the same concept."

Beck quirked a brow. "Hardly."

"How so?" Nix's shoulders tensed.

"There's nothing pretend about being named their fourth, for starters," Beck began, but Lake had had enough.

He grabbed Nix's hand once more and began dragging him toward the exit.

"Let go!" Nix struggled, but his heart wasn't really into it.

Lake could tell because, typically, his strength was better than what he was currently exerting.

Or maybe he'd merely used all his energy up while trapped.

He did not like that idea.

"We're going to find out who did this to you," he announced, pleased when that at least ceased the Songbird's squawking.

Nix allowed him to tug him along the rest of the way without fuss, quiet until they entered the attached building to the right. "And then?"

"Then?" Lake caught that anger and held it close to his chest. "Did they push you with both hands?"

Nix frowned. "I…think so?"

"Then I'll cut them both off at the wrists."

And watch as the culprit bled out on the ground.

CHAPTER 28:

The security room was empty when they entered, but that didn't deter Nix. His nerves had settled on the walk over, and he was trying not to allow the fact that a lot of that had to do with Lake's presence to linger on his mind.

At first, he'd suspected the Demon when Lake had stormed into the stall, but it'd quickly become evident that he was just as upset by what had happened as Nix was. He was also still dressed in his waif uniform, further proving he'd come from the field. That, added to the fact there was no reason Nix could think of for Lake to want to frighten him, it was clear someone else had done it.

But what exactly had it been meant as?

A prank?

A warning?

Since the person who'd shoved him hadn't stuck around to specify, Nix was left scrambling in the dark for answers, and he wasn't a fan of that at all.

"We can come back," Lake said when they entered the room and the security guard who was meant to be monitoring the screens wasn't there.

Nix ignored him, taking the seat himself, fingers already dancing across the keyboard. "Like hell. I want to know who did this to me."

"Are you afraid of cramped spaces?"

He shook his head, busting through the password

protection on the device.

"Are you hacking into the system, Songbird?"

"What do you expect me to do?" he shot back. "Wait?"

Lake sighed and moved behind him, dropping his hands onto Nix's shoulders, though he didn't attempt to pull him away from the computers. "Did you really learn how to do all of this because you wanted a job at Star Eye Holding? What does being able to hack have to do with creating video games?"

"I want to get into developing," Nix replied. "In order to do that, I had to learn programming skills. The hacking was sort of just…fun? I didn't break into anything too illegal."

Lake paused and then repeated, "*Too* illegal?"

"I never went near the club." Nix didn't have a death wish, and the last thing he'd wanted was to end up in prison. The change in topic did make him realize Beck hadn't followed them. "What happened to your cousin?"

Lake turned around and glanced at the closed door to the room. "I forgot about him. He must have had something else to do."

A professor at an elite university like this one probably had a ton of better things to do than chase after a couple of students. Nix didn't have any classes with Beck, but he'd heard about him once or twice from West and, obviously, occasionally from the news throughout the years.

"Here." He accessed the footage from the stables and rewound a little over a half hour until he saw himself enter on screen.

"Did you come to see me?" Lake asked. "You look upset, Songbird."

"I was more upset after when…Here!" He pointed as another figure slipped into the stables behind him.

"Well damn," Lake drawled. "That is a legitimate cloak."

The man catching up to Nix was dressed in a long black rope with a hood. It concealed everything aside from the tips of his brightly colored shoes. The pattern was orange with neon yellow soles.

They both watched as the Nix on-screen realized he was being followed and started to turn. Before he could all the way, the cloaked man twisted to his side and shoved him straight into the stall with both hands. The second Nix fell in, the man slammed the door shut, flicked the bolt lock, and turned on his heels.

"He's running," Lake snarled. "Like a little bitch."

Nix didn't disagree.

"He didn't say anything to you?" There was no audio included in the feed, but there hadn't exactly been time for the two of them to have a chat.

"No," Nix confirmed anyway. "Not a single word." No one else entered until Lake and his cousin did twenty or so minutes later. He clicked to switch feeds, going to the one that showed the front of the stables, but it wasn't much more useful. They saw both Nix and the cloaked man walk in, and then the cloaked man run out. Then nothing. He didn't stick around or return. "Do you think it was random?"

Lake snorted. "You don't actually believe that's a possibility, do you?"

Nix slumped into the chair and rubbed at his forehead. All the screaming and panicking he'd done had left him with a splitting headache and a sore throat. All he wanted to do was climb into bed and sleep today and all its shitty events off.

He froze, recalling why he'd come here in the first place.

"What is it?" Lake spun the chair around and settled his hands on the armrests when Nix didn't respond fast enough for him. He leaned in until their faces were close, openly searching Nix's expression. "Did you remember something?"

Lake might not have been the one to shove him earlier, but that didn't change the fact that his cousin was right. The only reason he was being targeted right now was because of his association with the Demons. Nix wanted to blame him, but he wasn't exactly innocent in all of this either.

He'd been the one to hack into the app, after all. If he hadn't, none of this would have happened.

Nix had been the one to start it.

"Is there even a hacker?" he blurted, opting to at least ask some of the questions he'd come all the way here for.

Lake's eyes narrowed. "Are you letting my cousin get to you?"

"You didn't tell me anything about being a fourth," Nix pointed out. "How can I be sure there isn't a ton of other shit you're keeping from me? Is the hacker real or did you make it all up in order to—"

His hand settled around Nix's throat and he tipped his head up. "You're clever, take a moment to think this through before making accusations. Who am I?"

Nix frowned, but when those fingers tightened, he rushed to answer, "Lake Zyair."

"Soon to be crowned Emperor of Tulniri," he said. "If I want something, I don't need to lie, or beg, or barter for it. I simply have to *take*." He shoved Nix away, scowling as he straightened. "I don't have to make up some story about an imaginary enemy to make you mine, Songbird. And let's not forget, you were the one who reached out to me first."

Nix dropped his gaze because hadn't he just been thinking that exact same thing?

"Are you scared now, is that it?" Lake surmised.

"I did have a dead animal put in my bag and now this," Nix stated, even though that wasn't it at all. Sure, he didn't like the idea that someone was targeting him, but it wasn't the highest issue on his list at the moment.

Could he trust Lake enough to tell him what he'd initially planned to though? He'd raced here without really considering all of the angles, and after Lake's speech just now...

What if he confirmed he was manipulating Nix?

What would knowing that for certain achieve?

What if he really didn't know anything about Branwen and Iris being the same person, and he got angry at Nix once he learned the truth?

"If I am," Nix tentatively began, already sort of knowing

what the response would be, but wanting to test it out anyway, "and I want to put an end to this thing between us still...?"

"Everything I told you last night still stands," Lake said.

"This doesn't change anything for you? Not even a little?"

"What, that you were attacked?" He hummed. "If anything, it only makes my stance on the matter more firm. We'll catch whoever did this to you, and I'll keep my word. Once we're back at the Roost, I'll ask West about your cousin's account."

"I have to ask you something," he began, licking his lips and wringing his hands in his lap. "You might get angry. Or I might. Depends on how this goes really."

"If this is another attempt to leave—"

"It's not," he said. "Despite my comment just now, I heard you last night. I know you're not going to let me walk away that easily."

"Try ever," Lake growled. "I won't let you walk away ever, Songbird."

Warning bells went off at that, but Nix locked them down since there was nothing he could do about that possessive note in the other man's voice. Instead, he focused on what needed to be done.

"My cousin's username was WildFlower." Nix felt his heart sink when Lake noticeably went still. "I had no idea, but apparently, she went by a different name while she was here. I don't even know how she picked it. To me, she's always just been Branwen, but apparently, to everyone on campus, she was—"

"Iris," Lake filled in before he could finish. "You're telling me that your cousin is Iris Cherith?"

"Her real name is Branwen Cherith," Nix corrected, but it seemed like Lake barely heard him.

"You don't share the same last name," he took him in, "or even similar features."

That caught his attention. "So you've seen her?"

Yejun obviously had been involved, but Nix had been so sure that Lake wasn't. Had he been wrong about that?

"Only in pictures," Lake stated, but when his eyes met Nix's there was a darkness there that hadn't been present before.

Survival instincts kicked in, and Nix shot out of the chair, backing away with his arms up between them. "I didn't keep it from you. I really only just found out myself."

"How?" Lake didn't move from his spot, but the tension filled the room, and it was clear he could pounce at any moment, that he was holding himself back. "Your explanation better be good."

"I found one of Yejun's paintings," he confessed. "That's when I recognized her, and before I came here to find you, I ran into Juri—"

"Who?"

"Juri, he's a junior here? He's another Legacy."

Lake shoved him hard against the wall, his hand back around Nix's throat. "If it's who I'm thinking of, he's a reject. After turning down the Demon title, it was pity from the Order that allowed him to still attend Foxglove. After he leaves this place? He'll be lucky to get a decent paying job anywhere on this side of the planet."

Nix frowned. "Just because he didn't want to be one of you?"

"You don't get to reject us," he growled. "Every action has consequences. Yours are no different."

"Lake—"

"So you spoke to a relative stranger about our business," he cut him off. "Someone other than me knows about this? Someone *before* me knew?"

Okay, he'd obviously botched this whole thing.

"Lake—"

"Do you have any idea what your bitch of a cousin did to Yejun?"

Nix grabbed onto his wrist despite the danger. "Don't call her that."

"I'll call her whatever the hell I want, Songbird," he practically snarled. "If you knew the details, you would say much worse about her, blood relative or not."

"What does that mean?"

"You don't need to know."

"Lake—" He tried to push away from the wall, hissing when he was shoved back and that hand tightened, hard enough now that it momentarily restricted his breathing.

Why were these assholes always throwing their weight around trying to choke him?!

No fucking wonder his cousin had betrayed them.

The second Lake's hold loosened, Nix couldn't help himself, the words shooting off his tongue like vitriol.

"You're all monsters," he snapped. "What the hell did you do to my cousin? What the hell did you make her do?! Did West try and smother her with his cock?! Did Yejun force her to pose nude for him?! You all think you're so high above the rest of us because of your connections to the club. You disgust me!"

"*I'm* the monster?" Lake's usually icy exterior cracked even more. "Iris almost got Yejun killed. She almost cost him everything. Yet you have the audacity to stand here preaching like she's some saint? Newsflash, Nix, you didn't know your cousin very well. You might not have known her at all. Don't take that out on me. She wrote you a letter telling you to come here? She practically gave you to us, but you want to defend her?"

"She didn't!" In her letter, she'd told him not to come. She'd told him...

Oh, but she'd known he wouldn't listen.

Of course she'd known.

Because even if Nix was now realizing that maybe Lake had a point, that didn't change the fact that clearly Branwen had still *known him*.

But loyalty was a complicated thing.

Right now, it didn't matter how much truth may or may not be in Lake's words. What Nix knew for a fact, maybe the only thing he was certain of even, was that Branwen was his cousin. For years, she'd been the only person he'd cared about as a friend.

"Get off of me!" Nix swung, his knuckles connecting the

side of Lake's jaw.

They both froze simultaneously.

The hit had probably hurt him more than the Demon, his hand radiating pain which he ignored, too afraid to move a muscle.

"When Yejun finds out you're related," Lake's voice cut through the silence like a sharp blade, but it seemed like he was talking to himself, "he'll destroy you. It won't matter that I've already named you our fourth. That won't be enough to stop him from tearing you to pieces and scattering your parts across the city."

Nix's mouth dropped open but he had nothing to say to that. So far, Yejun had been the kindest to him out of all of them but…He was learning he wasn't the best judge of character. Clearly, since in a matter of minutes, Branwen had gone from his closest confidant to a relative stranger.

"He'll take you from me." Lake's head turned, his eyes dark but slightly clouded over, almost as though he was too deeply lost in thought to focus on what was in front of him.

Which, unfortunately, was Nix.

"I can't blame him," the Demon continued, still in that low tone, "but I also can't allow it."

Nix cried out as he was yanked forward by the collar of his shirt, the material tearing under Lake's ministrations. He struggled as it was tugged down on the right, exposing him. Before he even knew what to brace for, Lake's mouth was on that meaty spot between his neck and his shoulder.

When his teeth clamped down, there was no hesitation. He chomped into Nix's flesh, tearing through skin, right down to muscle. He pinned Nix against the wall and held, growling when Nix's struggles continued and he cursed and sobbed against him.

The pain was bad, but it was nothing compared to the fear.

This wasn't the person who coaxed him into comfort over the video feed. Or even the man who'd stood by and watched as his friend pounded Nix's face with his cock. There was nothing sweet or collected in this, a version of Lake that seemed undone, cut off from that tight control he was so famous for.

That wasn't the only part that scared Nix, though. Bites were…ritualistic. Old. Practically unheard of in present society, but the meaning behind the action was glaringly obvious, even if Nix couldn't quite understand the why of it.

Hadn't he been promised this would all end on Demons Passing?

Then why…

Lake released him all at once, stepping back and rubbing his hand across his mouth. The move smeared blood across his face, and he watched as Nix slid to the ground before crouching in front of him. He pulled the material of the torn shirt out of the way again to inspect his handy work, humming to himself, an unmistakable glimmer of self-satisfaction in his green eyes.

"That's going to scar," he announced. "I marked you in a way that can't be ignored. Not even by Yejun."

Nix flinched and protectively lifted his arms in front of his face when Lake moved his hand to touch him. Even with everything else that had been done to him, this was by far the worst. He'd never been truly injured by another person before, and knowing it was someone like Lake, someone powerful and stronger than him, made it ten times more frightening.

He wished he'd stayed locked in the stables instead. That would have been better. So much better.

Lake shushed him and gently lowered his arms, keeping a hand over one of Nix's wrists so it remained in his lap. "Don't be afraid, Songbird. It's over."

"Please," Nix squeezed his eyes shut, hating how pathetic he was being yet unable to stop himself. "Please."

"I won't hurt you anymore," he promised, easing his knees down to the ground so he was caging Nix in. Carefully, he captured his chin, tipping his face up before his lips brushed against Nix's, featherlight. "Shh. Don't cry."

"You don't get to say that," Nix stated, but he didn't push the other man away. "You don't get to touch me like this after doing that to me either."

"I'll touch you how I please," Lake corrected, but there was no anger in his tone now, his voice still trying to soothe. "You can blame that precious cousin of yours, Nix. She's the reason we're both in this position now. She forced our hands."

"Liar."

"You can't tell Yejun about her yet," he warned. "This will be enough to keep him from killing you, but that doesn't mean he won't try and make your life a living hell. There's only so much I can do to stop him from that."

"Liar," he repeated with more venom. Now that the pain was starting to turn into a dull throb, his anger was returning full force.

"He's my best friend," Lake said, as if that should explain everything.

Suddenly, the door to the room opened, and a middle-aged man dressed in a security uniform stepped inside, pausing the moment he spotted them across the room.

"Get out," Lake ordered, not even bothering to turn to face him.

He hesitated briefly, then seemed to realize who Lake was. With a muttered apology, he stepped back and slammed the door shut, sealing the two of them in the room once more.

"I'll tell him myself once I figure out the best way to put it," Lake picked up the conversation as though the interruption hadn't happened. "Promise you won't say anything, Nix."

"And if I do?" There were still tears in his eyes, making his vision blurry, but he stubbornly glared through them at Lake. "What? Are you going to bite me again?"

"You know why I had to do that."

"No, I fucking do not."

He sighed. "You're native to this planet. *You know.*"

Nix didn't want to go there, and frankly, he didn't have the mental strength to do so at the moment.

"The only good thing about all of this is we're after the same person," Lake said then. "The same one who recruited your cousin. You wanted revenge on them, remember?"

"I wanted revenge on whoever hurt her," he corrected.

"That wasn't us."

"I don't believe you." How could he, all things considered? "I'm bleeding on the floor right now, thanks to you."

"I did that to protect you."

"Bullshit!"

"All right, I did that to protect you and as punishment for talking with Juri Ferd. You want something, you come to me. If I find out you're cheating—"

"We had a single conversation, Lake!"

"And that's where it'll end. You're mine." He poked at the still bleeding wound. "Officially and permanently."

Nix winced and finally gathered enough courage to slap his hand away. "Stop saying things like that."

"Like?"

"We agreed on ending this come Demons Passing."

"We agreed on no such thing." Lake stood and then extended a hand down to him, curling his fingers when Nix didn't make any moves to accept it. "Get up, Songbird."

"Why?"

"We've got places to be."

"Like?"

"Nix. If I have to lift you myself, it won't be pretty."

Ignoring his hand, Nix struggled to his feet, grimacing when Lake reached forward and adjusted his shirt to cover the bite.

"Let's move fast," Lake suggested. "The sooner we get this done, the sooner we can get back to the Roost and tend to your injury."

"The one you gave me?"

"Don't pout. One day, you'll thank me for it."

"Dream on." Nix wanted to argue further, but he really was spent now. "Where are we going?"

"Your dorm," Lake said, but before Nix could feel any sort of relief from that, he added, "To pick up your things."

"What?" He shook his head.

"You're moving into the Roost."

"No."

"I'm not asking, Songbird." Lake stepped in close, pausing when Nix tensed. "Put your animosity toward me right now aside. Someone is after you. The Roost is—"

"If you finish that sentence by claiming it's the safest place," Nix stated. "I'll bite you back."

Lake didn't seem nearly as offended by that as Nix had hoped.

"By all means," he kissed Nix's forehead and then retreated. "Mark me, Songbird. I won't stop you."

He didn't exactly stick around to give him the chance, though, either.

Nix debated refusing as he watched Lake head to the door, but knowing that would just lead to more suffering, he gave in. It wasn't like he was following the Demon straight to hell or anything anyway.

This was already it.

And he was already here.

ABOUT THE AUTHOR

Chani Lynn Feener has wanted to be a writer since the age of ten during fifth grade story time. She majored in Creative Writing at Johnson State College in Vermont. To pay her bills, she has worked many odd jobs, including, but not limited to, telemarketing, order picking in a warehouse, and filling ink cartridges. When she isn't writing, she's binging TV shows, drawing, or frequenting zoos/aquariums. Chani is also the author of teen paranormal series, *The Underworld Saga*, originally written under the penname Tempest C. Avery. She currently resides in Connecticut, but lives on Goodreads.com.

Chani Lynn Feener can be found on Goodreads.com, as well as on Twitter and Instagram @TempestChani.

For more information on upcoming and past works, please visit her website: **HOME | ChaniLynnFeener (wixsite.com)**.

Printed in Great Britain
by Amazon

53444ac3-db1b-4bfd-a9a1-d7ae9de28deeR01